CONSCIENCE AT THE CROSSROADS

This was the moment Rosalie had been dreading ever since she had come to the Duke of Solway's vast estate while her injured ankle healed. This was the moment that Rosalie had known was coming ever since the duke had stood with her under the mistletoe and his lips had come down on hers in a kiss she could not forget, try as she might.

Now as she saw the look in his eyes, the set of his jaw, she said, "I can guess what you have to say, my lord." She paused, and went on, "But you are a duke, and—and I'm only a dancer."

"That didn't prevent us from becoming friends," Gervase said.

Her gaze was steady and her voice calm as she said, "I believe you seek more than friendship."

The duke took her hands in his. "Rosalie, I'd try so very hard to make you happy."

If only she could tell herself he was lying, but she could not.

If only she could tell herself that she did not hunger for the happiness he offered, but she could not. If only she could say yes . . .

DANGEROUS DIVERSIONS

DANGEROUS DIVERSIONS

by

Margaret Evans Porter

A SIGNET BOOK

SIGNET
Published by the Penguin Group
Penguin Books USA Inc., 375 Hudson Street,
New York, New York 10014, U.S.A.
Penguin Books Ltd, 27 Wrights Lane,
London W8 5TZ, England
Penguin Books Australia Ltd, Ringwood,
Victoria, Australia
Penguin Books Canada Ltd, 10 Alcorn Avenue,
Toronto, Ontario, Canada M4V 3B2
Penguin Books (N.Z.) Ltd, 182–190 Wairau Road,
Auckland 10, New Zealand

Penguin Books Ltd, Registered Offices:
Harmondsworth, Middlesex, England

First published by Signet,
an imprint of Dutton Signet,
a division of Penguin Books USA Inc.

First Printing, April, 1994
10 9 8 7 6 5 4 3 2 1

1

A dancing Shape, an Image gay,
To haunt, to startle, and waylay.
—WILLIAM WORDSWORTH

London, 1810

Force of habit was so strong that Gervase William Marchant paused before crossing the threshold of the study, instinctively waiting for permission to enter. His thoughtful gaze rested on the leather wing chair near the window, now unoccupied.

Otherwise, the room was unchanged. The mahogany bookcases were crammed with calfbound editions of classical authors, biographies, travel writing, essays, and political treatises, and even in the gloom of late afternoon their gilded spines glittered enticingly. A set of folding library steps had been left open at the base of the tallest bookcase. Gervase could remember standing upon them as a boy, examining his surroundings from the superior perspective of an adult. His wise and patient father had never scolded him for playing in his well-furnished retreat, or chastened him for repeatedly spinning the large globes in the corner.

He strode the perimeter of the rich Persian carpet, examining the portraits of his ancestors that decorated the walls. Among those represented were a Royalist general, ennobled by Charles the First for his valor during the Civil War, and his Cavalier son, a court wit who had wed an illegitimate daughter of the martyred Stuart's merrier son. The youthful Gervase had been fascinated by tales of their exploits on the battlefield and at Whitehall, and in later years he'd read their names in his history texts.

Now, as in childhood, he regretted that he bore no resemblance to his forebears. His eyes were gray rather than romantically dark; he had ordinary brown hair, neatly cropped, not the flowing ebony tresses of the earlier Marchants. The only feature he'd inherited, albeit in a slightly improved form, was that proud and prominent nose. His plain black coat compared unfavorably with their brightly colored satins and velvets; it lacked the broad cuffs so liberally embellished with silver thread embroidery. No lace adorned his white shirt, he didn't carry a silver sword, and the gold signet he wore was not as impressive as the large jewels upon his ancestors' fingers.

He sat down at the writing desk where his father's thoughtful and carefully reasoned speeches had been composed. He nodded in the direction of the bust of William Pitt, mounted on a pedestal on the other side of the room, as if it were animate and might respond in kind. But the marble face of the late Prime Minister remained fixed, and the sightless eyes maintained their unwavering stare.

Opening the top drawer, he took out a sheet of writing paper and laid it upon the olive leather desktop.

At that moment a dark-haired boy bounded through the doorway. "Here you are!" he cried. "I've been searching all over. Parry says you're going to your club tonight!" His intense blue eyes blazed with accusation.

"Yes, that's true," Gervase replied, his hand moving to an oblong footed tray his grandfather had commissioned from Paul de Lamerie, a celebrated silversmith. It held an inkpot and pounce-box, a penknife case, and a compartment for pens, all engraved with the arms of the Duke of Solway. Selecting a pristine white quill from the top drawer, the possessor of that illustrious title began to pare its tip with the tiny knife. "But first I must write your sister. Care to add a line or two yourself?"

"I haven't time," the intruder responded. "Do pay attention, Ger. I've something vastly important to tell you."

The duke laid down his pen. "What is it, Nin?"

"Robert the footman was describing the aquatic show at Sadler's Wells, a grand spectacle called *The Spectre Knight*. I looked in the papers and found out that it's playing tonight," the youth concluded significantly.

"I'm quite sure it will be repeated," said Gervase, his tone as firm as he could make it.

"But you said I might have a treat before you send me back to Harrow."

Unable to deny it, he doubted the wisdom of making so generous an offer to his cousin and ward. "I wasn't specific about *when* you might have this treat."

Without a doubt Ninian Peverel favored the handsome gentlemen of the portraits. In addition to black curly hair, milky skin, and the haughty Marchant nose, he exhibited the stately bearing of one who had inherited an earldom at the age of two. His height was average for a boy of twelve, and Gervase supposed his thinness resulted from incessant activity, for he was a voracious eater. Those persons who had been acquainted with his mother, the great beauty of her generation, never failed to notice that she had passed her remarkable looks on to her son, but Ninian's oval face was saved from girlish prettiness by the impish sweep of his brows and a determined chin indented by a deep cleft.

"You can't say no," he continued serenely, "because I've already ordered the carriage and it's waiting in the street. The theater opens at half past five, and we'll want good places. Don't forget to bring money—a box seat costs two shillings."

When he went to the window, Gervase discovered that his town coach was standing in Park Lane, its caped driver on the box and a liveried footman at the door. He hardly knew what to say, and he missed his father more in that helpless moment than when he'd stepped into the study. Not that Ninian had minded the late duke any better than he did the present one, Gervase reminded himself.

He wore a beleagured expression as he considered his options and his fingers raked his brown hair, disarranging his valet's careful handiwork. This would be his first night in London after an absence of many months and he'd intended to spend it at White's Club in St. James's. And yet he knew it would be risky to leave Lord Swanborough at Solway House without amusement—or adequate supervision.

"You are a pestilential brat," he announced, and resigned

himself to his fate. Apparently there was no way to avoid
passing the evening at a theater renowned for its lavish
spectacles incorporating a famous tank of water. "What are
we to do about our dinner?"

"That's no problem. There's a jolly tavern across from
the playhouse where I went last year with Justin. Or we can
eat at the theater. A man sells food and drink during the intervals."

"Delightful," said the duke, his tone a clear indication
that he regarded the prospect as anything but.

During the subsequent journey from Solway House to
the northern suburb of Islington, Lord Swanborough entertained his guardian with a description of the performance
he had witnessed when his sister's husband had taken him
to Sadler's Wells.

"Don't most boys your age prefer Astley's Amphithe-
atre?" Gervase asked.

"Pooh, dancing horses can't compare with naval battles
and aqua dramas," Ninian said disdainfully.

"I gather Justin took you to the Wells as a favor to Miranda."

"He wanted to go. It was his first time, and afterward he
said Astley's is nothing to it."

"Ever the diplomat," Gervase murmured. "I sometimes
wonder whether Viscount Cavender would have married
into our family if the responsibility of looking after you had
fallen to him."

"Justin likes me," Ninian said blithely. "But I think he
would have wed Mira even if he didn't. When I was at
Cavender Chase for Easter they were always taking long
walks together and kissing in corners when they thought no
one could see. And now she's going to have a baby."

"Are you implying that one necessarily leads to the
other?"

Grinning, the boy answered, "I know better. Lord Phillip
Wanslow got a village girl with child last term. He's six-
teen and has lain with five different women, or so he
claims. He told us everything about it—before he was expelled."

"And to think my father sent you to Harrow to become a proper young gentleman." Gervase, who had attended Eton, was all too aware of the dangerous effects of public schools, yet he blessed the existence of the one in Harrow-on-the-Hill. On the first day of Michaelmas term, he would be rid of his wild and naughty ward, and a welcome peace would then fall upon his bachelor household.

Exasperated though he often was by Ninian, Gervase had to pity one whose relatively brief history was so full of sorrows and tragedy.

The late Lord Swanborough, a famous sportsman, had remained unwed into middle age, when he began his courtship of Lady Hermia Marchant. The earl owned a neighboring estate and was familiar with the beauty's idiosyncrasies: the despondent moods, the persistent melancholy, the frequent fits of weeping. Her fond brother, the Duke of Solway, exhibited scant enthusiasm for the match but hadn't prevented it.

Unfortunately for the couple, the birth of a daughter was not immediately succeeded by the son Lord Swanborough desperately wanted, and regular miscarriages shattered the countess's fragile nerves and delicate health. After a decade of touring spas and watering places, she presented her husband with his heir, an ordeal so detrimental to her state of mind that she withdrew to Bath, hoping to find a cure. The following year the earl died from an excess of drink and disappointment, leaving little Lady Miranda and her infant brother Ninian to the guardianship of their Uncle William. The youngest peer of the realm had inherited a handsome fortune, Swanborough Abbey in Leicestershire, and a celebrated pack of foxhounds, all held in trust for him until he reached his majority.

That happy day, which Gervase desired far more than the person who would derive the material benefit, was nine years off, and he hoped he possessed enough fortitude to meet the difficulties ahead.

Ninian had demonstrated scant respect for his authority during a summer stay at Pontesbury, Gervase's estate in Shropshire. Since their arrival in London earlier that day, the willful youth had managed to tyrannize the Solway

House servants. Parry, the hitherto unflappable Welshman who had been elevated from underbutler to butler when his predecessor chose to remain in the service of the widowed duchess, already exhibited signs of strain.

Too many houses, too many dependents, and entirely too many responsibilities, Gervase thought glumly. As the carriage rolled through the Islington Road turnpike gate he vowed to forget the weighty responsibilities that had devolved upon him at his father's death for the space of an evening. Perhaps, like Lord Cavender, he would enjoy the sort of entertainment offered at Sadler's Wells.

The theater, a substantial brick building with many gables and projecting wings, sat amidst a grove of elms and was enclosed by a low wooden fence and regularly spaced lampposts. It stood on the north bank of the New River, into which several hopeful fishermen were casting their lines. Gervase envied them their peaceful pursuit, for he enjoyed angling and had passed many a pleasant hour outwitting elusive trout and greyling.

After his coachman halted in the yard of the Myddelton's Head Tavern, he and Ninian descended. Observing the crowd at the entrance of the playhouse, Gervase handed the footman eight shillings.

"Secure the best box seats you can find, Robert, and hold them while his lordship and I are dining." With an understanding smile, he presented the man with several more coins, adding, "Find a seat of your own in the gallery, if one can be had, and buy yourself some beer."

Ninian railed at Gervase for choosing a private parlor in preference to the common room, but he said dampingly that he had no desire to eat in the company of actors and tumblers.

"But Grimaldi the clown might be among them!"

"I doubt it very much," Gervase said when they sat down at an unoccupied table. "A player of his stature would hardly risk overeating or drinking too much before going on the stage. It might adversely affect his performance." He passed the bill of fare to his cousin.

Ninian's prodigious appetite prompted him to select the pigeon pie, bread pudding, and a cherry tart. "What's the time?" he demanded as the waiter cleared away the first of his empty plates. "The program begins at half past six, and we mustn't be late."

"We won't be, so stop bolting your food."

Despite his recent elevation to the pinnacle of the aristocratic hierarchy, Gervase hadn't been a duke long enough to disdain a simple meal, so long as it was well cooked and amply seasoned, and that was precisely what the kitchens of the Myddleton's Head offered. Watching his ward chase a morsel of crust with his fork he realized that he was actually looking forward to *The Spectre Knight,* which would surely be more interesting than the droning debates carried on at White's. Several years ago, when his name was proposed for membership in his father's club, he had been suitably gratified. But he didn't yet feel at home there. He hadn't yet determined to what extent he would involve himself in politics, nor was he especially fond of gaming or gossip.

When Ninian and Gervase took their seats in the stage box Robert had hired for them, the opening ballet was in progress. Turgid music rose from the orchestra pit as the dancers glided across the stage. The female soloist, decked out in a diaphanous spangled gown, pirouetted prettily. Her male counterpart carried a trident, which he waved continually; a short tunic revealed his muscular limbs. When the principals retired to the wings, the ladies of the corps de ballet moved forward, all clutching combs and hand mirrors. Twined about their bare shoulders were long greenish vines, and shorter strands were woven into their unbound hair.

"What is the subject of the piece?" he asked Ninian, who clutched a playbill.

"It's an underwater ballet," the boy replied. "I *think* those girls are meant to be mermaids, and the stuff wrapped around them must be seaweed. The man with the pitchfork thing is Neptune, and the lady is his Queen. Her real name is Madame Louis. Do you suppose she's French?"

"All the best dancers are French. Or Italian."

"I wonder why."

His dread of unanswerable questions caused Gervase to

sigh. "I'm sure I can't say. But I do know that our actors are reputed to excel those of all other nations."

Neither of them was sorry when the dance ended and the pantomime began. It was a humorous piece with a simple plot, and featured London's most popular comedian as Clown.

In one scene Josepsh Grimaldi delivered a sharp kick to old Pantaloon's rump, and the audience roared with laughter. A gentleman in the pit shouted, "That's our Joey! Give 'im another one!"

"I wonder how much time Grimaldi takes to clean his face each evening," Ninian said during the ensuing interval. "All that white and red paint must be a bother to wash off."

Gervase shifted in his seat. "Having a good time, Nin?"

With a shrug, his ward replied diffidently, "The ballet was nothing great, but the panto was amusing. I wish the aqua-drama would begin—that's what *I* came to see." He gripped the rail in eager anticipation and described the vast water tank that the manager of Sadler's Wells had built beneath the wooden stage. Upon this artificial lake, he informed his cousin, miniature boats were floated, villains met their doom, and valiant heroes rescued lovely ladies from drowning.

Charles Dibdin, the author of nearly all the plays he produced and the lyricist for the songs, had based *The Spectre Knight* on Sir Walter Scott's popular poem "Marmion." The result was highly melodramatic, and its climactic scene was set within Fingal's Cave on the Isle of Staffa, faithfully depicted by an ingenious scenery painter. A sentimental conclusion had a powerful effect upon the females in the crowd, and many a handerchief was in evidence by the time the curtain dropped upon the final tableau.

"How I should love to watch them fill the tank," Ninian commented. "The water is pumped in from the New River, you know. D'you think we might go under the stage and have a look at the waterworks?"

Gervase examined his timepiece. "It's eleven o'clock already, Nin, and well past your bedtime."

"Do let's stay till they've cleared away the scenery." His

eyes darkened to blue-black and he thrust out his chin stubbornly. "I don't wish to go yet."

"Stop trying to bully me, you young devil."

"Don't be such a stick, Ger. Say yes."

For the second time that day, Gervase's resolution failed him. "We'll stay for a little while, if you promise not to get in anyone's way and agree to leave when I say it's time—with no argument."

Ninian's mouth had flown open in instinctive protest, but after a pause he said instead, "Oh, very well."

Curious stares from players and stagehands followed Gervase and Ninian as they prowled the labyrinthine corridors behind the stage. One harassed-looking individual, upon being informed of their desire to have a look around, offered to fetch Mr. Harris or Mr. Dibdin from the treasury, where they were counting up the night's receipts.

Gervase replied that this wouldn't be necessary, and his steely eyes dared Ninian to protest.

"But don't you want to see the water tank?" the boy asked plaintively as the man hurried down the hallway.

"Not if it entails disturbing the manager or the proprietor. I suspect all of these busy people are as eager to go home as I am."

"If anyone objects to our looking about, you can tell them who you are," Ninian suggested. "There's a door at the end of the hall," he crowed when they rounded a corner. "I'm sure it must open onto the stage."

"Are you?" Gervase asked wearily. His sense of direction had deserted him long ago. "I'll try this one."

The door nearest him lacked a handle, but a single shove was sufficient to open it. The chamber, dimly lit by a flickering taper on the high mantelshelf, was occupied by a young woman in a gauzy green gown. She stood beside a window, her hand resting on the sill as she stretched one leg out before her. The instant she saw Gervase, she lowered it hastily and regarded him with dismay.

"Forgive me," he said, "I didn't mean to intrude."

Before he could withdraw, she moved in his direction,

her heart-shaped face showing alarm. "You won't tell anyone you found me here?" she asked softly.

"Of course not," he assured her.

"Mr. Dibdin won't let us have a proper green room," she explained, "and he would fine me if he knew I came here to practice my steps." Her voice carried a faint accent, and she tended to lisp her sibilants.

It was too dark for Gervase to determine the precise color of her enormous eyes, which were set beneath arching brows and fringed by dark lashes, but he perceived that the fluffy hair tumbling about her shoulders was light brown. She was small and slim, but her fragile appearance was belied by a nicely rounded figure, much of which was revealed by her insubstantial draperies.

"The devil's in it, Ger," announced Ninian, stepping into the room. "That door at the end of the hall is locked."

"The custodian has already bolted it," the girl told him. "There's nothing much of interest behind the scenes, only the pipes and water cisterns."

"I *wanted* to see them," Ninian informed her loftily.

"By now Mr. Wheeler will have made his way to the attics," she said apologetically. "Perhaps you and your father can come back another time."

Gervase hastened to make it clear that he was the boy's guardian, not his parent. "We had hoped to have a look at the pumps and the stage machinery, but if the person in charge has departed, then we must do the same."

Ninian, peering curiously at the young woman, asked suddenly, "Weren't you a mermaid in the ballet? I remember! You're the one who climbed on the rock to do that little jumping step. How d'you keep your balance?"

"Not very well, most of the time," she answered on a laugh. "The *entrechat* is almost impossible to perfect, and is even more difficult when one perches on a cliff."

"Come along, Ninian," Gervase urged his ward. "We mustn't keep the lady from her practice, lest she make a mistake the next time and blame you for it."

But his cousin had no intention of departing just yet. "I'm an earl," he stated impressively. "Wouldn't that convince the custodian to take me under the stage to look at the tank?"

"Not necessarily" was her frank reply.

"D'you think we might arrange a tour?"

Her expression was thoughtful as she regarded her inquisitor. "The men who work inside the tank during the performances have been complaining that the water has gone bad—it smells after a few weeks of use. Would your lordship like to watch the stagehands pump the old water out and replace it with fresh?"

"Wouldn't I just!" Ninian declared fervently, gazing at her as if she were a fairy who had granted his dearest wish.

"Mr. Garland, the machinist and stage carpenter, is a particular friend of mine. I'm sure he'd let you observe his operations and would also show you whatever else you wish to see. I'll speak to him tomorrow."

Gervase bestowed a grateful smile upon her. "If he is willing to oblige us, you may send a message to Solway House to let us know the day, Miss—" He paused for her to supply the surname.

"My name is Rosalie."

Ninian, demonstrating his impatience with proper introductions, asked her whether she'd ever gone into the tank herself.

Rosalie shook her head. "Some of the actors use it when the water is clean, which it rarely is, but I've never done so. Mr. Dibdin would disapprove of mixed bathing parties." Her eyes twinkled. "He's very strict with the company, and even conducts prayers before each performance."

"What a bore," Ninian responded.

"Nin," said his guardian, "thank Miss Rosalie for offering to make the arrangements for your tour, and bid her farewell. It's nearly midnight."

"Is it?" the dancer asked in surprise. "I'd best hurry home, else my landlady will think the worse. She waits up until all of her lodgers from the theater return, and I'm always the last."

Gervase had already extracted a calling card from his case and he presented it to her, admiring the graceful curve of her arm as she held it up to the candlelight. "Is your lodging house very far from the theater?"

She returned his gaze warily, patently suspicious of his motive for asking so personal a question. "I live quite near, your grace."

Her defensive attitude precluded an offer to see her safely to her door. "Come along, Ninian," he repeated in his sternest voice.

His cousin bowed to the young woman, saying with uncharacteristic gallantry, "I'm vastly pleased to have met you."

With similar formality she executed a curtsy. "Your lordship is most kind."

"You'll let us know soon about seeing the water tank?"

"Indeed I shall," she promised, smiling at his zeal.

Gervase laid one hand on his cousin's shoulder and steered him toward the door. Before exiting the room he cast a backward glance at the pretty dancer and saw that she was biting her lower lip as if to stifle a laugh. He could only hope it was Ninian who amused her, and not himself.

In the morning Gervase was able to eat his breakfast in peace. According to his Welsh butler, Lord Swanborough had departed for Hyde Park at an early hour with his cherished miniature sailboat tucked under his arm.

"He went alone?" Gervase inquired.

"I made sure that a footman accompanied his lordship," Parry said calmly. "Robert is most popular with him because his brother serves in the Royal Navy. And Robert himself witnessed Lord Nelson's departure from Portsmouth before the Battle of Trafalgar."

"Did he? Well, I only hope he can keep my cousin away from the docks. The duchess lives in fear that he'll run off to sea."

"I hardly think so, your grace, now that Robert has informed him about ship's rations. My lord Swanborough is very particular about his food."

Gervase had heard Ninian's criticisms of the Solway House cook, and surmised that he had also aired his grievances to the butler. "Only one week more," he said heavily, wondering if he would survive it, "and I shall turn him over to Dr. Butler and the masters of Harrow."

A short time after deserting the breakfast room, Parry returned with the silver letter tray. "This was just delivered for your grace."

The direction inscribed on the square of folded paper was written in a feminine hand, one unfamiliar to Gervase. He tore through the seal and flattened out the single sheet. "My lord Duke," it read, "Mr. Garland of Sadler's Wells will be honored to receive both your grace and Lord Swanborough on Saturday at midday. Your obedient servant, Rosalie de Barante."

"Did the lady bring it herself?" he asked the butler.

"The footman will know. Shall I inquire?"

"Never mind, it makes no difference."

He returned to the study to carry out yesterday's uncompleted tasks. After seating himself at the leather-topped writing desk, where a stack of letters awaited his attention, but he ignored them in order to write Lady Cavender in Wiltshire. His pen moved steadily, producing line upon line of news, until he heard a curious noise from the hall. When it was repeated he was able to identify it as a moan from the housekeeper, warning him that Ninian had returned from his outing in a less than respectable state.

A moment later his ward appeared, and the muddied clothes and tangled black curls confirmed that he'd spent a busy morning.

"What a grand time I had," Ninian declared. "But I desperately need a larger boat than *Victorious*."

"Soon you'll be at school," Gervase pointed out wryly, "where I trust you'll spend your time more productively."

"I suppose I can bear Harrow, if I'm allowed to view the waterworks at Sadler's Wells before I go back." When Gervase handed over the note that had arrived in his absence, he snatched it greedily. "Her writing is pretty," he commented after reading the brief message. "It looks like she trims the point of her quill very fine. What sort of name is de Barante?"

"French."

Ninian's face fell. "D'you really think so?" he asked in dismay. "I like her. I don't want her to be *foreign!*"

"It might not be the case," Gervase said soothingly. "Many dancers take stage names."

"You said all the best ones come from France," Ninian recalled. "Though I suppose she might want the public to believe she's French." He tucked the paper into his pocket and made an unceremonious exit.

Gervase completed his final paragraph and signed his name. Setting the letter aside, he examined the morning's post and found nothing more interesting than some invitations which he would probably refuse, with false regret.

Conscious of his new and unwelcome prominence, he had no desire to remain in town longer than was absolutely necessary. At some future time, perhaps after he'd wed some lady as yet unknown, he might learn to enjoy balls and routs and exhibitions. But for the present, he wanted only to hasten back to the country.

He'd passed his summer of bereavement in peaceful seclusion at his Shropshire manor house, dividing his time between riding his acres and studying newly published works on modern farming methods, free from all social obligations save a twice-weekly visit to his mistress in Shrewsbury. It was autumn now, the season for shooting his well-tended preserves, fishing the streams, and chasing foxes with the Swanborough Abbey huntsmen, all of which pastimes he could enjoy at Haberdine Castle, his ancestral estate in the heart of the shires.

London represented temptation and trouble, besides being a reminder of a time when Gervase had seriously disappointed his fond parents. For most of his life, Solway House had been no more to him than a superior hotel with a well-organized staff and excellent food, and he would not be sorry to leave it.

Politics and society could wait, he told himself. In his opinion, they were the business of older and wiser men.

2

There was a star danced,
and under that was I born.
—WILLIAM SHAKESPEARE

On Saturday morning Rosalie Delphine de Barante woke
from a dream of Paris, the city of her birth. Her subcon-
scious mind had carried her back to a past she seldom
dwelled upon, to days filled with laughter and frolic. To a
distant time when her mother, also a dancer, had been the
darling of the French nobility.

Nothing, she thought dully, was a greater contrast to the
lost grandeur of the ancien régime than her present abode,
an upper floor apartment in Owens Row. The tiny chamber
in which she slept and the cramped parlor made her long
for her childhood home, a spacious suite of rooms in the
Rue du Hazard, conveniently near the Paris Opéra.

Rosalie climbed out of bed, and the floorboards protested
as she crossed to the washstand. She was conscious of the
persistent pain in her right ankle, always at its worst early
in the day. The demanding entrechat admired by Lord
Swanborough several evenings ago had compounded an injury that refused to heal. Even so, she continued to perform
the step.

After bathing her face with cold water, she put on a silk
dressing gown edged with some of the rich Valenciennes
lace brought over from France and went into the adjoining
room. She'd tried to make it attractive as well as habitable,
for her soul cried out for beauty, but her lack of funds
hadn't permitted any drastic alteration. The chintz curtains
were so faded that their pattern was barely distinguishable,

and she regretted her inability to replace them, or refurbish the worn sofa, its seat cushion flattened from overuse. She'd acquired a pretty hearth rug and the chipped vase in which she kept fresh flowers from a street market. A few colored theatrical prints hid the worst of the marks scarring the walls. Upon the shelf of the mantel stood a porcelain figurine modeled after her mother.

While she was extracting a few wilted blooms from the vase, a maidservant arrived with her breakfast.

"Lawks, miss, I was sure you'd be dressed by now," Peg Reilly declared, depositing the tray on a low table between the sofa and the fireplace. "The other ladies went down an hour ago, to do their shopping, I s'pose. It's a scandal how they waste so much of their money on fripperies!"

"They have more of it to waste," Rosalie said. "Actresses are better paid than dancers."

"Don't you be jealous, now," the girl remonstrated as she tied back the curtains. "They've none of 'em performed at an opera house, or any other grand theater. And for all their fine airs and graces, nary a one has ever lived in France!" With quick efficiency she dusted off the tabletops, then went into the next room to make the bed.

Rosalie was glad to have a friend in the house, for the landlady was militantly disapproving of her theatrical lodgers and the performers were themselves disinclined to confide in each other. The fact that she'd come from Paris was a marvel to the downtrodden servant, who never tired of hearing about her adventures and listened avidly to harrowing tales of the Great Terror, her pale eyes round with amazement. Peg was thrilled when she learned that Rosalie had actually seen Napoleon Bonaparte, not once but many times, although she refused to believe that he bore only a slight resemblance to the hideous monster so regularly depicted in print shop windows.

Rosalie's breakfast consisted of a boiled egg, bread and butter, and a small pot of coffee so black and strong that Peg, whom she'd taught to brew it to her taste, wondered how she could drink it. Her profession required that she take good care of herself, for food and rest were essential for preventing the illnesses and fatigue which destroyed many a dancer's career. Thus she lived a Spartan life, eschewing all personal luxuries and many of the pleasures she had known in happier, more prosperous times.

The new day promised to be busier than usual, despite the fact that she had no rehearsal. She intended to visit the theater and remind Mr. Garland of his appointment with Lord Swanborough and the Duke of Solway. She had accepted a rare invitation to a social function, an afternoon party at the home of a former opera dancer now respectably wed to a man of fortune. And most important of all, she was scheduled to perform in the ballet that evening. Out of consideration for her feet—and her aching ankle—she would have to travel to Golden Square and back in a hackney. Coach fares, like food, depleted a significant portion of her income.

When she finished her meal, she went back to her bedroom to begin her toilette. Successfully taming her golden brown curls, which had a tendency to escape pins and combs, she arranged them in a simple knot at the back of her head and coaxed the short, wispy strands into decorating her temples and forehead. She opened the door of the wardrobe, wincing at the loud complaint from the rusty hinges, and looked over her dresses, seeking one that would be appropriate for her various activities. Her choice, a jade cambric gown with a pink bodice and trimmings, made her changeable eyes appear more green than blue. She completed her ensemble with a simple straw bonnet designed and trimmed by a fellow emigrée, her reticule, and a pair of kid gloves which had seen better days.

Leaving her lodging house, she followed the footpath beside the New River. The weather was bright and clear, not uncommon for late September, and her walk to the theater was pleasant. She rather looked forward to another meeting with the duke and his ward. Although she seldom encountered aristocrats, she was far from being discomfitted by them. In her infancy she'd sat upon the silken lap of Marie Antoinette, the martyred Queen of France. And her mother's patron, the exquisite Duchesse de Polignac, had doted upon her, providing such tokens of affection as silver apostle spoons and a coral teething ring.

When she approached the grounds of Sadler's Wells she heard the cries of children as some or all of the manager's eight offspring played in front of their house. The prolific Mrs. Dibdin occupied a prominent place in the company as both leading lady and premier songstress, and she appeared on the boards as regularly as her frequent confinements permitted. Her antipathy toward the other female players was rooted in bitter jealousy. Each season saw the departure of the very best singers, for none could dare to outshine the lady and expect to remain in her fond husband's employ.

A man was seated upon a low bench near the stage door, filling the bowl of a clay pipe with tobacco. "Good day, Wheeler," Rosalie greeted him.

"A fine one it is, Miss Rose, every bit as sunny as midsummer."

"Has Mr. Garland arrived?"

Mr. Wheeler nodded. "He's inside with the stagehands—they'll soon be pulling up the floor."

When he questioned her presence, she explained, "Some acquaintances of mine are coming to examine the waterworks."

The doorman gave her a sour look. "Shall I give them my opinion of our manager's famous innovation? You won't remember, 'twas before your time, but Sadler's Wells used to be renowned for clever pantos and pretty ballets and daring rope walkers. Nowadays it's all aquatic spectacles, and if not for them the theater would likely fail."

"People also come to see Mr. Grimaldi," she pointed out.

"Aye," he agreed. "Clown Joey and that tank of putrid water—that's why Mr. Hughes gets rich, and Mr. Dibdin and his wife can give their fine dinners and parties. Not that they're any worse than their partner Mr. Barfoot, who chases after all you ladies." Mr. Wheeler frowned and shook his gray head. "This theater brings in a full two hundred pounds a night when all the seats are taken, yet those fine gentlemen pay their golden goose of a clown a mere twelve pounds a week."

"Oh?" Rosalie earned less than half that amount and felt she was lucky to get it.

"Don't never say 'twas I who told you. And bless him, he's worth far more than that to the managers, for he's as hardworking as he is popular." Glancing in the direction of the turnpike road to London, Mr. Wheeler said, "Here's a carriage now—must be your friends coming." The handsome coach was drawn by four fine horses, and both the man holding the reins and the servant perched beside him wore gold-braided livery. "Fine company you're keeping these days," he commented, not unkindly.

Lord Swanborough, the first to emerge, rushed toward Rosalie.

The duke followed at a more sedate pace, and greeted her by saying, "We didn't expect to find you on the premises, Mademoiselle de Barante."

"Have you a rehearsal?" the earl demanded. "Will I be able to watch it?"

"No rehearsal today, my lord," she answered. "I've come to introduce you to Mr. Garland, if you will but follow me into the theatre."

She led both visitors to the auditorium. The lamplighters were replacing the old candles of the lowered chandeliers with new ones, and portly Mr. Wren busied himself with replenishing the stock of food and drink he would sell to the playgoers that night. On the stage, workers had already begun raising the platform with ropes and pulleys, revealing the tank of water beneath it.

Lord Swanborough couldn't wait for Mr. Garland to be presented, but began a conversation as readily as though they were lifelong acquaintances. The gentleman listened patiently as the young peer bombarded him with eager questions. "Come along with me, my lord," he said in his friendly way, "and I'll show you how the pumps work, and many other wonders."

"Don't you wish to go also?" Rosalie asked when the duke remained by her side.

"Not in the least," he replied bluntly.

"Lord Swanborough was talking so fast that I never had

an opportunity to make Mr. Garland known to your grace," she said sorrowfully.

He consoled her by replying, "It's just as well, for I've no desire to compete with Ninian for his attention." Smiling down at her, he added, "I'm sorry you felt it necessary to come. You must have other more important things to occupy you today."

"I'm entirely free until this afternoon," she assured him. His impeccable manners and elegant attire were as impressive as his height and his good looks, and his physique was sufficiently muscled and athletic to command the respect of a dancer. But he seemed very much out of place in the murky, empty theater, prompting her to say, "I believe your grace will be most comfortable in Mr. Barfoot's box while you wait for his lordship. It overlooks the stage and is high enough that you can watch the tank fill."

He accompanied her to the box lobby. "Unlike my cousin, I care very little for the mysteries of the water tank," he said, coming to a halt, "and on a day so fine I prefer to be outdoors. I've always heard about the tea gardens at Islington but can't recall ever visiting them. May I take you there?"

The offer was flattering and tempting, yet she didn't feel she ought to accept. "Lord Swanborough won't know where to find you," she pointed out.

Gervase didn't regard this as an impediment. "I'll leave word with the doorkeeper, and he can tell Ninian where we've gone."

Without much difficulty he managed to overcome her reluctance, which he considered unusual in a dancing girl—his limited experience had taught him that the majority of her kind were all too eager to consort with noblemen. Recalling her wariness at their first meeting, he hoped she wasn't nervous of him. But as they walked together to the gardens, she gave him no real reason to suppose that she was.

His initial impression of her beauty survived the merciless glare of the sun. Her long-lashed eyes were greenish blue, and the fringe of curls hanging over her brow was light brown. She was as tiny as she was lovely—her head didn't even reach his shoulder—with a slender waist and perfect posture. He also noted that her attire was neither new nor fashionable, proof that she hadn't yet made her fortune on the stage.

As soon as they reached the gates of Islington Spa, he paid the requisite entrance fee. When he commented on the absence of pleasure-seekers, his companion said knowingly, "Tomorrow there will be a crowd. On Sundays it is very busy and gay."

"Do you come often?" he asked, taking her down a serpentine pathway bordered by late-blooming flowers.

"Less often than I'd like," Rosalie replied. "*Il faut de l'argent*—it is necessary to have money, and only when I'm reasonably plump in the pocket can I afford to come here. If I'm in the mood for a ramble, I generally go to Sadler's Wells Field, for that costs nothing."

Here was another indication that she was poorly recompensed for her labors. "How long have you danced at Sadler's Wells?" he asked.

"This season is my sixth," she responded. "I hadn't planned to return but changed my mind because the ballet master desperately needed me to fill out his corps. Last year Miss Gayton left to marry a clergyman, and now we have a problem with poor Miss Bates, one of the small-part dancers." Her voice lowered to a confidential murmur. "Mr. Barfoot, who owns a share of the theater, *preys* upon the females in the company. He has a child by Miss Bates, whose place I must fill whenever his wife attends a performance. As long as she continues living under Mr. Barfoot's protection, Mr. Dibdin can't dismiss her, which Mrs. Barfoot is forever demanding that he do. It's an awkward situation."

"I can see how it would be," Gervase said sympathetically.

The surrounding landscape was thickly wooded with elm, laburnum, and shrubbery and rendered even more picturesque by classical urns and pedestals. At a bend in the gravel walk they came upon the spring of mineral water that had given birth to the spa, and he suggested that they make use of a strategically placed stone bench.

He could tell by the way she perched beside him, as though she might bound up again at any moment, that inertia was an unfamiliar state. Her rapid speech and dancing eyes made up for the fact that her body was at rest, and her answers to his questions were punctuated with hand gestures, a Gallic habit which he considered quite charming.

"I gather you've been a performer for quite some time," he said.

"All of my life," she responded matter-of-factly. "I began as an opera dancer in Paris—I was born there."

"You haven't much of an accent."

"I once did," she said with a laugh. "My mother was a *soloiste* with the ballet of the Paris Opéra, and when I was still a very young child I danced there, too, in the great patriotic spectacles that were produced in the aftermath of the Revolution. I portrayed pages and Cupids and cherubs until I was old enough for the corps. During the Peace of Amiens we came to London. Papa was an Englishman, a violinist and composer, and he'd heard that the theaters here were eager to acquire foreign artists—he regarded himself as such after twenty years in France. He joined the orchestra of the King's Theatre, but by that time Maman had stopped performing. Mr. d'Egville, the ballet master, hired me in her stead, but as a coryphée rather than a principal dancer. I was thirteen."

She fell silent and gazed down at her feet, the points of which poked out from beneath her skirts. Gervase noted that they angled outward; having received instruction in the rudiments of dance for purely social purposes, he recognized the first position.

"At so young an age most girls are in the schoolroom," he commented. "Did you mind working so hard?"

"I was thankful that I was able, especially when Papa became ill and had to resign his position. After he died I was my mother's sole support. Her health also declined and I lost her in 1805, a year of many trials. Mr. d'Egville left the opera house—the mangers, and especially the critics, disapproved of his using the children from his dancing academy in his ballets. He found employment at Sadler's Wells and encouraged me to join him, in the belief that Mr. Dibdin's theater would be safer and more suitable for a girl still in her teens and alone in the world. But I haven't been as happy here as I was there and I mean to go back, if I can."

Gazing at her profile, Gervase said, "It is no less dangerous now than it used to be."

"That makes no difference," she told him firmly. "My career as a dancer may last only a decade more, if as long, and I'd prefer to spend it with the best ballet company in London. And the pay at the King's Theatre is better than at the Wells. I'm twenty-one years old now, and have no interest in the gentlemen who frequent Fops' Alley. Entanglements of that sort are not for me."

It was a great pity, he thought, that a girl so young and lovely should be concerned about sordid matters like making money and eluding backstage gallants. He deemed her integrity all the more remarkable because it contributed to her poverty. She could live far more comfortably as the pampered plaything of a male admirer, for she was enticing enough to have her share of offers. When he remembered how he'd found her hiding in a dark room late at night, practicing her steps as if her life had depended upon it, he was glad he'd invited her to come to the spa gardens for a brief respite from work and worry.

"I hope you will excuse my making a familiar remark on such short acquaintance, Mademoiselle de Barante, but I imagine that the life you lead can be a lonely one."

She bowed her head in acknowledgement, and the brim of her straw bonnet hid her expression when she replied, "I can't deny it. I do have some friends—the Grimaldis are very kind to me, and Mr. d'Egville—but none of the dancers in the company are close. There's too much jealousy in our ranks."

They soon abandoned the bench and Lord Swanborough found them wandering through a shady arbor.

After describing the many wonders Mr. Garland had shown him, he suggested that they order some tea. "I'm thirsty as the devil."

"It's no wonder, if you chattered to your guide as ceaselessly as you've been doing for the past few minutes. Mademoiselle de Barante, will you join us?"

"I'm not sure I can, your grace. What is the time?"

Extracting his gold watch from the pocket of his silk waistcoat, he answered, "Half past one."

"I do have that engagement in town," she admitted, "though it's the casual sort of party where people drift in and out. I don't suppose the hostess will feel slighted by my tardiness."

Ninian, who had preceded them along the path, suddenly spun around to say, "Gervase and I will take you in the carriage."

"*Non, non,*" she protested, her cheeks pink. "Your lordship is most kind, but it isn't necessary."

"You *can't* refuse."

"I agree," Gervase said, and her troubled eyes met his. "If not for you, my cousin wouldn't have seen the waterworks. You must let him repay his debt and reciprocate your generosity by providing you with transportation. Where does your friend reside?"

"In Golden Square. But—"

"It's settled," he interrupted gently. "Ninian is determined to befriend you, and I'm so very reluctant to trample his first charitable impulse that I really must insist upon your accepting his offer."

Her grateful smile was a sunbeam lighting up her lovely face, and Gervase regretted that Ninian was its recipient.

Of the dozen persons scattered about the sunny drawing room, Rosalie was acquainted with no more than half, yet she felt quite at ease among them. Hearing the language of her native country, she could easily imagine herself at an artistic salon, an institution which had survived the turmoil of the Revolution, the Reign of Terror, and the many changes imposed on France by the Directory and the Consulate. Last night she had visited Paris in her dreams, and now she fancied she was there again.

"How glad I am that you are here at last, petite," Rosalie's hostess said warmly.

At the height of her fame, Mademoiselle Parisot had been the toast and the scandal of London, adored by the public and condemned by the clergy for wearing costumes that revealed more of her charms than they concealed. Since her marriage to the wealthy Mr. Hughes she had kept herself covered in public, but she smiled no less constantly than she'd done from the stage of the King's Theatre.

"James d'Egville has been asking about you for the past hour. See how eagerly he comes to greet you!" Mrs. Hughes indicated a swarthy, well-dressed gentleman moving toward them. He had wavy dark hair and long side-whiskers, and the pronounced arch of his eyebrows gave him a look of perpetual surprise. "I promised you she would be here, *mon cher*," the former dancer told him triumphantly.

Rosalie held out her hand to James d'Egville. "How have you been, sir?"

"What's more important," he said gruffly, "is how you are going on."

"*Très bien, merci.*" Her right ankle throbbed in contradiction, but she knew better than to mention her aches and pains to any former or prospective employer.

"*Pauvre petite,*" her hostess sighed, placing one hand on her famed bosom. "I want to weep, knowing that you dance for the *canaille* who visit the Sadler's Wells. Delphine would never have permitted it."

"You are forgetting, Parisot, that I used to be ballet master of the Wells," d'Egville interjected, "although I share your belief that our Rosalie is destined for better things. What are your plans, my dear? Will you spend the winter season at Astley's theater in Wellclose Square?"

Rosalie shook her head. "I mean to try my luck at the new playhouse in Tottenham Street."

"But why not at the opera house?" Mrs. Hughes clutched the gentleman's arm. "Please, you must convince Signor Rossi to have her in his company."

James d'Egville studied Rosalie, his brows moving higher still. "Is that your wish?"

"There can be no question!" Mrs. Hughes cried. "You must meet the signor, petite—I will introduce you *maintenant*. He does not make ballets as lovely as *mon cher* James, and I hear complaints that he favors the Italian dancers, but you will not mind that. At least you will again perform before audiences of true taste and style, and for an artiste anything else is *insupportable*! Come with me."

With a backward glance at d'Egville, Rosalie allowed herself to be borne to the other side of the room. Three persons stood before the window, a gentleman of middle age flanked by a vivacious brunette and a stocky young man whose vacant expression became animated the moment he spied Rosalie.

He darted forward to take both her hands in his own and went down on one knee, raising them to his lips in homage. "*Ma belle,* I dare not hope you remember me, but I have not forgotten my first partner. How many years it has been!"

"More than I care to admit," she declared, smiling down at him. "You haven't changed, Armand Vestris. In our student days you were as famous for your *galanterie* as for your *grands jetés*!" She noted the jealous sparks flying from the brunette's black eyes, further proof that the Frenchman still had the habit of choosing his partner of the season for his mistress.

When Armand rose, he faced the frowning lady and said softly, "Fortunata, you must not be alarmed. She was never my sweetheart, she had not enough courage to go walking with me when I begged and pleaded. For her, it was always work, work, work. *Chère* Rosalie, I present Signorina Angiolini, the *première danseuse* of the opera ballet." Turning to the other gentleman, he explained, "I knew Mademoiselle de Barante in Paris, Signor Rossi. She was a pupil of *mon père*, and of Dauberval."

The ballet master inclined his head. "The name is familiar."

"*Bien sûr*, you will have known her mother, Delphine de Barante."

"*Sí, sí,*" the Italian replied, examining Rosalie more closely and with heightened interest. "You are the dancer d'Egville has mentioned to me so often, a coryphée of great promise."

But the ballet master did not engage her in conversation. Addressing his countrywomen in their own tongue, he escorted her to a nearby sofa, leaving Rosalie and Armand together.

"All winter and spring, and last year *aussi,* Fortunata and I have danced together at the opera house," he told her. "Did you not see us?"

"I'm afraid a ticket is beyond my means," she answered candidly, "though I sometimes read about your performances in the newspapers." The critics had been unkind to the Frenchman at first, but he'd won them over with the athletic power of his dancing and his ability to spin on one foot like a top.

"When Parisot told me your parents had died, I was so sad for you."

"I've been without Maman for five years now."

"Last season, a French gentleman came backstage to ask me if I'd been acquainted with La Belle Delphine. He had followed her career in Paris, I think, and was *très désolé* when he spoke of her. I cannot recall his name. Remercier? *Non,* it was something else." After a pause, he shrugged. "It matters not. So tell me, *ma belle,* why do you not dance at the opera house?"

"I left when d'Egville moved to Sadler's Wells and was never invited to return. I hope he'll recommend me to Rossi, should there be a vacancy in the company next season. And Oscar Byrne would probably vouch for my ability, if I asked him."

"I, too, will have a word with the signor," Armand promised her. "And you may also rely upon Deshayes."

"Didn't his wife retire from the company?" Armand confirmed this with a nod, and she begged him to tell her all the gossip. "I've been buried in Islington and hear so little news from the King's Theatre. Is it true that Monsieur Boisgerard opened an academy and is training young opera dancers?"

"He did, but *les enfants terribles* were banished from the stage not long after they first appeared. The English do not like to see the little ones kept awake so late at night!"

"Nothing has changed, then, for the public used to object when d'Egville introduced his own students into the corps."

Rosalie sighed. "It is strange to me, for no one complained when I appeared in ballets as a child."

"In Paris," said Armand loftily, "there is altogether more appreciation for true art. At the King's Theatre the audience talks through the opera, they hiss when they dislike a character, and they interrupt with their clapping at the most inappropriate times—*ils sont bêtes sauvages!*"

Laughing, Rosalie told him, "You would despise the Sadler's Wells audiences far more, I fear. And the salary."

"Come back to my theater, *chérie*, and you will soon be rich enough to buy silk gowns, and jewels to match your eyes," Armand said extravagantly. "Parisot made over twelve thousand pounds during her career, not all of it from her lovers. The managers would pay you well, at least three hundred in your first year."

"As a coryphée?"

"*Mais non,* you will be a *soloiste!*"

The vision conjured by his eager words was most appealing. The Opera season lasted from late December to early August, not quite eight months, and three hundred pounds was triple what Rosalie earned for the nearly the same period at Sadler's Wells. To resume her interrupted career as an opera dancer was her dearest dream. If it ever came true, she would be able to afford a pleasant and comfortable lodging, preferably within an easy walking distance of the theater. No more hackney coaches, she thought exultantly.

Her spirits soared as high as her hopes, and while she circulated among her former colleagues she prayed that she would soon be able to rejoin them on the stage of the King's Theatre in the Haymarket. Bearing in mind that she was supposed to perform in a matter of hours, she watched the clock, and when it was time to return to Islington she sought out her hostess to make her excuses.

"Departing so soon!" Mrs. Hughes said in dismay after Rosalie expressed her heartfelt thanks for a delightful afternoon.

"I really mustn't linger, madame, for I'm dancing this evening."

"Ah, then I won't try to keep you. But wait, there is

something I want you to see—can you guess what? Come with me to my boudoir."

As Rosalie followed her friend up the staircase to a small room furnished with a dressing table draped in pink silk and several French rococo pieces. A large oil painting in a gilt wood frame hung upon one wall. It depicted a slim female in Gypsy costume, her arm forming a graceful arc as she held a tambourine decorated with crimson ribbons high above her head. The scene, a Paris street, was also familiar to Rosalie.

"I thought you would like to look at it again," Mrs. Hughes said quietly.

"Oui," Rosalie whispered, focused on her mother's laughing face. "It was a great relief to me that you wanted to own it. So many of her pictures went to collectors."

"She didn't sell them all?"

"We kept the other Fragonard, and most of the portraits Monsieur Greuze painted of me when I was a child. Maman was quite sentimental about those, and they weren't especially valuable."

"You must never let them go, or the other things Delphine left to you. Any exquisite object—a painting or a porcelain ornament, or even a tiny scrap of lace—can be a source of joy."

"I know."

"And never forget, you have the power to make others happy by performing. Remember how you used to feel hearing your papa play his violin, or watching Delphine dance? They were so talented. And so proud of you, as are all of us who knew their hopes for your success. *Chère* Rosalie, do not make the mistake of wasting such a valuable legacy."

"I won't," she promised. Looking at the colorful canvas one last time, she added, "I can't."

3

Sends Nature forth the daughter of the skies
To dance on earth, and charm all human eyes.
—WILLIAM COWPER

Despite his unwillingness to dance and his preference for
the sober colors of protracted mourning, the Duke of Solway received cards of invitation from all of London's
prominent hostesses. He accepted only a fraction of them,
for he derived no pleasure from standing about in overheated ballrooms, feigning interest in the young ladies trying so desperately to attract his notice.

But his peace of mind was no longer disrupted by his
ward, whom he had delivered to Harrow. He was now free
to devote himself to his favorite solitary pursuits—reading
the papers and writing letters to his steward at Haberdine
and to his mother in Shropshire. When the weather permitted, he drove in the park, and if he had no social commitments he visited one of his clubs or dined with his closest
friend, the Marquis of Elston.

Lord Swanborough had been at school for less than a
week when Gervase received a scrawled note of despair.
Harrow was a prison, the masters were brutes, and he'd
been flogged twice without cause. Knowing Ninian's talent
for provocation, his guardian was inclined to doubt this, but
he resolved to pay a Sunday visit to Harrow-on-the-Hill.

He wrote to inform Ninian of his intent and received a
brief missive in response, demanding that he bring Mademoiselle de Barante.

His ward's admiration of the dancer perplexed Gervase
as much as it frustrated him. He didn't know where she

lived, or whether she might be willing to call upon a rude schoolboy she'd met only twice in her life. But the probability that a disappointed Ninian could create an unpleasant scene was reason enough to find out if she had any objections to the scheme, and to overcome them if necessary.

After penning a note of regret to Lord Elston, with whom he had made a tentative pact to attend a ball, he dispatched a footman to Sadler's Wells to hire a stage box. Sitting through a ballet performance, he decided, would be less tiresome than to an evening of insipid small talk with those damsels who had failed to snare a husband the previous spring.

He had just finished dressing for the theater when Parry announced Lord Elston's arrival. "Tell Timothy to bring the carriage around in ten minutes," he instructed the butler before going downstairs to face his friend's criticism for the abrupt change of plan.

The blond gentleman waiting in the green salon had already supplied himself with a glass of port. "I'm sure your new fellow fills his position admirably," he said, "but I do miss old Richards."

Taking up the decanter, Gervase replied, "My mother's need is greater than mine, and I had no wish to rob her of a faithful retainer. Richards trained Parry, so the house runs as smoothly as it ever did. I've no intention of entertaining anyone but you."

"Yet you spurn my company with no explanation. Have you an assignation with some fair creature?"

"I'm going to Sadler's Wells."

This announcement startled the marquis out of his customary composure. After a restorative sip, he said, "You must be joking."

"Not at all. This is a favor to Ninian, who has become attached to one of the ballet dancers."

"He's rather young to begin his career as a rake," Damon Lovell commented. "And when one considers the sterling example of conduct set by his guardian, the circumstance is even more incomprehensible. Your interest in carousing was singularly short-lived, as I recall."

"My appetite for wine, women, and so forth certainly never matched yours," Gervase said lightly.

"Oh? I wonder. It seems to me that your restraint arises more from consideration for your family's feelings than from disinclination. Although a disappointment in love could also be responsible for your monkish existence."

"A certain fair female in Shrewsbury could refute that characterization of me."

"How intriguing. Has someone finally eclipsed Georgiana in your affections?" Observing the duke's frown, Damon said, "We needn't talk about her if you'd rather not, though I admit I'm curious to know what caused the rift."

"I suppose you deserve to know," Gervase replied. "You are her friend. You even introduced us."

"Did I? Do forgive me, for I meant no harm to either of you." Wagging his golden head, the marquis commented, "That affair was a nasty business from the beginning."

"And Georgiana's final affront was decidedly the worst," Gervase volunteered. "After concealing my guilty pleasures from my parents for a considerable period, I bravely informed them of my desire to marry the twice-widowed Lady Titus, whose second husband died after dueling with one of her former lovers. Although they accepted the news stoically, I know it broke their hearts."

"You never proposed to her," Damon said gravely.

"Fate conspired against me on the very night I intended to make my offer. We'd arranged to meet at a party, but I was detained and arrived much later than I expected. Whereupon I learned that my beloved had departed in the company of another. I went to her house in Clifford Street straightaway, but the maid refused to let me in. She did, however, confirm my worst suspicions. My response to an act of infidelity so flagrant that it sickened me was to return to Solway House and make myself profoundly drunk. As it happened well over a year ago, I'm fairly certain my recovery is complete."

"Evidently, if you keep a mistress in Shrewsbury and are chasing after this creature at Sadler's Wells," said his friend. "I always believed that you had more in common with your Stuart ancestors than you let on. Charles the Second was notorious for his amours with play actresses."

"I told you, Mademoiselle de Barante is Ninian's friend." With a sly smile, Gervase added, "You could come with me and see her for yourself. Or is mixing with the common herd too far beneath your lordship's dignity?"

"Not if the dancers are pretty enough," Damon replied, draining his glass.

Spectators, laughing and chattering as they waited for the performance to begin, crammed the pit and gallery of the playhouse. One of the seats in Mr. Grimaldi's box, which commanded an excellent view of both stage and audience, was occupied when the two noblemen sought their places. The stranger's fashionable but flashy attire and the cheerful, hearty way he welcomed their arrival told Gervase that he was a scion of the prosperous middle class. His sandy hair was curled and pomaded in the newest and most fashionable style. His waistcoat was a riot of color, a number of fobs and seals dangled from his watch chain, and his plump hands were weighed down by heavy gold rings.

"Thought I would be sitting here all alone," he greeted the gentlemen. "Name's Benjamin Beckmann. How d'ye do?"

"Quite well, thank you," Gervase responded. Damon's aloof silence and his rigid features expressed his distaste at sharing the box with a social inferior. "I'm Marchant, and this is Lovell," he said, using their family names rather than their titles to preserve anonymity.

"Pleased to make your acquaintance." Mr. Beckmann embarked upon a long commentary in which he praised the manager of Sadler's Wells for the introduction of water dramas and stated his admiration of Clown Grimaldi. "And the dancing—well, my friends, wait till you see those pretty girls in their little short skirts." Angling his florid face toward Gervase, he added, "I've got my eye on one of 'em, I confess."

From his cheerful admission that he'd come into money upon his father's death, Gervase inferred that he was dissipating it on expensive diversions. Knowing all too well that

Damon was capable of snubbing the vulgar, voluble young man, he was relieved when the curtain began to rise.

The audience murmured approval of the setting: a leafy arbor with a real waterfall in the background. Seated beneath the dome of a small white temple was a female in classical attire, and as she raised one arm the orchestra began to play.

A trio of performers wearing pastel gowns floated out of the wings, followed by a pair of men in tunics and flesh-colored tights who sported about in a manner more athletic than graceful. A tiny boy costumed as a cherub appeared and joined the lady on the dais. The last dancer to join the revels was Rosalie de Barante, her arms filled with pink and white roses which she presented to the lady as an offering. Her curling hair was unbound and she wore a coronet of blossoms; her draperies were pale green, embroidered all over with leaves and flowers.

As she danced a *pas de trois* with the two men, Mr. Beckmann elbowed Gervase. "That's Mamselle de Barante, the very one who's taken my fancy. A real dasher, ain't she?"

Damon, seated on his other side, spoke for the first time. "It's Botticelli's 'La Primavera' brought to life. Venus, Cupid, the three Graces, Mercury, Zephyr, and Flora. Which is young Swanborough's inamorata?"

"Flora," Gervase whispered.

He suspected that their slight acquaintance had prejudiced him in her favor, but in his opinion her performance was superior. The beauty and fluidity of her body in motion was impressive, and she seemed to live and breathe the music. While dancing she looked so joyful, so free—altogether a different being from the earthbound girl who had candidly admitted her troubles to him at their last meeting.

When the performers froze in a final tableau, Mr. Beckmann clapped loudly. Grinning, he said, "Don't mind telling you, Marchant, I'm smitten. Look at that figure, those legs!"

The young man's raptures were wearing thin with Gervase. Damon interrupted them by pronouncing, "A charming pastoral, almost worthy of an opera ballet. A pity that the audience appreciates the attributes of the dancers more than the dance itself."

As they waited for the pantomime to begin, Gervase listened absently to Mr. Beckmann's discourse, wondering all the while whether it was a good time to seek out Rosalie de Barante and where he might find her. He rose and excused himself, carefully avoiding his friend's accusing blue eyes.

By now he was familiar enough with the theater to make his way from the box lobby to the backstage corridor. A hopeful visit to the room in which he'd first seen the dancer was disappointed, and he continued the search. His persistence was rewarded by a timely encounter with the stage doorkeeper.

"Hullo, sir," the man said, recognizing him. "Come to see the panto?"

"Actually, I need to speak with Mademoiselle de Barante. Could you help me locate her?"

"Miss Rose?" Leaning forward, Mr. Wheeler said in a conspiratorial hiss, "She wanted to practice, so I let her into the scene painting room—though Mr. Dibdin would sack me if he ever knew it. Wait here and I'll fetch her for you."

A few minutes later Rosalie joined him. Her wobbling steps caused the silk flowers sewn to her costume to quiver and prompted Gervase to ask if she had sustained an injury.

Disregarding his concerned query, she said softy, "You shouldn't be here. Mr. Dibdin doesn't permit us to receive visitors backstage. We aren't even supposed to speak with each other during the performance."

"Then don't say another word," he told her, keeping his voice low, "because you can answer me with a nod or a shake of the head. My ward—and I—would be very much obliged if you'd consent to visit Harrow School on Sunday. Ninian insists that you accompany me when I go to see him. Can you, or is it too great an imposition?"

A faint laugh escaped her rouged lips. "Your grace makes it difficult to reply, pelting me with so many questions at once. Yes," she said with a brisk nod, "I'll visit him. And no, you aren't imposing."

Gervase smiled his relief. "I'm glad."

"I can't imagine why Lord Swanborough should ask for me. I thought he cared only for the waterworks."

"I confess I'm a bit surprised myself," he admitted. "In general he dislikes strangers."

"You don't object to my going?" she asked curiously.

"Why should I?"

"Because—well, because I am a stage performer, and not at all the sort of female his lordship's family would wish him to befriend."

"Do you know," he said, his sober expression belied by the light in his gray eyes, "it never even occurred to me that you might be a bad influence. In truth, it's far more likely that Ninian will corrupt you."

Again she laughed. "I'll be on my guard against it." After glancing over her shoulder, she said nervously, "Mr. Dibdin sees us—I cannot stay, else he'll fine me for talking." She turned to go, then faced him again, her head cocked sideways. "At what time on Sunday must I be ready?"

"I'll come at noon. Where should we meet?"

"At my lodging in Owens Row," she whispered. "The fifth house down."

When Gervase returned to his seat the pantomime, *Bang Up, or Harlequin Prime,* was in progress. He answered Damon's curious look with an inscrutable smile, and turned his attention to the stage. Although he and his friend were members of the Four-in-Hand driving club, neither of them took umbrage when the piece satirized the coaching mania. Mr. Beckmann laughed the loudest, slapping his knee at Mr. Grimaldi's antics.

The clown wore a skullcap to simulate baldness, and his motley consisted of a short tunic, its brightly colored dots contrasting with the striped shirt underneath, thigh-length spotted trousers, and white breeches tied at the knee with ribbons. His winking, rolling eyes served him well, and he could provoke laughter merely by screwing up his whitened face.

The audience cheered when he stepped forward to sing "Tippety-witchet," a popular ditty Mr. Dibdin had composed for him.

> This very morning handy,
> My malady was such,
> I in my tea took brandy
> And took a drop too much!

After a few drunken hiccups, he warbled the next verse.

> Now I'm quite drowsy growing,
> Because this very morn,
> I rose while cock was crowing,
> Excuse me if I yawn.

Drawing a snuffbox from his pocket, he held it up.

> But stop, I mustn't chatter hard,
> My head aches if you please,
> One pinch of Irish blackguard,
> I'll take to give me ease.

He mimed taking snuff, inhaled deeply, and immediately let out an explosive sneeze. After two more verses he bowed to the appreciative crowd and exited the stage.

Gervase, having succeeded in his errand, was prepared to depart, but Damon persuaded him that they ought to stay for the aqua drama. "After all," he said, "it's the form of entertainment Sadler's Wells is so famous for."

The first scene featured a revolving model of the planetary system, and a transformation in which the man in the moon became the Harlequin of the piece. The clown's return inspired boisterous applause, and he leaped and pranced across the stage, playing his usual pranks on the other members of the company. In a departure from his characteristic laziness, he sought employment with an astrologer.

"Oh," Grimaldi cried to his public after the wise man had offered to cast his horoscope, "he's going to tell my fortune!"

"Thou wert born under the planet Mercury," the ancient gentleman intoned, "and therefore by disposition thou'rt a *thief*!"

"Who d'you call thief?" Grimaldi demanded, his eyes bulging with outrage.

"Thou wert not in the sign of Taurus born, nor Leo, Virgo, or Libra."

"Go to the *library*?" the Clown repeated, to the great amusement of the crowd.

"Pisces, Aquarius, Capricorn disown thee, also Scorpio and Sagittarius."

"Sausages? Oh, I likes to eat *them*!"

Mr. Beckmann let out an explosive guffaw, and Lord Elston's face was softened by an amused smile.

The troop of dancers, Rosalie de Barante among them, made a brief appearance while the wooden platform of the stage was raised behind the curtain for the final spectacle: an illuminated temple floating upon the water.

"You'd best warn young Ninian that he has a rival," Damon advised Gervase when they left the theater.

"Are you referring to that overdressed mushroom?" he asked.

"I'd call him a blustering bag of wind but won't dispute your description, for it is similarly appropriate. After your mysterious disappearance, he entertained me with a recital of his plans for the little dancing girl. He intends to have her for his mistress."

"He's got no chance of winning her favors, of that I'm certain."

"Your confidence raises certain questions about your earlier claims of indifference," Damon drawled. "Did you really come to Sadler's Wells on young Swanborough's behalf, or your own?"

Annoyed by his friend's damning assumption, Gervase made no reply.

"What does Napoleon look like?" Lord Swanborough asked, lifting a forkful of meat pie to his mouth. "Did you know him well?"

"The first time I saw him, I was a little girl and he was a young general," Rosalie answered.

Immediately after their arrival, his lordship had lured his visitors to the King's Head, a tavern in the High Street. So far all Rosalie had seen of Harrow was the exterior of its buildings, and she doubted she would see much more. The earl had made it quite plain that he abhorred his school.

"Where did you meet him?" he prompted her.

"In my godmother's home. She owned and managed a popular theater—all of literary and artistic Paris flocked to her rooms above the Café de Chartres. Famous politicians frequented her salon as well: Danton, Robespierre, Marat. Bonaparte and his friend Barras were great admirers of the tragic actor Talma, as famous in France as Mr. Kemble is here, and knew they could meet him at Madame Montansier's. In those days the Emperor was a thin, pale, awkward man in a uniform. Since then he has filled out, but when I last saw him he still had the same dark hair and very black eyes."

Ninian lifted his head. "When was that?"

"In 1801, the year before I came to England. I was dancing at the Paris Opera that season, and occasionally he and his wife attended the performances." Rosalie accepted the cream pitcher from the duke and followed his example by pouring a dollop over her trifle.

"Tell me about Napoleon's wife."

"Ninian, you really must give Mademoiselle de Barante an opportunity to eat her dessert."

Rosalie assured the duke that she didn't mind his lordship's questions. "Josephine was no more beautiful than her husband was handsome, for she had the sallow complexion of a Creole, and bad teeth. But she always wore such perfect gowns. All the women of Paris tried to dress as elegantly as she, but few succeeded."

"Will you return to France someday?"

Rosalie considered the earl's question briefly, then shrugged. "I can't say. But I've no relations in Paris nor any friends—so many of the dancers from the Opera are also living in England now. I suppose I'd go home if there were a Restoration, although that doesn't seem at all likely."

Ninian reached across the table for a plate of cakes. "Cousin Edgar is fighting in the Peninsula, and he thinks Boney will be routed soon."

"My brother serves on Lord Wellington's staff," Gervase explained.

"How lucky you are to have family," she said.

"Am I?" He directed a pained glance at his ward.

"I always longed for brothers and sisters and cousins. Except for Armand Vestris and the other students at our dancing academy, I knew no one close to my own age, and we were too busy working to have much time for play."

"What did you do for fun?" Ninian inquired.

"We thought dancing was fun. When we had the time, and if the day was fine enough, we strolled in the Jardin des Tuileries. Sometimes in the evening we made up a party and went to the Tivoli Gardens—rather like your Vauxhall. Monsieur Greuze, the painter, was a friend of mine, practically a grandfather to me. I used to accompany him on his promenade from his apartments in the Louvre to the Palais Royale. I would put on my very best dress, and he wore his black coat trimmed with gold lace. We always stopped at Café Frascati for ices, and afterward he'd let me choose whatever I wanted from the bookstalls."

"I *hate* to read," her inquisitor said venomously.

"That," Gervase interjected, "explains your lamentable lack of progress in Latin and Greek."

"What are your favorite books, mademoiselle?"

Blushing, she fidgeted with the cream pitcher and butter plate, realigning them and then changing them back to their original positions. "Your guardian might prefer that I not tell you."

"Nasty books?"

"Well, French ones," she admitted, not quite daring to meet the duke's amused gaze. "Novels and poetry." Desperate to change the subject, she began to question Lord Swanborough about his favorite pursuits.

"I like rowing my boat on the lake and sailing my miniature ship, *Victorious*. In summer I bathe in the pond near Haberdine, and in winter we go skating, if the surface freezes hard enough."

"What is Haberdine?"

"Ger's castle in Northamptonshire. I've got a house, too," Ninian informed her proudly. "It's called Swanborough Abbey. He administers the estate and manages my foxhounds. I quite like hunting, but I'd rather have my own sailboat than a dozen horses! If only I weren't an earl I could go to sea and no one would care."

"You wouldn't wish to if you'd ever crossed the Channel," Rosalie told him with conviction.

Gervase broke in upon his cousin's demands for an explanation. "I daresay Mademoiselle prefers not to discuss her experience, if it was an unpleasant one."

"How could it be?"

"Well," said Rosalie, striving for delicacy, "not everyone is comfortable being on the water when the waves are rough. Neither I nor my parents, or any of the other passengers on the packet from Calais to Dover, *enjoyed* the journey."

A short time later the threesome exited the King's Arms. When the duke excused himself to confer with the headmaster, Ninian offered to take Rosalie to the Fourth Form room, where pupils past and present had carved their names or initials into the wood-paneled walls and on the backs and seats of the benches.

"How many boys attend this school?" she wondered aloud.

"I don't know," he said diffidently. "Two or three hundred."

"You must have many friends."

"My best mates were taken away two years ago. We organized a great rebellion—I stole the key from Peachey the custodian so we could open up the birch cupboard and put the whips they flog us with on the fire. The older boys managed to blockade the road to London. None of the post coaches could reach the school and the masters couldn't write to the parents for days! But after they restored order they became much stricter with us. Now there's no blanket tossing, and we aren't permitted to throw bread at the new boys if they try and enter the hall. That's our private club, where we plot against the masters, and tell jokes. Shall I tell you the one I heard the other day?"

She nodded.

"What man shaves more than ten times a day?"

Rosalie pondered this. "I can't imagine."

"A *barber*," he announced triumphantly, and waited expectantly for her laugh. After she obliged him, he said, "Here's a puzzle for you to solve. Suppose a man standing on the bank of a river has with him a wolf, a goat, and a basket of cabbages. He wants to take them all across with him but his boat is only big enough to carry him and one other thing. Therefore, he must take them over one at a time and in such a way that the wolf has no opportunity to devour the goat, and the goat cannot eat up the cabbages. What should he do?"

"*Nom de Dieu,*" she said helplessly. "It will make my head ache to think of an answer. I'm afraid I'm not very clever."

"Shall I tell you? First, he takes the goat over. Then he returns and takes the wolf, leaving it on the other side. He carries the goat back and leaves it to take his cabbages. Lastly he goes over again to fetch the goat. That way, the wolf is never left with goat, or the goat with the cabbages."

His sudden desire to show Rosalie the lake and games field saved her from another such trial.

The persistent throbbing in her ankle had not troubled her all day, and she suffered no pain during their walk. Though she was gradually warming to the aristocratic youth, she considered him less engaging than Joe Grimaldi, the studious and well-conducted son of the comedian. Lord Swanborough's erratic behavior indicated that he had little in common with her friend Joe.

Some lads tossing a ball near the water's edge waved at him, but he ignored them. "They're in the First Form," he informed Rosalie, lifting his cleft chin in disdain. "Little babies, who cry for their mamas and their nannies."

"What do you do to make them cry?"

"The same things the big boys did to me when I first came here."

"You and your fellows are a pack of bullies," she commented in a voice of disapproval.

"The masters are the bullies," Ninian contradicted, his azure eyes flashing defiance. "The only Trojan at Harrow is Jem Martin, who arranges things for us. He'll find a horse if someone wants to slip away for some hunting, and he looks after *Bluebell*. He just finished painting her for me."

He took her to a small building where cricket bats, footballs, and fishing tackle were stored. In the middle of the unswept floor was a wooden rowboat glistening with a fresh coat of blue paint.

"Next time you come to visit, I'll take you out on the lake," Ninian promised when she'd had ample opportunity to admire his most prized possession.

They found the duke waiting for them in front of the brick house where Ninian lodged. The phaeton was in readiness; the liveried groom held the team of four gray horses.

Although Gervase presented his ward with a half guinea as a parting indulgence, he said sternly, "Your housemaster's story was most damning, and Dr. Butler is so displeased that he gave *me* a lecture. If you hate floggings, Nin, I advise you to conform to the rules of discipline. Your deportment had better alter significantly, or I'll remove you from school and consign you to a tutor's care. I doubt if you'd enjoy that."

"Not much I wouldn't," Ninian growled. "You won't tell Aunt Elizabeth what Dr. Butler said?"

"I haven't decided about that yet."

The duke offered Rosalie his hand, and when she was comfortably settled she said farewell to Lord Swanborough.

"Do come again, mademoiselle," the boy sang out as the carriage rolled along the street.

After successfully negotiating the steep hill upon which the school and village were situated, Gervase said, "I hope he didn't weary you with his tiresome questions."

"Not in the least," she answered promptly. Seeing his frown, she stifled an inquiry about the headmaster's report. His face was so grim that she feared his dissatisfaction with his ward extended to her. She folded her hands in her lap and waited for him to speak again, reluctant to intrude upon his reverie.

Until now he'd exhibited an affability so unforced that she judged it to be habitual; as at their previous meetings, he had treated her courteously and kindly. If she hadn't been aware of his name and title, she would have cause to doubt that he was her social superior. For the first time she was conscious of their differences in background and modes of living, and she marveled that she had ever felt relaxed and easy in his exalted company.

They had traveled a considerable distance in silence when he finally said, "Ninian never had much respect for authority at the best of times. With my father gone and my mother living in Shropshire, he thinks he needn't mind anyone."

"How long has Lord Swanborough been an orphan?"

"He isn't one." Looking over at her, he explained, "Despite the fact that his mother is living, he was left to my parents' care when his father died. Lady Swanborough suffered a mental decline shortly after Ninian's birth and resides at Bath in the care of an eminent physician. Although she has steadily improved, she'll never return to the Abbey or be able to take care of herself—or her son. My cousin Miranda, who married Viscount Cavender at the first of the year, is fond of her brother, yet I can't foist him upon a pair of newlyweds in happy expectation of their first child."

"He is an odd boy," Rosalie acknowledged.

"And always was. Mother and Father ruled me and Edgar and our sisters with a firm hand, but they spoiled Ninian. I've been his guardian since last spring, and at first I believed I would be the one to put a stop to his naughty tricks and curb his tendency to ride roughshod over everyone he meets, but so far I've failed miserably. He still has his way in all things. As you have seen, he's fearfully persuasive."

Eyeing his strong profile, she said, "And yet you don't seem to be a person who is so easily persuaded."

"Not easily, but inevitably." He heaved a sigh. "Have you any advice for me?"

With a regretful shake of her head, she replied, "I never had any brothers or sisters, and my experience of little boys is limited to Joe Grimaldi, who is very good. I am slightly acquainted with Mr. Dibdin's children," she added direly, "and have no desire to know them better. They are all so horrid and noisy that I try to avoid them, and I wish *they* would go away to school."

"Ninian is turning me old before my time," he confided. "He has made himself so odious at Harrow that I shudder to think what sort of mischief he'll tumble into at Oxford or Cambridge."

When he returned her to the house in Owens Row she regretted having to bid him farewell and hoped her feelings weren't apparent to him. His cousin had injected some much-needed excitement into her life, and the duke was the most distinguished gentleman she'd met since coming to England.

Though she judged it unlikely to happen, perhaps they would meet again somewhere. When trying to stage their next encounter she decided it should take place at the opera house, after the most brilliant performance of her career. Her arms would be filled with floral offerings, testimony to her talent and popularity, and he would be exquisite in his evening attire. The sea of her male admirers would slowly part, permitting him to approach her. . . . And then she remembered that such ambitions, professional and personal, were hopelessly unattainable.

She would never succeed in becoming a famous and popular dancer because she lacked her mother's artistry. She might possess a pretty face and a good figure, but she viewed her own charms as less than dazzling and hardly sufficient to attract a handsome duke. And even if they could, in her heart she knew that she would never welcome his advances.

4

A lovely apparition, sent
To be a moment's ornament.
—WILLIAM WORDSWORTH

The leading players at Sadler's Wells enjoyed the traditional perquisite of a benefit performance at the close of the season, and the profits they derived supplemented their weekly earnings. In October the most popular pieces in the repertory were repeated for the purpose of enriching Mr. Grimaldi, Mr. Ridgway, and Mrs. Dibdin. Rosalie maintained an easy friendship with the two actors and hoped their nights would be successful, but her wishes with regard to the manager's wife were rather less charitable.

One day, after her dismissal from rehearsal for a new dance, she was accosted by the company's premier comedian, whom one critic had called a living jest book.

"Miss Rose, I hope you will let me take you home with me for tea and a visit with my wife. I promised her I'd ask—oh, a week ago at least, but till now I've not had the chance." Years of constant grinning had etched deep lines around his mouth and eyes, and they were particularly noticeable when he said soberly, "Our paths seldom cross at rehearsals, and soon as the curtain comes down after the panto I must dash away to the Covent Garden playhouse."

"You'll wear yourself out if you don't take care, sir."

"My Mary says the same—not that she doesn't work just as hard, looking after our young Joe and playing small parts at Drury Lane."

Rosalie gladly accepted his invitation, for she owed Mrs. Grimaldi a visit. Throughout the long walk across the fields, Joseph Grimaldi spared no effort to amuse, and if he was as weary as she was he gave no sign of it.

He'd known many a tragedy during his thirty-two years, the worst of them the loss of his beloved first wife Maria, who died in childbed. In his desperate grief he'd been comforted by the actress Mary Bristow, and she now presided over their modest but comfortable dwelling in Baynes Row. Despite Joseph's reputation for penny-pinching, both he and the second Mrs. Grimaldi tended to live above their means. Their combined salaries from three theaters—Sadler's Wells, Drury Lane, and Covent Garden—barely covered the expenses of a town house, a country property, the horse and gig, and the education of their only son.

Mary ushered her husband and their guest into the parlor and gave the servant orders to bring food and drink. Young Joe, a miniature version of his father, shook hands with Rosalie in his polite fashion. As well as being dark-haired and small for his age, he was agile and quick-witted.

Although Rosalie's envy of her friend's elegant silk gown was tempered by the suspicion that the dressmaker hadn't yet been paid, she was quick to compliment it. Within a short time the tea tray arrived; accustomed to solitary meals, she reveled in the Grimaldis' merry jokes and lively discourse.

Eventually the comedian excused himself and retreated to the room where he kept his butterfly collection and at his mother's urging, Joe scampered back to the nursery. The two ladies then passed a pleasant half hour devoted to theatrical gossip.

After they had voiced their mutual dislike of the Dibdins, Mary said, "Has Joey told you that he has been engaged to perform at the Theatre Royal in Birmingham next month? I was afraid he might miss our son's eighth birthday, but it turns out he needn't leave till after the celebrations. You're coming to Joe's party, I hope?"

"Of course. And you must depend upon me for any assistance you require."

"Thank you, I'll keep it in mind. Well, I daresay the provincial audiences will be delighted to have my husband in their midst, and goodness knows we need the money.

I'm also eager for some news of my sister Louisa. She's with the Birmingham company this season."

"We miss her at the Wells," said Rosalie. "She is by far a better Columbine than Mrs. Dibdin, and charmed her Harlequin off the stage as well as on it. Will Miss Bristow and Jack Bologna make a match of it, do you think?"

The other woman shrugged. "I wish I knew, for I'd like to see her married. And you, too, Rose—it troubles me that you live so alone. But I suspect your circumstances might improve, having heard some intriguing reports of fashionable gents lurking backstage."

With a shake of her head, Rosalie replied, "You were misinformed. It was but one gentleman, far too grand for me, and his ward, only a few years older than your Joe."

Unwilling to boast of so slight an acquaintance, she hadn't discussed the Duke of Solway and Lord Swanborough with anyone and was reluctant to begin now. She had already accepted the unlikelihood of meeting that noble pair again. His lordship's curiosity about her theater had been satisfied, and he had other diversions now that he was at school. And the Sadler's Wells entertainments were not sophisticated enough to turn his guardian into a regular visitor.

Continuing their discussion of professional matters, Mary asked, "Where will you be dancing this winter?"

"I've already found a place at the New Theatre in Tottenham Street and begin rehearsals there within a fortnight. In fact, I'm having a costume fitting with Madame Ferrier this evening. The first ballet is *Flora's Sports*—a pastoral not unlike the one I danced at the Wells this autumn."

"So you won't have to leave Islington after all?"

"It appears not. As yet I've received no summons from Signor Rossi, not any word from d'Egville about returning to the King's Theatre. So you needn't seek another French teacher for Joe," Rosalie added brightly, to cover her disappointment. "Does he still make good progress in his studies?"

Mary Grimaldi beamed her pride in her son's attainments. "Indeed, and he likes his school, which is the same one his papa attended as a boy. He often talks of the time you visited our farm at Finchley to speak French with him, and hopes you will again. Did you know that we're calling the house Tippety Cottage now, after Joey's song? Oh, I *do* hope we can keep the place, being there is so good for him—and all of us."

After promising to return soon, and often, Rosalie left Baynes Row for her appointment with the elderly female who sewed her costumes. Darkness had fallen by the time she reached Madame Ferrier's lodging, a dilapidated house in Pentonville Road. The building was occupied by a variety of tradespeople, and its rooms were as dim and uncomfortable as Rosalie's.

The Frenchwoman, formerly a dresser at the opera house, helped the dancer out of her clothes and into a partly finished stage dress. Constructed from pale green muslin, it had a stomacher front and emerald-colored piping at the seams.

Twitching the full skirts, Rosalie commented, "A modest garment for the ballet. I'm not used to so many petticoats, or so conservative a décolletage."

"Is this not as you wanted, mademoiselle?"

"*Absolument*," she assured the seamstress, "for the audiences at the Tottenham Street theater aren't accustomed to naked limbs and bare bosoms."

"Ah," sighed the Frenchwoman, "I remember well the dresses I made when you were at the King's Theatre. The material thin enough to show *le corps et les jambes,* and draped so one breast was exposed." Her hands moved to Rosalie's waist and she pinched the loose fabric. "You have become thinner."

"Have I?"

The gray head bobbed slowly. "I sewed to your measurements—or as they were in the spring. How shall this be finished? Some gold lace to trim the neck, *peut-être*?"

"I think a tiny cluster of silk flowers just here," said Rosalie, indicating the top of her bodice.

"*Bon.*" Madame's swift, impersonal fingers began unlacing the front panel.

"When will it be ready?" Rosalie asked when she slipped her own gown over her head.

"Within two days. Do you wish a glass of wine before you go, mademoiselle?"

She declined, saying apologetically, "This has been too busy a day. *Je vous assure,* I will stay longer when I return for my costume."

During her solitary walk homeward, she found the Duke of Solway intruding upon her thoughts, as he sometimes did when she was too weary to consider her work or her uncertain future. Apart from being handsome and wealthy, his grace exhibited only a few of the qualities she associated with French noblemen. Rather than flirting with her as though she were a potential conquest, he'd treated her as a rational being, worthy of respect despite her profession. British aristocrats, it seemed, were more democratic in their outlook than the dispossessed nobility of France, because so many of their titles and fortunes were of comparatively recent origin. The present generation of peers had abandoned the rigid social code of their fathers and grandfathers. They made friends of actors, consorted with prizefighters, copied the attire of their grooms, and admired radical politicians. Not unlike the *jeunesse dorée,* the gilded youth of the Directory, who had flaunted the latest fashions in clothing and haunted the Paris theaters as patriotic fervor inspired a greater appreciation for the arts.

Her consideration of the duke gave way to memories of her musician father. He'd instilled in her an appreciation for the rights of all men at a time when his adopted nation had struggled with a concept so alien. For the past eight years she'd lived in his land, one of peace and plenty—and inconsistency. The English admired French clothes and furniture and art, yet to them French people were objects of distrust and ridicule. And even though she was no longer sensitive about the satiric caricatures lampooning France's victorious leader, she hadn't relinquished her innate national pride—or her national guilt.

One of her earliest memories was of the sad, worried face of Marie Antoinette. The most painful one was her mother's tearful announcement of the poor Queen's death.

So many people had perished, and when the horrors of the Revolution were succeeded by the still more heinous acts of the Terror, it had seemed to Rosalie that the end of the world was imminent. Her heart and mind had been loyal to the Royalist cause, even though she had frequently personified the republican spirit on the stage of the Paris Opera. A few creative artists, her mother among them, had flourished: ballets, operas, plays, and paintings had effectively communicated political ideals and rhetoric. Anyone wise or desperate enough to follow the lead of the party in power had been allowed to live and work without hindrance. Thus Rosalie and her parents had managed to survive.

Circumstances had forced her to be a hypocrite, and her conscience was still uneasy about her inability to choose a single side and support it to the death. As she crossed Waterhouse Field, she mourned those who had paid the ultimate price for their convictions. And she feared her failings would disappoint that attractive duke with the wise gray eyes.

"What the devil have you been doing?" Gervase demanded of the individual standing on the threshold of his study.

"Swimming in the Serpentine," replied Ninian, who resembled someone salvaged from a shipwreck rather than a juvenile peer of the realm. He was wet from head to toe, and his thin frame was wrapped in the dark blue coat of a Solway House footman.

"In October?"

The boy shrugged and the coat slipped from his shoulders. Righting it, he replied, "It wasn't so cold as you might think. When the *Victorious* capsized I had to rescue her, and after I was in the water there wasn't much point in coming out straightaway."

Gervase transferred his gaze to Robert the footman, in whose charge Ninian had departed for Hyde Park. "While his lordship changes into some dry clothes, you will explain how this disaster came about."

"It wasn't *his* fault," Ninian stated emphatically before retreating.

Lord Swanborough's expulsion from Harrow had

marked the beginning of the most disruptive and disheartening week of Gervase's experience. He had put off writing an explanatory letter to his mother, not knowing what to tell her. His home was rife with contention; thus far Ninian had offended the chef, frightened the housekeeper, and created an unpleasant scene in a bookshop. Now he'd made a spectacle of himself in Hyde Park.

"Your grace, I would've gone for the boat myself if I'd realized his lordship meant to go in the water. 'Twasn't till I heard the ladies scream that I knew what had happened, he was that quick. They thought he was drowning. One was so shocked that she fainted on the grass. The park keeper tried to make the earl come out, and so did I, but as your grace knows—"

"I know all too well," Gervase said grimly. "I'm sure you did your best, Robert."

"Yes, your grace, and I'll do better next time."

"Grateful though I am for your good intentions, I devoutly hope there won't be a next time."

The footman backed out of the room, his face a study in despondency.

After mulling over the problem of his ward, Gervase concluded that the only way to ensure Ninian was sufficiently prepared for university was to engage a private tutor. Harrow had been his playground and his platform, and during his brief career at that hallowed institution he'd distinguished himself only in his ability to infect other pupils with his waywardness. Loathing all subjects equally, he'd so stubbornly resisted any effort to educate him that his knowledge of Latin and Greek was a disgrace for a boy his age, and his deplorable deficiency in history and mathematics needed to be remedied.

"How does one go about hiring a tutor?" he asked Lord Elston that night when they met at White's Club in St. James's.

"I haven't the foggiest notion," the marquis replied blandly, wandering toward a table in the coffee room. "I should think you advertise. But I can't believe a pasty-faced parson will be able to control young Swanborough any better than you do. Clearly he's a hopeless case—you had better foist him upon the masters of Eton."

"I thought of that," Gervase admitted, "but I should find myself in exactly the same predicament a few months hence. Besides, as an Etonian, I am reluctant to inflict Ninian upon *my* school."

"What about marriage?"

Startled, he stared at his friend. "Whose marriage?"

"Yours, of course. A drastic measure, I agree, but females have a way of imposing order and discipline—so I have inferred from observation."

"I thought you gave up matchmaking after you paired my cousin Miranda with your cousin Justin," Gervase commented, his tone neutral.

"I'm not proposing any particular young lady. I trust you to know who'll suit you best."

Gervase chuckled. "I don't dare leave Ninian unsupervised long enough to go looking for a wife. Besides, there's no certainty that he would approve of my choice. The only female who has ever taken his fancy is that opera dancer, Mademoiselle de Barante. He talks about her all the time. For years he refused to learn anything useful or necessary, but all of a sudden he's adamant about studying French. Says he wants to converse with her in her native tongue so she won't feel homesick. Admirable of him, but quite unnecessary, as she has lived in England for nearly a decade."

Damon commented, "You are rather well informed for one who consistently denies any interest in the lady."

Shaking his head, he replied, "I know next to nothing about her, only that she and Maman danced at the Paris Opera. She uses her mother's surname rather than her father's English one, so I presume she was love-begotten." Seeing his friend's frown, he said in quick defense, "It's not as if it was her fault."

"I quite agree."

"Then why are you scowling?"

"I was remembering how you dragged me to Islington, a vicious act for which you're not yet absolved."

"I didn't notice that you were so very bored," Gervase

retorted. "You said the ballet was as good as you've seen at the King's Theatre."

"*Almost* as good," Damon corrected. "The experience might have been a pleasanter one had it not been soured by that chap Beckmann, who talked me into a stupor."

"Not that I need one, but that's another reason to hire a tutor. He would take on the responsibility of accompanying Ninian to the playhouse. You'll let me know if you hear of a promising individual, won't you?"

"You may depend upon it," the marquis said cordially.

But it was Miranda, Lady Cavender, who discovered the ideal candidate. Gervase, after informing her by letter of her brother's latest scrape, received a reply in the next post. Her ladyship reported that the local vicar's son had taken orders; he was a brilliant scholar who would be without preferment until his father retired from the living. Because Viscount Cavender had no other parish in his gift, and she wondered if Gervase might employ the estimable young man as a secretary or librarian.

Gervase penned a summons to Mr. Jasper Duffield, trusting Miranda to warn him about Lord Swanborough's character and shortcomings, and he provided a bank draft to cover the costs of a journey from Wiltshire to London.

His mind free of care, he spent a pleasant evening at White's, dining and drinking and conversing with his father's friends, who had accepted him into their circle. They were congenial company, if a trifle dull and sedate.

He left St. James's for Solway House close to midnight, and he was astonished to find the senior members of his staff gathered in the entrance hall as if waiting for his arrival. When he relinquished his hat and gloves to Robert, he noticed that the footman's hands were shaking. Parry appeared to be slightly more at ease, but he had a habit of concealing his emotions.

"Your grace," the butler said quietly, "I deeply regret that I must impart some disturbing news."

Gervase's disquiet, which had been in abeyance for several hours, instantly revived. "What has Lord Swanborough done now?"

"He ran away, your grace." Parry dismissed the gaggle

of footmen and housemaids watching from the top of the service stairs, and followed his master to the salon.

"When did you discover that he'd gone missing?" Gervase asked.

"His lordship went up to his room after dinner, carrying your grace's newspaper. Susan, the chambermaid who waits upon him, came to me about an hour ago to report his failure to answer her knock when she wanted to turn down his bed. She and Robert searched all the upstairs rooms. The earl wasn't hiding in the cellars or the mews, or in any of the places we thought likely. I'm afraid he must have left the house on foot, slipping out while the staff and I were dining belowstairs."

"I expect so. Did you say he'd been reading my paper?" After considering this possible clue to his cousin's whereabouts, he said heavily, "Send a message to the carriage house, that John must not unharness the horses yet. I believe I know where Lord Swanborough has gone."

The first item on the Sadler's Wells program that evening had been the ballet. Rosalie, after completing her performance, was pressed into service as dresser to the actresses appearing in the principal entertainment, *The North Briton*. It was a new drama written by Mr. Ridgway, one of the company's leading actors, whom she liked well enough to help in any way he required.

She ignored Mrs. Dibdin's constant carping about an ill-fitting gown, and busied herself by pinning up the lace trim that dangled from Miss Jellet's bodice. For some time afterward, she tried to keep Master Aubun the Infant Phenomenon and little Miss Worgman from getting in the way of the adult players.

When the play was finally over, she helped the ladies out of their dresses, staying behind to hang each costume on its peg. By the time she emerged from the stifling canvas enclosure that served as a dressing room, she looked forward to the day when she'd have one place of employment rather than two. Until Mr. Dibdin dismissed his company later in the week, she must divide her time and her energies between ballet rehearsals at the New Theatre in London and her performances at the playhouse in Islington.

She bade Mr. Wheeler a weary good night at the stage door and left the building. The coachyard was deserted, for the playgoers and the performers had long since departed. To make up for lost time, she diverted from her customary path along the river and took the quicker way across the lawn, pausing occasionally to draw a refreshing chestful of cool air. The stars sparkled and danced in the clear autumn sky, and the elm leaves dislodged by the light breeze wafted gently to the ground.

"Mamselle de Barante!"

Upon hearing a shout behind her she halted abruptly. Turning around, she saw that a gentleman was following her. When he came closer she discovered that he was a stranger, despite his knowledge of her name. His substantial frame was squeezed into a fashionably cut coat and pale, tight pantaloons, and a high collar framed his full face.

Lifting his hat to her, he revealed a crop of fair, curly hair. "Ben Beckmann, your most obedient servant. Pray let me escort you home—so fair a creature shouldn't be walking alone at this hour."

"I'm safer than you imagine," she countered. "The watchmen from the Hatton Garden Magistrate Office patrol the theater grounds at regular intervals."

"Only let me walk with you for a little way then, as far as Islington Road," he pleaded. "I've been wanting to meet you for many weeks. I'm your greatest admirer."

Hoping to dissuade him, she answered, "I'm too fatigued to be good company, sir."

"Oh, I don't care about that. I'll do the talking—in fact, I waited just so I could speak to you. For weeks I've been wanting to ask if I could call upon you. You're my favorite dancer in all London." He paused, then blurted, "Damn it, m'dear, I'd like to be your friend, your very special friend." His pudgy fingers closed around her arm.

The avid light in his eyes alarmed her, and his bulk was intimidating. "Mr. Beckmann, please be kind enough to release me."

"I'm hoping you'll be kind to me. Just one kiss, m'dear, that's all I ask."

As his arm circled her waist, a shadowy figure emerged from the trees and raced forward to deliver a swift and brutal kick to his shin.

"Let her go, or I'll do it again!" the Earl of Swanborough cried militantly, holding up his clenched fists.

A bewildered Rosalie stared at her rescuer. *"Mon Dieu,"* she gasped. "What are you doing here, my lord? You should be at school!"

"The headmaster expelled me."

"No wonder," Mr. Beckmann huffed. "Young devil, I'll teach you go about kicking people!"

"Just try it, you fat baboon," Ninian retorted. "If you move one step closer I'll have you thrown in prison—and don't think I can't. I'm an *earl*!"

Rosalie nearly laughed at the ludicrous expression of chagrin on her admirer's face.

"Call off your watch pup, mamselle," he muttered. "I meant no harm. I just thought we might—" Glaring at Ninian, Mr. Beckmann fell silent.

"If you don't want trouble, you'd better go away now," the boy warned him.

"Indeed he should," agreed a gentleman whose low, controlled voice was familiar to both Rosalie and Ninian. "Or I, too, may resort to violence."

5

Her feet were much too dainty for such tread!
                    —WILLIAM SHAKESPEARE

The duke's arrival alarmed Rosalie no less than had the earl's attack upon her infatuated swain. *"De mal en pis,"* she muttered under her breath, for the situation had most definitely shifted from bad to worse.

To her surprise, he greeted the other gentleman as an acquaintance, saying coolly, "Good evening, Mr. Beckmann. We meet again."

"Oh, hullo there—sorry, but I've forgot your name. Lovell, ain't it?"

"That was my friend. I'm Marchant, and I'm curious to know what you did to excite my cousin."

"He was being nasty to Mademoiselle," growled Ninian, his fists clenched purposefully.

The duke placed a restraining hand upon his shoulder and glanced at Rosalie. "Is that true?" he asked her.

"Lord Swanborough exaggerates," she replied as calmly as she could, thankful that the darkness hid her blush.

"But he tried to kiss you," Ninian protested, "and I knew you didn't want him to. He's too ugly."

Replacing his tall hat upon his woolly head, Mr. Beckmann said, "I'll leave you now, mamselle. But I look forward to continuing our discussion at some other place and time, when we can be more private. Good night, Marchant." He retreated with undignified haste.

Ninian frowned at his guardian and asked with intense displeasure, "How the devil did you find me?"

"Parry told me he'd seen you with my newspaper, and I deduced that its account of some spectacle enticed you here. Have you been enjoying yourself?"

"Not as much as I expected to," the boy said bluntly. "There wasn't a water show tonight, only a melodrama. But Mademoiselle danced."

"My carriage is in the yard of the Myddelton's Head. Wait for me there."

Ninian shook his head. "I want to talk with Mademoiselle."

"Do as I say—*now!*"

The earl's hunched shoulders and hanging head aroused Rosalie's pity and emboldened her to plead for merciful treatment. "Please don't be too severe with him, your grace. He meant well."

"I daresay, but his method of rescue was unnecessarily rude and crude." He studied her silently, then asked, "Have you known Beckmann long?"

Did he suppose she'd courted the gentleman's attentions? Seeking to clarify her integrity, she told him, "I never met the man before tonight. Is he your friend?"

"Hardly that," he replied, his expression grim. "Lord Elston and I shared a box with him when I last had the pleasure of visiting Sadler's Wells."

Rosalie attempted a smile. "Maman used to warn me that attracting unwanted followers was one hazard of our profession."

"Beckmann is not likely to return, but Ninian and I will see you home nonetheless." Before she could protest, he said firmly, "You must let us do what we can to save your precious feet."

He must have been conscious of her discomfiture, for during their walk through the grove he said no more about Mr. Beckmann. As if trying to put her at ease, he asked a few questions about her life in Paris.

"My parents made regular visits there before the unfortunate upheavals made travel to France too dangerous. I wonder if they ever saw your mother dance."

"It is possible. She was many years with the Opera, and so popular a performer that all the most famous artists invited her to sit for them." Looking over at him, she confided, "I am called Rosalie in memory of Monsieur Fragonard's daughter, who died as a child. Like Monsieur Greuze, he was a friend of Maman's and painted her several times, dancing in a grove *en le style de* Boucher. One such picture was very well received—in it she wears a gown like a pink cloud and a garland of roses in her hair. It was titled 'La Belle Delphine.' After my father's death, Maman had to sell all but one of the Fragonards. We needed the money."

"Who has them now?"

"Madame Parisot took one, and Sir George Beaumont bought the other to add to his collection."

"The next time I visit his house in Grosvenor Square, I shall look out for 'La Belle Delphine.'"

"Oh, do you know him?" Coming to a halt, she placed her hand upon his arm. "Perhaps your grace would do me a favor."

"Anything in my power," he responded gallantly.

"I am quite anxious to know whether Sir George also possesses a certain Greuze painting, one called 'Mischief.'"

"What is the subject?"

"Me," she said simply. "As a child I posed for a series of works in which I personified innocence, grace, purity, and mischief. Monsieur Greuze always referred to them as 'La Petite Bergère,' 'La Petite Danseuse,' 'La Petite Ange,' and 'La Petite Gitane.' The critics regarded them as sentimental, and when none found buyers he offered them to my parents. When Maman died and I had to pay her funeral expenses I delivered 'Mischief,' the Gypsy picture, to Mr. Christie. I'm certain it sold because I received a bank draft with his signature. I've always wondered if Sir George acquired it, and I would be so very grateful if you could find out for me."

"I will."

"How kind you are! I can't imagine what it would be, but if there's anything I can ever do for you . . . " As he gazed into her eyes, she ran out of words, and it dawned upon her that he might expect a more tangible reward than mere gratitude.

When he placed his hands on either side of her face, her

heart raced. Then it seemed to cease beating altogether when he leaned closer and gently kissed her lips.

"Now you're thinking I'm as bad as Beckmann," he said, his voice tinged with amusement. "Come along, lest my cousin accuse me of monopolizing you—which I am, to my shame."

This casual apology only made her feel worse. Deeply wounded by his apparent assumption that kisses like the one he'd bestowed were commonplace to her, she accompanied him to the waiting coach.

Lord Swanborough insisted that she take the place beside him, forcing her to sit directly across from the duke, whose speculative gaze was singularly unnerving. At the end of their short drive, the earl bounded out to unfold the steps for her, holding out his hand to assist her descent.

Still flustered by his grace's watchful presence, she misjudged the distance from the bottom step to the pavement and lost her balance. Her right foot paid the price.

Immobilized by pain, she summoned a false, stiff smile in response to his lordship's effusive farewells. After waiting for the carriage to turn the corner of Islington Road, she hobbled over to the area railing, which provided necessary support as she began a slow and agonizing progress toward the door.

Worse than her physical discomfort was the blood-chilling realization that if she couldn't walk, she would definitely be unable to dance.

The effort of entering the house made her weak and queasy. The looming staircase presented a trial she was not at all prepared to meet, for her ears were ringing and tiny pinpoints of light had begun to cloud her vision. Sinking down upon the bottom step, she closed her eyes. How could she ever rehearse that new ballet at the Tottenham Street theater tomorrow?

From far away she could hear Peg's panicked shriek. "Come quick, someone—oh, do *hurry*! Miss Rose has fainted away!"

The Tower guns fired at midday on the twenty-fifth of the month, which concluded the King's fiftieth year on the throne.

The celebrations marking His Majesty's achievement were less ostentatious than those of the previous October. A commemorative medal had been struck and festive bunting was draped in public places; patriotic persons stuck wreaths of laurel on their hats, and children gathered in the park to set off squibs and firecrackers. But most of the shops remained open, and the King's failure to show himself in Windsor or London lent credence to the rumor that Princess Amelia, his most beloved daughter, was gravely ill.

In the evening the Duke of Solway and Lord Elston attended a Jubilee Ball at the Argyle Rooms and discovered that the sad story making the rounds of the ballroom had cast a pall over the event. Gervase was more perturbed by the arrival of Lady Titus, the widow with whom he had dallied the previous year.

Her spectacular beauty had helped her to overcome the defects of common birth and an early marriage to an obscure army officer, and during her first widowhood she'd been mildly notorious for her liaisons. Eventually she enticed the elderly Sir Algernon Titus to the altar, only to lose him a few weeks later when he was mortally wounded in a duel with Lord Blythe—her former lover—who had subsequently wed Gervase's cousin Nerissa.

Even though she was no less lovely than he remembered and her brown eyes were still soft and inviting, the lavishly endowed body tempted him no longer. Her betrayal of his trust had slain his passion and his affection in one terrible blow. When he saw her coming out of the supper room on the arm of her latest cavalier, a uniformed Guardsman, he was comforted by his indifference and accepted it as proof that his recovery was complete.

He made no attempt to avoid meeting her in the overcrowded ballroom, and even entered into a discussion about the royal family.

According to Lady Titus, who had heard it from her Guards officer, a London jeweler had been dispatched to Windsor Castle by royal command. "Princess Amelia wished to have a choice stone set in a ring as a last gift to her poor papa, with the inscription, 'Remember me when I am gone.'"

The musicians struck up the tune of a popular dance, and she regarded him hopefully, prompting Gervase to say, "You must ask Damon to partner you. I still mourn my father."

"It makes no difference," she said tartly, "for I lost my taste for dancing after you deserted me."

"No reproaches, Georgiana."

"But you never allowed me to explain, or to defend myself."

"I don't need explanations."

"Gervase," she continued relentlessly, "I feared that your parents had persuaded you to cast me off!"

"And rather than waiting to find out the truth, you took advantage of an opportunity to be unfaithful to me. Are you so determined to review what happened that night? You never used to care for ancient history."

She lifted her golden head, saying pensively, "I have never ceased to regret my actions, and would welcome the chance to make amends."

"I'm afraid you'll have scant opportunity, for I won't be in town much longer. I'm departing for Northamptonshire immediately after my debut in the House of Lords and don't expect to return before spring."

Her chin shot higher, and in a threatening tone she declared, "Then I shall rely upon Lord Elston for consolation during your absence."

"Be warned, Georgiana, he also requires fidelity from a mistress. You don't want to make that fatal mistake again."

Accepting the failure of her attempt to rouse his jealousy, she said with artful carelessness, "Have a pleasant journey, your grace. I daresay we shall next meet during the season."

He related the substance of this conversation to the marquis later while they shared a bottle of cognac from the Elston House cellars.

"She's a damnably attractive woman, despite her lack of sound judgment," Damon opined. "I've always been fond of Georgiana, but I do pity her. To think that she might have been your duchess, had she behaved herself!"

Gervase shuddered. "I was a fool to consider marriage."

"It's no wonder she was casting out lures tonight. You are a very notable *parti*—there are so few bachelor dukes below the age of fifty. But your fortune is probably a greater attraction to Georgiana than the title. She has very little money and far too many debts, with only her house in Clifford Street as a token of Algy's misplaced affection."

Determined to change the subject, Gervase asked, "Are you still so friendly with that set of art connoisseurs as you used to be?"

"I only tolerate Thomas Hope, but remain on reasonably good terms with Sir George Beaumont. Why should you want to know?"

"I'm trying to locate a Greuze painting of a young Gypsy titled 'Mischief.' I'd like to buy it."

"If you're setting up as a collector of French pictures, I can put you in the way of acquiring a charming Watteau that will soon be offered for private sale. It's a better value than some insignificant Greuze."

"I'm not making an investment." Meeting his friend's curious stare, Gervase explained, "I intend to restore it to the former owner." Precisely why he was so determined to spend heaven only knew how many hundred guineas on a gift for a dancing girl, he wasn't prepared to admit. He didn't entirely understand it himself.

By organizing and regulating Lord Swanborough's days and nights, Mr. Jasper Duffield had earned the respect of Gervase and all his servants. The hitherto ungovernable youth rose at a respectable hour—earlier by far than his guardian did—and spent two hours at his studies before having a late breakfast. He and his new tutor were generally absent from Solway House during the afternoon, and by evening his energies were sufficiently depleted to make him an unexceptionable companion.

Arriving in the dining room one morning, Gervase cast a benign smile upon the bespectacled young man who had restored peace to his household. "Good day, Mr. Duffield. I'm eager to hear your report of yesterday's edifying excursion."

Ninian speared a large portion of bacon with his fork.

"We saw the Elgin marbles. Antiquities are terribly important, aren't they, Jap?"

"Indeed, my lord, and I'm happy that you've learned to share that opinion." The brown-haired gentleman laughed more often than might be expected of a tutor, one reason that his first week as Lord Swanborough's preceptor and chief companion had been a triumph. By dispensing with formality he'd been able to keep his pupil's attention, and the instructive rambles in and around London had been both entertaining and enlightening.

"Just remember," Ninian added slyly, "I only went because you agreed to take me someplace *I'd* like to visit. I've made up my mind to take you to Sadler's Wells so you can meet Mademoiselle."

"The theater has closed for the season," said Gervase.

His resolution unimpaired by that bit of information, Ninian responded, "Then Jap and I will take her to the spa gardens." Turning to Mr. Duffield, he added, "Mademoiselle may be French, but she's very nice. *And* pretty."

"So I understand, my lord. If you've finished your tea, you may return to the schoolroom to continue writing your essay."

After a final swallow, Ninian set down his empty cup and abandoned the table. He not only obeyed the gentleman's instruction, he did so without argument and that, thought Gervase, was a great improvement.

"Am I permitted to take his lordship to Islington, your grace?" Mr. Duffield asked his employer. "It would certainly be possible to combine a tour of the New River waterworks system with a lesson about Roman aqueducts."

"How inventive," Gervase said approvingly. "No, I don't object to Islington, but Ninian mustn't disturb Mademoiselle de Barante. If he insists upon visiting her, you might remind him that she rehearses during the day."

Gervase, sharing his ward's preoccupation with the dancer, had also been tempted to call upon her. His failure to do so was rooted in guilt over his behavior at their last meeting. Kissing her had been no great crime, he argued to himself, but he couldn't quite shake off the suspicion that she'd regarded it as one. Finding her precious painting and returning it to her, whatever the cost, seemed the most suitable means of making amends.

He retreated to his library, where the morning paper awaited him. All the news from Windsor was bad, for the King, after receiving the engraved ring from his dying daughter's hand, had succumbed to sobs and tears. Since then he had reportedly been "unwell"—a suspicious epithet and one alarmingly reminiscent of his former spells of madness.

The royal physicians issued regular bulletins describing His Majesty's health, and as the week progressed they abandoned any attempt to conceal the unhappy truth. The fearsome malady had recurred, and the King's anxiety about Princess Amelia had plunged him into a dangerously volatile state.

Parliament convened at Westminster on the first of November, despite the fact the monarch was unable to sign a commission to extend prorogation, or carry out the duty of addressing both houses. The government crisis intensified on the following day, when Princess Amelia's sufferings ended. Her father's illness was by then so far advanced that his recovery was in doubt, and the Lords and Commons could only vote upon a proposed adjournment of a fortnight. In the interim the Whigs closed ranks around the Prince of Wales and clamored for a Regency bill, while the Tories interviewed the doctors again and again in the hopes that they would give the favorable report that might forestall so drastic a measure.

Denied his formal presentation to the Upper House and lacking a strong motive for remaining in London, Gervase fell prey to the long-suppressed urge to travel to Haberdine Castle. The political debates being waged in the gentlemen's clubs and the ladies' drawing rooms could not compete with the bucolic delights of Northamptonshire. Privately he believed that a Regency was inevitable, but he preferred to keep his opinions about it to himself until he was required to cast a vote.

One gloomy afternoon while he was out exercising his grays, a whim prompted him to drive in the direction of Islington. As the phaeton approached Owens Row, he wondered about the chances of finding Rosalie de Barante at home.

Gently twitching the reins, he guided his horses into a turn. Seeking to justify the visit to himself, he decided that he required some additional information about the missing Greuze canvas to assist his search.

He halted before her lodging house and left his team in the groom's capable hands. He approached the door, tapping it with the silver butt of his whip, and after a lengthy interval a pale, scrawny maidservant appeared.

"Can you tell me if Mademoiselle de Barante is receiving visitors today?" he inquired.

"Miss Rose? She's gone away, sir."

"When do you expect her to return?"

The girl stared at him blankly. "She never said she would. I'm hoping she *does* come back, but I don't think she'll want to, not if she can't dance anymore."

"Is she ill?"

"That's what I feared when I found her lying at the bottom of the staircase," she replied obscurely. " 'Twasn't till after the mistress sent for the doctor that we learned Miss Rose had sprained her ankle. She never told us how. After keeping to her bed for a week or more, she made me pack up her trunks and send them to the mail coach office. As far as I know, she left town that very evening, with her right foot still wrapped in a bandage."

If only he'd allowed Ninian to visit her, Gervase thought with dismay, or done so himself, he would have learned about this tragedy. "Haven't you some idea where she may have gone?"

"Not I, sir. The clown's wife—Mrs. Grimaldi—sometimes sat with her, she might know. The other performers living here weren't that friendly to Miss Rose, so she wouldn't have told them nothing."

"If you don't mind, I'd like to come inside and talk with you. What's your name?"

"Peg Reilly," she answered as he entered the vestibule. "I always carried Miss Rose's breakfast to her, and looked after her rooms. They've not been let to no one else yet, if you'd like to have a look."

"I would, thank you."

"She took away all that was hers—the flower vase and the prints and the little china statue of her mum." Peg preceded him up the narrow staircase. "She was French, you know—*is* French," she corrected herself. "I mustn't speak as if she's dead, though I do think she wanted to be at first. Once I found her crying, and it wasn't just from the pain. I never saw her look so sad, not even when she used to tell me about the guillotine."

Gervase halted on the topmost step. "The guillotine?"

"And the murders. When she lived in Paris, one of her friends was stabbed with a knife when he was sitting in the bath—at least, I think she knew him. Some of them she knew, and some she didn't." Pausing before a door halfway down the corridor, she opened it and said, "You may go in, sir."

He was appalled at the small sitting room and the meanness of its furnishings—a scarred tea table, a couple of plain chairs, and a sofa with faded upholstery. Floorboards creaked beneath him as he moved about. After a cursory examination of the only other chamber, in which he found a bed, a cracked mirror, and a wardrobe that had seen better days, he returned to the shabby parlor.

It pained him to discover that the lovely, vital dancer had lived in such drab and dismal surroundings. The relief of knowing that she had escaped the squalor would have been great if he could be sure that she'd found a more comfortable refuge. The concern that it might even be worse gnawed at his conscience.

The expression on Peg Reilly's plain face was sad and worried, corresponding exactly with his own emotions.

Feigning absolute confidence, he declared, "I'll find her, never fear, wherever she has gone. And now, if you please, I'd like to know where Mrs. Grimaldi lives."

6

Fallen from her glory, and too weak to rise.
—WILLIAM COWPER

Rosalie eyed the knitting needles hopelessly, trying to summon the courage to pick them up again. Her unfinished handiwork was lumpy and ill-formed, resembling something altogether different from the stocking it was meant to be. Not even the most desperate mendicant, she thought glumly, would welcome such a gift.

Drawing her shawl closer about her shoulders, she realized that the parlor seemed colder because the fire was dying. She grasped the poker and wielded it with the energy of one who had been sedentary for a fortnight, but her efforts produced more smoke than flame. In Gloucestershire wood was cheaper and more readily available than the coals she'd been accustomed to in London; ensuring that the logs burned properly could be a tricky business.

Her ineffectual stabbing and prodding ceased when a middle-aged woman whose white cap concealed most of her graying blond hair entered the room and intoned, "What do you think you're doing?"

"Stirring the fire," she answered meekly.

"I left you that handbell for a reason, Rosie."

"But Annie is too deaf to hear it, and I refuse to summon my only aunt like a servant."

"Better that than setting the house afire, which you're in danger of doing. Give me the poker."

After Rosalie surrendered it, her relation knelt down to remedy the damage. "There now," she said with satisfaction as she worked the bellows. "If you aren't warm again in a few minutes, I can fetch a blanket."

"Thank you, Aunt Tilda." With a regretful smile, Rosalie held up the lump of coarse wool. "You see how poorly I'm getting on with this. Should I pull it apart and begin again?"

Shaking her head, Matilda Lovegrove answered, "Best give it up as a bad idea. You needn't repine, because I never expected you to take on my work. This is supposed to be a holiday."

Rosalie made a face.

"You need a good rest, Rosie. If you'd taken better care of yourself, that ankle wouldn't have been damaged so severely. Didn't the doctor say that you aggravated an earlier sprain which never healed properly?"

"The doctor said a great many things." She studied her right foot, bound with a strip of linen and resting on a hassock.

Matilda patted her shoulder. "There's no need to fall into one of your despairing moods just because I'm determined to keep you chairbound for another few days. I know I sound like a crotchety spinster, soured by too many years of teaching flighty, ignorant young women, but I believe you should stay off that ankle for as long as possible. You're young and strong, and you'll dance again."

"But not in time for the opera season." Rosalie could feel tears of frustration gathering. During her long period of inactivity she'd had time to think too many gloomy thoughts, mostly about the seeming impossibility of rejoining the prestigious ballet company belonging to the King's Theatre.

Her dismal journey from London's General Post Office had begun at eight o'clock one cold November evening. After rocking and jolting past innumerable towns and hamlets, the mail coach reached Oxford, and two hours later a sleepy Rosalie had boarded the Bristol coach for Gloucestershire. The early morning fog had filled the valleys between the Cotswold hills, and her despair had deepened at the sight of bare tree limbs, and the clouded sky; even the sheep along the roadside had looked gray and unattractive. Half faint from sitting up all night, she had hired a post chaise in Fairford, where the mail set her down, and during her journey to Bibury she had wished for a hot brick to warm her feet.

She had astounded her aunt by limping up to the door, pale and tired. Chilled to the marrow of her bones, she had desperately needed Matilda's firm, fond embrace and repeated assurances that all would be well.

Both ladies were descended from a prosperous landholder who left his farmhouse early in the last century and settled in Bibury, where he acquired a dwelling appropriate to his social and financial standing. When Mr. Lovegrove's grandson David demonstrated an aptitude for the violin, he'd sent the boy to the best teachers he could afford, first in London, then in Paris. Matilda, blessed with a golden voice, also received musical instruction but her parents had opposed her plan to sing professionally. In her girlhood she'd been allowed to perform at private gatherings, eventually accepting the position of voice instructress at a select female seminary in Bristol.

Her acquaintance with her niece began when David Lovegrove first brought his French wife and thirteen-year-old daughter to Bibury to meet his family, and subsequent encounters had taken place in sickrooms and at funerals. Matilda hadn't resigned her teaching position until after both her parents were dead, at which time she took possession of their house on the banks of the River Colne. She'd offered to share it with her widowed sister-in-law, but Delphine de Barante, entirely devoted to furthering Rosalie's dancing career, had been reluctant to leave London for a remote Cotswold village. So the spinster lived alone, supported by her own savings and the annual rents from the Lovegrove farms. On Sundays she walked to St. Mary's Church to take her place in the family pew, and during the week she kept busy gardening and calling upon her neighbors, and each year she invited friends from Bristol to join her for the Bibury Races.

"I don't want you to make the same mistake I did when I was about your age," the older woman went on. "I was supposed to sing at a party, and when I took a cold in the head I only made it worse by continuing to practice. I was able to perform, but not as brilliantly as I'd intended. Let that be a lesson to you."

"Signor Rossi *does* expect brilliance in his dancers," Rosalie interjected. "A few weeks ago I might have convinced him that I could meet the standard of perfection set by Armand Vestris and Oscar Byrne and Signorina Angiolini. Not now. Perhaps never. Oh, I wish I'd never become a dancer!" she cried pettishly.

"Do you think you would prefer the humdrum existence of most married women, or being an old maid like me?"

"I don't know, but I wouldn't mind having a *soupçon* of your Lovegrove respectability," she admitted.

"Whatever can you mean?" her aunt wondered.

"I've become a target for presumptuous gentlemen," she confessed. "On the night of my accident I was preyed upon twice. First by a rude stranger, and then by—by an acquaintance of mine. You can't imagine how distressing it was."

"Well, my face never inspired any painters, but I had my fair share of admirers. Lord, how long ago it seems." Moving to the window, Matilda pulled back the wooden shutters, then turned to say with fond pride, "Lovely as you are, I can't be surprised that a pair of bold young bucks would court your favors. Who were they?"

"The rude one was Mr. Beckmann. Fortunately Lord Swanborough, the boy I've been telling you about, chased him away. As for the other man—well, I may have been partly to blame for what he did." Rosalie's lips curled in a reminiscent smile. "*Entre nous,* I haven't much experience managing gentlemen. Maman scarcely let me out of her sight when we first lived in London. She accompanied me to classes and rehearsals and was always backstage during performances at the opera house. In Islington I've been fairly safe, because Mr. Dibdin is so opposed to his actresses and dancers having followers. Not that I want any," she added. "I intend to keep my promise to Papa."

"You haven't been tempted to break it yet," Matilda said shrewdly.

"*N'importe.* My will is very strong, and I learned early the discipline of keeping a vow. I attended a convent school, until it was burned down, and my godfather was an *abbé*."

"By all accounts he was a shockingly worldly man, despite his calling."

"True," Rosalie acknowledged.

"David really should have taken you to church after he brought you to England."

"Sometimes he did—so I could hear the organ music!"

"As far as I can tell, despite your vow of chastity you're not a proper Papist, and you're a most improper Anglican. To you, the only difference between a Roman priest and an English parson is that one can't marry and the other can. The result of your religious upbringing is deplorable."

"Papa was a freethinker," Rosalie said in defense. "He used to say that good and evil were concepts, not absolutes, and that what is right for one person could be entirely wrong for another."

"Evidently his morals became muddled after so many years of living in a country run by radicals and atheists."

"But he did believe that some sort of religious faith was better than none at all. He also said any document outlining the Rights of Man should grant a person the freedom to choose his church as well as his government. It's a wonder he was never thrown into prison," she said thoughtfully, "for he wasn't one to keep his opinions to himself."

Matilda laughed. "A Lovegrove trait, I'm afraid. And here's my opinion—you should put that pitiful piece of knitting aside. Your spirits need lifting, not lowering, so I'm going to fetch that novel one of my neighbors loaned me."

Rosalie did as she was told. But her troubled mind refused to concentrate on Miss Owenson's tale. For a long time the book lay upon her lap untouched while she stared at the flames leaping in the grate.

For too many weeks she'd ignored that recurring pain in her ankle, hoping regular exercise would have a beneficial rather than harmful effect. Now she was forced to acknowledge the truth of Matilda's accusation that her injury was worse and her recovery slow because her joint had been in poor condition. And the cure was even more dangerous than the sprain itself, because prolonged inactivity was a dancer's greatest enemy. Already her arms were growing weak from disuse, and when she flexed the muscles of her thighs and calves, they were no longer taut and firm.

Yet even if she never performed again, her body would retain the structure imposed upon it by years of training. Her legs were permanently and unnaturally turned out from the hips, forcing her arched feet to point diagonally rather than straight ahead.

The quiet and calm of Bibury made her restless, and the foretaste of her future depressed her. Day after day she sat in her invalid's chair by the parlor window, and when she wearied of gazing at the view of river and corn mill she watched the arrivals and departures in the adjacent innyard. She pined for the excitement of London—the busy streets crammed with carriages, the shops whose goods were beyond her means, the theaters where she had performed.

Frowning down at her bandaged ankle, she prayed that a few more years of dancing were left to her. To give up her work, to lose her only talent at twenty-one, was a fate too dreadful to contemplate.

Bibury, which lay at the center of a triangle formed by the larger towns of Northleach, Fairford, and Cirencester, possessed a Jacobean manor house, an ancient church crowned by a square bell tower, and a tidy inn. The Swan and its outbuildings stretched along one bank of the slow-moving River Colne, spanned by a solid stone bridge with a triple arch.

The landlord, impressed by the private traveling carriage at his front door, stated his hope that Gervase would be stopping for the night. "Or do you require horses for the next stage to Gloucester, sir?" he inquired, proudly indicating his large stable and coach house.

"I'm not positive about my precise plans," Gervase replied. "But my postilions require food and drink, also my valet."

"And for yourself, sir?"

"I want nothing at the moment, for I must first call upon Mademoiselle de Barante. Perhaps you are acquainted with her?"

The landlord shook his balding head. "Can't say I know anyone of that name."

"Has *any* young lady lately come here from London?"

"Miss Lovegrove has her niece to stay, and I've heard she lives near London. Works at a theater, though you wouldn't think it to look at her. Such a quiet little thing she is. Always was."

"Where might I find Miss Lovegrove's house?"

The man directed Gervase to the dwelling adjacent to the inn, which was built from the same pale weathered stone. It had tall chimneys at either end, sash windows, and a slate roof. Trusting the efficient Webster to reveal his identity to the proprietor of the Swan and its staff, he left the inn.

Well-tended shrubbery encroached upon the Lovegrove door, and the brass knocker gleamed from a thorough polishing. The spare, elderly female who answered his determined rap had difficulty hearing or understanding him. After he repeated his request to speak with Mademoiselle de Barante, she bade him enter and mumbled that she would fetch her mistress.

Despite its simplicity, the furniture was well made, with the patina that resulted from decades of careful attention. In the parlor, a cosy room with thick wooden beams and a colorful Persian carpet, he found substantial proof that he'd come to the right house. Four oil paintings hung upon the walls, and three were studies of a girl whose delicate features, golden brown curls, and melting eyes were so accurately limned that she was instantly recognizable.

In one oval-shaped portrait the young Rosalie cradled a lamb, her draperies arranged to reveal one budding breast. Another canvas depicted her as a pink-cheeked cherub with fluffy white wings. The third was a full-length portrait of her in a ballet costume.

Gervase recognized the fourth and largest painting as the work of Fragonard. A smiling brunette lady whom he knew to be Delphine de Barante held up her frothy blue skirts to show off her shapely ankles and pointed toes.

Hearing footsteps, he turned hopefully toward the door.

A tall woman stepped into the room, her expression not entirely welcoming. "I am Matilda Lovegrove," she informed him. "Annie says you asked to see my niece. May I ask how you knew she was here?"

"Her friend Mrs. Grimaldi told me."

"Pray be seated, sir," she said in a dry voice. "There is something I must make you understand."

Her eyebrows drew together, reminding him of the stern governess who had terrorized his sisters, and he did as she commanded.

"As my only brother's only child, Rosie is very dear to me. She is neither friendless nor helpless, and I warn you, I won't stand idly by and let some unprincipled man of the town plague her half to death. Yes, she confided in me, I know very well how distasteful your advances are to her. If you seek a mistress, sir, you would do better to court a less respectable dancer."

"I don't—and I didn't follow her to Bibury to make advances," he said adamantly.

"I'm not finished," she interrupted, her eyes glinting. "I can tell from your dress and your demeanor that you were born a gentleman. Let me tell you, sir, lurking in the dark and *pouncing* on a young female is hardly my notion of gentlemanly behavior!"

"Before you reach for your birch rod, ma'am, let me assure you that I am not Benjamin Beckmann. Mademoiselle de Barante can corroborate it."

"In this part of the world she is called Miss Lovegrove," Matilda corrected him. "Who are you, then?"

"Gervase Marchant, but like your niece I often employ a different style. I'm also known as the Duke of Solway."

The effect of this speech was not what he had hoped or expected, for Miss Matilda Lovegrove continued to frown at him. But the violence of her antagonism abated, and gave way to a semblance of civility. "I hope your grace will overlook my rudeness, not that your rank would excuse your behavior if you *had* been chasing after her."

"I'm not," Gervase said smoothly. "My interest in Mademoiselle de Barante—or Miss Lovegrove, as you prefer—is charitable rather than dishonorable. I feel a certain responsibility for the accident which caused her to lose her place at the Tottenham Street playhouse. My cousin, who is also my ward, precipitated it."

"Her ankle is much better, and I trust she'll be back on the stage by Candlemas. Sooner, if she has her way."

"But I didn't come only to inquire about her recovery," he went on. "I'd rather tell her the other reason in private, if you will permit."

She pressed her lips firmly together as she considered his request. "I suppose I can't object to that," she said at last, "so long as Rosie doesn't mind. She's lying down in her room just now."

Climbing to his feet, Gervase said, "I don't wish to disturb her rest. Should I return later?"

For the first time, the woman smiled at him. "That is most considerate, your grace, but I can't imagine she would thank me for sending you away. If your grace will excuse me for a moment, I'll tell her you've come."

Within a few minutes she was ushering him up the staircase and into a spacious chamber that was a vast improvement over the cramped rooms of the Islington lodging house. The green curtains at the windows and around the bed complemented a set of tapestry-covered chairs. Rosalie occupied the windowseat, a patchwork blanket draped across her lower body. Loose brown curls framed a face much paler than Gervase remembered, or could approve.

"Here's your visitor, Rosie," Matilda Lovegrove announced before withdrawing.

As the young woman began to rise he said quickly, "Please don't get up."

Complying with his wish, she sank back against the pillows. "I regret that your grace felt it necessary to journey into Gloucestershire on my account."

"As I'm on my way to Pontesbury, my Shropshire estate, it was easily arranged. But had it required a much greater effort, I would have found you." After accepting her invitation to be seated, he said, "I wish I'd learned about your mishap sooner than I did."

"In truth, I was reluctant to tell anyone," she replied. "If James d'Egville or Signor Rossi heard about my sprain they would consider me spoiled goods, to the detriment of my future career. So I left London as soon as I was able to travel."

"Yes, I found that out when I visited your lodging house. Peg Reilly was ignorant of your whereabouts, but she directed me to Mrs. Grimaldi. I understand that you were hurt when Ninian helped you down from my carriage."

"I should have been more careful."

"That you weren't is partly my fault, I think," he told her gravely. "I distressed you that night, didn't I?" When she looked away, thereby confirming his conjecture, he went on, "My pride has received blow upon blow since then. I accept that you might conceal your acquaintance with a duke from Peg, and I don't know to what extent Mrs. Grimaldi is in your confidence. But the fact that you failed to mention me to your aunt is only slightly less wounding than her suspicion that I was Benjamin Beckmann!"

Still avoiding his eye, she toyed with a corner of the blanket. "To link your name with mine, however innocently, was too great a risk. Gossip, even when untrue, can do a great deal of damage."

"I commend your good sense, Miss Lovegrove." When she glanced up in surprise, he said, "I've been told I must call you so, here in Bibury."

"This was Papa's home, and the local people would think it odd if I didn't acknowledge my parentage. Maman was always Mrs. Lovegrove whenever we came here to visit. It used to make her laugh whenever she heard her rightful title, she was so unaccustomed to it."

"They were married, your parents?"

"But of course."

"Yet you use the surname de Barante."

"I did so at the urging of my mother, who wanted me to benefit from her fame. Your grace isn't the first to assume that I'm baseborn. Several Sadler's Wells performers are— Mr. Grimaldi, Master Carey, even our strict and stuffy Mr. Dibdin." Eyeing him curiously, she said, "Aunt Tilda told me you wanted to discuss a private matter."

"I do—thank you for the reminder. Miss Lovegrove, I have a proposition to lay before you. When Mrs. Grimaldi told me, among other things, that you have been teaching

French to her son, it occurred to me that you might take on the task of instructing Ninian in that language."

"Does his lordship *wish* to study French?"

"He has said so, provided you consent to be his teacher."

"But I've never been bookish, and I'm not at all clever. I can't imagine that I would be very effective in a schoolroom."

"This wold be a temporary appointment," he elaborated, "lasting only until you are well enough to rejoin the ballet company. Ninian and his new tutor, an excellent man, are presently at Haberdine Castle and will remain there through the winter. Naturally I would cover the expenses of your journey to Northamptonshire to join them, and also pay for your return to London when you feel ready to dance again. And you'll receive a generous salary."

"Hardship pay?" she asked suspiciously.

Smiling, he answered, "I won't deny that Ninian can be a difficult charge, but I feel sure you'll be a good influence on him. He said I must tell you that he'll *try* to behave himself. Because he and I are largely responsible for your present difficulties, we decided that we owe you an alternate form of employment. I ask only that you consider my offer, for I'm not here to press you into making a hasty decision. May I call upon you tomorrow—not to hear your answer necessarily, but to see how you go on?"

"If—if you wish," she said hesitantly. "It is your grace's intention to remain in Bibury, then?"

"Judging by appearances, this is a charming place to break a journey."

"It is certainly quiet," she conceded.

"That will suit me very well. During my university days I visited this district on a fishing holiday, and we spent a most enjoyable week at Fairford. I suspect there's equally fine sport to be had in your river, provided I can beg or borrow some tackle."

Her gaze wavered again at his approach, and faint color tinted her cheeks when he extended his hand, saying, "Till tomorrow, Miss Lovegrove."

A quarter of an hour later Gervase was installed in a comfortable chamber in the quiet wing of the Swan Inn, which had the added advantage of facing the windows of Rosalie Lovegrove's bedroom. He recognized her green curtains.

The landlord, discomposed by his guest's exalted title, sought assurance that the accommodation was satisfactory. "I had the great honor of serving tea to the duchess, your grace's mother, several years ago," he informed Gervase proudly. "She stopped for refreshment and a change of horses."

"I should like to cast for trout tomorrow, if the weather permits. Would it be possible to arrange the loan of a fishing rod?" Gervase asked him.

"Indeed, your grace, I'd be honored if you used mine," the man offered. "And my lures as well."

"You are most generous, but I prefer tying my own. I rely on you to direct my man Webster to a shop where he can procure the necessary materials."

After a respectable supper of roast capon and pigeon pie, Gervase set to work. Webster had obtained silver and gold thread from the village seamstress, and the landlord's wife had provided needles, scissors, sealing wax, and some rust-colored feathers plucked from the fowl she had sacrificed for his dinner. Gervase applied himself to the familiar task, his eyes unwavering and his brow furrowed in concentration as he assembled the bits and pieces into careful copies of plain hackles and great duns and palmer flies.

His mind was as busy as his fingers. A thoughtful assessment of his brief interview with the dancer led him to the conclusion that she would probably turn down the position he'd offered. And that one imprudent, impetuous kiss would, he suspected, be the reason for her refusal. Somehow he must find a way to allay her concerns about his intentions.

She hadn't admitted to holding him or Ninian responsible for her plight, but he'd read the truth of it in her mobile face. And though she had maintained her composure at his false impression of her illegitimacy, she had surely been pained by it.

So much of her life, past and present, was still a mystery to him, but to court her confidences would be to risk involving himself. She was a curiosity, and a beautiful one at that, but for both of their sakes he would have to remain detached, he told himself, replacing the unused hooks in the landlord's well-stocked tackle box.

After extinguishing the branch of candles, he moved to his window to stare at the one across the way, curtained and lit like a miniature stage. He stood there until he caught a tantalizing glimpse of Rosalie in her nightgown, then backed away so she wouldn't see him spying on her.

Did she braid her hair before retiring, or did she bundle it into a bedcap? While he readied himself for his own repose, he pondered the insoluble question, which teased him until he finally drifted off to sleep.

7

Footing it in the dance that fancy leads.
—WILLIAM COWPER

By the following morning the Lovegrove ladies were still discussing the Duke of Solway's remarkable visit, and its purpose. Matilda shared Rosalie's view that his grace's offer of employment was an act of charity but disagreed that as such it should be refused outright.

"After you went to bed I studied his family in my father's old *Debrett's*," she said, her knitting needles clicking busily. "The Marchant lineage is most impressive, going back to the Tudors and the Stuarts. Your duke is eight-and-twenty, with a brother, Edgar, and two sisters called Imogen and Ophelia. Do they also live at this castle of his?"

"The sisters must be married," Rosalie replied. "Lord Edgar Marchant serves in the Peninsular army."

"I also found an engraving of Haberdine Castle in a book of views, and it looks to be a grand old pile. I must admit, it would be a nice change of scene for you. The little earl may not be a model of deportment, but he can't be much worse than the stage children you've known. And afterward you'd be entitled to an employment reference, which might be useful."

"Signor Rossi won't care for that."

"One never knows," Matilda said sagely. "Of course, you needn't work at all if you don't care to, for I'd gladly keep you here with me. This house and all the tenanted farmland will belong to you someday, and I can think of no good reason why you shouldn't enjoy the benefits during my lifetime. If you want to stay, that is, and I don't think you do." Watching Rosalie flex her foot, now free of its bandage, she added, "The dance has ever been your obsession. I remember Davey used to say you wanted to dance before you ever learned how to walk."

"He spoke the truth," Rosalie admitted, almost apologetically.

"Still," her aunt went on, "you should go to Northamptonshire, if only till the New Year. Look on it as a holiday, your chance to see more of the world than the interior of a theater or an opera house. You cannot reasonably expect to dance before then, not even if Signor Rossi invited you to join his company."

"I don't know what to do," she sighed, thinking only of the thing she was meant to do and couldn't.

At midday a servant from the Swan delivered a rush basket containing a brace of trout and a large grayling and presented them with his grace's compliments. Matilda ordered Annie to prepare them for the evening meal, and penned a note to the Duke of Solway inviting him to dine.

Rosalie was as indecisive about what she should wear as about accepting or turning down his offer.

Matilda, after changing into a gown normally reserved for Sundays, approved her choice of rose-colored kerseymere with creamy lace at the collar and the cuffs.

"You'd better go into the parlor and light the candles," she advised. "It's growing dark already, and our guest will soon be here. I must take the best wineglasses out of the china cupboard and dust them off. Annie is too busy in the kitchen to do it herself."

With everyone occupied elsewhere, the scullery maid had the honor of showing the Duke of Solway into the parlor, where Rosalie was hastily plumping the sofa cushions. The formality of his attire surprised her; his white neckcloth was beautifully arranged, and silver buttons adorned his black coat.

"Thank you for the fish," she said, and his amused smile made her wish she'd chosen a less prosaic opening remark.

"November isn't an ideal month for angling, but here it seems not to matter. I've already considered returning in

May. My host at the Swan says he has taken trout as large as ten pounds during the spring and summer." When Rosalie moved to draw the curtains, he told her, "I'm delighted to see you on your feet again, Miss Lovegrove."

"I scarcely limp now," she said with pride, "though I'm not steady enough yet for *tendus* and *développés*. And I have no stamina at all."

Matilda, entering the room in time to hear this, frowned at her niece. "You've made a fine recovery, Rosie, but you're at least a month away from practicing your dance steps."

Said their guest, "She might accompany me on my next fishing expedition. I mean to try my luck at that wide bend in the river, north of the village, so she wouldn't have far to walk."

"If this dry weather holds, I see no harm in it." Matilda turned to Rosalie. "But you must dress warmly and sit upon a blanket or two, because the ground will be cold from the frost."

"I'll be careful," she promised, cheered by the prospect of an outing after so many days within doors.

But when the duke's gray eyes met hers, communicating his pleasure at her agreement, her soaring spirits abruptly descended. Rather than being flattered, as she ought to have been, she was reminded of the time he'd kissed her, and fear obscured her delight. Were his visit, his offer of employment, and his invitation to watch him fish the beginnings of an elaborate and devious seduction plot?

Although an overcast sky disappointed Rosalie, Gervase informed her that the weather couldn't be better for his purposes. "The breeze is in the proper quarter, too," he said brightly. "As my father always said, 'Wind out of the south blows bait to the fish's mouth.'"

In his brown coat and beige twill trousers, he bore no resemblance whatever to the elegant beau of the night before. He carried a long, single-handled rod with a butt made of ash wood and a brass reel and a landing net; a willow fish basket with a leather strap was slung over his shoulder.

Their short walk to the chosen place was more exhausting than Rosalie had expected, and she was grateful when he stopped to let her rest. While sitting upon the edge of the stone bridge, she explained that it had been built by subscription, and her grandfather had contributed to the funds.

The duke's interest in local landmarks resulted in several questions about several attached houses with sharply gabled fronts, which she identified as Arlington Row. "The buildings were built several centuries ago to store wool and were later converted to weavers' cottages," she explained.

When they reached their destination he helped her spread some blankets upon the grass, well beyond the shadows cast by the willows, and she sat down to watch his preparations. Attached to the long silken line was a shorter one made of gut, to which he fixed an artificial fly before dipping it into the river to take out the curl. Then, keeping the point of his rod upright, he sketched a broad circle in the air and flung the line forward. The fly drifted down to settle upon the water.

His lean body was taut and his eyes focused on the river as he stood upon the grassy slope. Rosalie, recognizing his passionate intensity, was amazed that so ordinary an activity could be its inspiration. The fanaticism of the sportsman, she thought, equaled that of the dancer.

He addressed her in an undervoice, saying, "One should always cast upstream, so the current will carry the line along. I'm keeping it on the stretch, and every so often I'll pull back to twitch the fly."

After several minutes of silence, he said even more softly, "Ah, a rise."

Holding her breath in anticipation and sitting very still, she studied his maneuvers.

He jerked the pole upright and cried triumphantly, "He's caught now, so I can let him run a little." Soon he began to wind his reel, walking backward as he did so. "A heavy one. Pass me that landing net, I'll need it presently."

She hurried to his side with the requested article, and when he pulled his catch out of the water she exclaimed, "It's larger than those you caught yesterday!" Unable to watch him stun the fish, she shut her eyes, and afterward held the basket open so he could place it inside.

"I usually get good results with my red-brown flies. I may try a palmer fly next time—that's how I caught the grayling. They're fatter and better at this season than trout."

The duke's first catch was his best one, but he brought in two grayling and another trout so small that he returned it to the water. After he admitted to feeling a trifle hungry, Rosalie unpacked the generous meal of cold chicken, bread, cheese, and chilled wine pressed upon him by the landlord's wife. While they dined together, seated upon the thick pile of blankets, she felt oddly at peace despite the uncertainty of her future—and his precise intentions.

"Yours is splendid country," Gervase declared.

Smiling, Rosalie replied, "My trips to Bibury have been so infrequent that I'm only slightly less a stranger here than you, your grace."

Leaning closer, he asked, "Couldn't you perhaps call me Gervase when we're alone together?"

"Non, non," she protested nervously, lapsing into French. "You are a duke, it would not be—*convenable.*"

"Why not, if I've given you leave? I don't much like to hear 'your grace' from anyone, as I inevitably associate that mode of address with my late father. Try my name, just once," he challenged her.

"Gervais," she essayed, eliminating the final consonant and giving strong emphasis to the second syllable.

"Sher-vay," he repeated. "It sounds far nicer in your language."

"Most words do." She wondered if he was about to kiss her again, and what else he might do if she let him.

"Paris must seem very distant when you are here," he said idly. "Do you miss it?"

"Occasionally."

"I gathered from my conversations with your Islington friends that you were there throughout the Revolution."

"I was born the year it began, on a hot summer day a fortnight before the Bastille fell. As a very young child, I witnessed the evil done in the name of liberty, fraternity, and equality."

His sympathetic questioning elicited many a secret she'd kept locked away. She related the harrowing tale of her godfather, the Abbé de Bouyon, who had been seized by a mob and hanged from a lamppost. She told him about the actors of the Théâtre Française, arrested and thrown into prison to await trial and certain death. But a clerk in the Prosecutor's Office, a former player himself, had intervened; he destroyed the indictment papers, and eventually all were released.

Her voice softened when she spoke of her beloved godmother, Mademoiselle de Montansier. "Although she had enjoyed the favor and patronage of Marie Antoinette, after the fall of the monarchy she embraced the cause of the people and produced plays promoting Republican virtues. But her patriotism couldn't save her, for she was falsely accused of being part of a Royalist plot to burn down the Bibliothèque Nationale. She was denounced to the Commune by an enemy and was sent to prison by some of the gentlemen who had frequented her salon above the Café de Chartres."

"Did no one step forward to defend her?"

Rosalie shook her head. "She spent nearly a year in Petit Force. We went to her, Maman and I—the Committee of Public Safety permitted visitors. I was terrified that the guards wouldn't let us leave when our hour was over, that we'd be trapped inside. I still have nightmares about it." She looked down, startled, when his hand covered her own.

"It was a difficult and painful time to grow up," he said gravely.

"Fear was everywhere, it ruled the city. My parents were also under a cloud of suspicion. Maman had so often performed in the royal theater at Versailles—so beautiful, she used to tell me, all gold and ivory and blue. At heart she remained faithful to the monarchy, though she pretended otherwise. As long as the Opera remained open she continued to work, and I remember her coming home in tears many nights, in despair about having danced for the very men who had ordered her Queen's death. Republican, Bonapartist, the *jeunesse dorée*—she pleased them all, and her popularity kept us alive."

"What about your father?"

"In theory he supported the Rights of Man—by British

standards he was a radical—but the atrocities committed by the politicians disgusted him. And in his own way he was a patriot. When Francoeur, the manager of the Paris Opera, staged an anti-English pantomime, Papa resigned his place in the orchestra as a protest. But we didn't starve, because he made money by composing and giving violin lessons, and Maman received a large salary. By that time I was dancing, too."

A sudden gust of wind showered them with golden willow leaves, and he reached out to pluck one from her hair. "You've led a most interesting life, Rosalie de Barante. Mine seems dull and tame by comparison."

She gazed back at him silently, envious of that calmer, easier existence.

As he rose from his recumbent position he declared, "I'm going to teach you how to cast a line, mademoiselle. You should learn quickly enough after watching me all morning." Evidently he took her acquiescence for granted, because he immediately handed her the rod.

Holding it helplessly, she asked, "What must I do?"

"Don't worry, I'll show you." He opened his leather pocketbook and removed an artificial fly with red feathers and a black body wound with silvery twist. While he attached it to the line he explained, "This is a lesser hackle."

"They've got such silly names," Rosalie commented.

"Grasp the rod here, just above the reel." In helping her find the proper position on the butt, his hands touched hers intimately and his breath fanned her cheek. "There, that's right. Remember to keep your back against the wind. Good. Now try to cast—yes, that's fine. Don't jerk the pole, but let your line drift downstream."

Nothing happened.

Gervase encouraged her to reel in and begin again. "Keep your eye on the fly at all times, and if you get a—"

"It moved!"

"Steady now, the fish is likely to nibble once more. Can you feel him yet?"

"I think so."

"Let him run, not too far, and then I'll help you bring him in."

"But he's gone," Rosalie wailed, tugging at the road. Nearly half of the line had disappeared.

"The devil! He took the fly, and the hook as well—the only Number Six." Looking down at her woebegone face, he added kindly, "A minor annoyance, but no harm done. I can make a hasty repair, and then you must try again." He sorted through the tackle box for a spool of horsehair and anther of gut, then lengthened the remaining line. "This Number Eight hook will serve," he announced, and began to tie it on.

Patience, Rosalie decided, was a necessary virtue for the angler. Following her instructor's example, she quickly recovered from her disappointment and before long was casting sufficiently well to win a commendation.

Her delight was boundless when she managed to catch a small chub, which she landed with Gervase's assistance.

"I hope you aren't tired of dining on fish," he teased as she placed it in the basket.

She laughed. "*Jamais*! Besides, I've not had the pleasure of eating one I caught myself." Several unruly curls had escaped their pins, and her cheeks were flushed from excitement and the effects of the chilly air. She didn't care about the mud stains on her gown or the willow leaves clinging to her shawl. She felt truly alive for the first time since the night of her accident.

They argued over who should carry the basket, and all the way back to her house they congratulated each other profusely on the success of the outing. Matilda was in the parlor, head bent over her knitting, and after she had listened to them boast of their achievements, she announced that a letter had just come for Rosalie.

"It's so weighty that I had to pay another eight pence," she said, passing it to her niece.

The duke declined her invitation to take a chair. "I've just remembered that I have some necessary letters to write today myself." With a smile and a nod for each of the ladies, he departed for the Swan, leaving the basket of fish behind.

"I think this is Mary Grimaldi's hand," Rosalie reported after studying the writing on the cover. She sank down upon the footstool and broke the seal of missive. "Two letters!" she exclaimed when a second sheet of paper fell into her lap. "By two different people, both strangers." She scanned the shorter one. "This comes from an attorney, writing on behalf of a gentleman who wishes to arrange a meeting with me," she reported.

"Not that nasty Mr. Beckmann, I hope," said Matilda darkly.

Rosalie shook her head. "He's called Lemercier, and wrote the other letter. The lawyer gave both to Mary Grimaldi to be forwarded. Poor woman—half of London has turned up on her doorstep since I left town. Monsieur Lemercier has wanted to meet me ever since he came to England last year, and requests that I contact him or his *avocat* when I return to London. He knew my parents in Paris." Looking up from the sheets spread across her lap, she murmured, "Etienne Lemercier."

"Are you acquainted with him?"

"The name seems familiar, but I can't think why. I don't suppose I owe him any reply. I hope not, for I've no desire to begin corresponding with every Frenchman who remembers Maman and Papa, or is suffering from *mal du pays.* Homesickness," she translated for her aunt.

While Rosalie continued to study her letters, Matilda asked, "What answer did you give the duke about the position he offered?"

"He never asked for one," she said absently.

"Have a care, Rosie. Don't offend him with your capriciousness."

"Of course I won't. When I refuse him, I'll be gracious and civil." Glancing up at last, she heaved a small sigh. "You still think I ought to accept."

Matilda resumed her knitting. "I do. Certainly I would have difficulty turning down an opportunity to spend Christmas at a duke's castle. If it's your career you're so concerned about, how much harm can a few more restful weeks do?"

"More than you realize, Aunt Tilda. My time would be better spent in London. James d'Egville is capable of preparing me for any ballet, however complicated, and—"

"And before you know it you'll be laid up with another sprain," Matilda predicted.

"If you think I mean to give up dancing now," Rosalie said with rising impatience, "you're deluding yourself. Not yet. Not until I've proved to d'Egville and Rossi and Armand Vestris and—and the rest of the world that I'm talented enough for the opera ballet!" On that defiant note she stalked out of the room, her clenched fist mangling the letters.

Early the next morning Rosalie, covered by her warmest pelisse and wearing a sturdy pair of shoes with two pairs of thick stockings to keep her feet warm, left the house. Determination to increase her strength with exercise motivated her every step, but before she reached the center of Bibury her heart was pounding and her legs ached.

The Church Road led her first to the peaceful cemetery where her grandparents rested and on past the grassy village common, occupied by a flock of gray geese. She nodded to the servant girl scattering corn for the vicar's hens and continued along Packhorse Lane until she reached the Pigeon House, so called because of the medieval dovecot adjacent to it. Pausing to catch her breath, she heard the mournful cries of the birds within.

Never had she felt more earthbound or less like a gravity-defying sylph. Her chest heaved, she could barely lift her leaden feet, and her knees were wobbly and unreliable. Matilda had suggest Ladyhill Covert as a pleasant place to roam, but Rosalie knew she would have to put off going so far until another time. She faced an equally taxing journey home.

She turned back, covering ground less rapidly than when she'd set out. The thorny hedgerow along the road and the blasted tree in a meadow were neither as pretty or picturesque as those she'd seen on painted canvas backdrops, she thought gloomily.

In an effort to elevate her spirits, she hummed the minor accompaniment to the mermaid ballet she often performed at Sadler's Wells but lacked the energy or the daring to attempt the *bourée*, *glissande*, and *arabesque* in the middle of the High Street. Not that anyone would have noticed. Even at that ridiculously early hour the men were working at their looms or opening their shops or cutting wood, and the cottage women were occupied with their various tasks.

The only other person abroad that morning, she soon discovered, was the Duke of Solway, who stood upon the older of the two bridges across the Colne, gazing down at the slow-moving water below.

"Come and look at this water vole," he said at her approach. When she joined him he pointed to a small brown rodent scurrying through the fallen leaves along the riverbank.

"Just like a *petit rat*," she commented when the creature darted into its muddy burrow. Realizing that the duke was without his rod and tackle, she asked, "Why aren't you fishing this morning?"

"Because I intend to depart for Shropshire within the hour."

She was so unprepared for his announcement that she stared mutely back at him.

"I wish I might stay longer, but my mother expects me at Pontesbury by tomorrow or the next day, and I mustn't disappoint her." Facing her, he asked whether she'd reached a decision.

At that moment, frustrated and discouraged by her own frailty, she was tempted to accept his charity. "Aunt Tilda urges me to say yes," she admitted.

"From the outset of our brief acquaintance, she struck me as an astute woman."

"But," she went on, "I am more inclined to refuse."

"Allow me to present some enticements that might persuade you. The castle has a ballroom where you can practice your dancing. Its servants, who have been with my family for many years, will treat you as they would any guest. Ninian has promised not to be naughty, but if you should be unhappy or uncomfortable, you'd be free to leave. The appointment will last only as long as you want it."

She could think of no arguments to counter his, nor did she remember just why she'd been so reluctant. "If I found out about a place at the opera house, or another theater, I'd have to go to London."

"Of course. That is understood." He withdrew a leather purse from his coat pocket and removed five ten-pound notes, interrupting her protests and reminding her of his earlier promise to pay her posting fees. "I suggest Banbury as a good place to stop for the night, as it's forty or so miles from here, nearly half the distance to Haberdine. The Red Lion is the best inn."

Rosalie stared down at the fortune he had pressed into her gloved hands. Fifty pounds—the largest sum she'd ever seen at one time, enough to live on for at least half a year. "I'm accustomed to traveling in the mail coach," she said, her eyes growing larger as he began counting out additional banknotes. "It's less expensive than a post chaise."

"Keep these for your return fare to London." Smiling down at her, he added, "You'll be glad to have some running away money if Ninian troubles you with his tricks. Write to me if you encounter any problem at all, though I doubt you will. This piece of paper has my direction in Shropshire and also the name of my London solicitor, who will know where I am at all times. Have you any questions?"

Striving not to drop the riches he had showered upon her, she gazed back at him in confusion. "Dozens, only I can't recall what they are."

He touched her cheek. "You've no cause for concern, Rosalie. Remember, you survived the Revolution and the Reign of Terror. By comparison, teaching my cousin to speak French should be easy enough." After replacing the purse, he extended his arm, saying, "Permit me to walk you home, for I must say good-bye to the other Miss Lovegrove. And I'd like one last look at those Greuze paintings."

Rosalie took him to the dormant garden behind the house, and when he'd addressed his farewells to her aunt, they went into the parlor. His thorough and thoughtful examination of the three canvases, two of which showed her in a state of partial undress, made her self-conscious.

"You must have been a well-behaved little girl to sit still

for so long," he commented. "I once had my likeness taken, and it was an excruciating experience."

"It was never easy," she answered. "When Monsieur made the initial sketches for 'La Petite Ange,' the halo kept falling down over my eyes, and the angel's wings were quite heavy. The lamb in 'La Petite Bergère' looks sweet and gentle in the finished picture, but I was all over bruises from his sharp little hooves. Posing for 'La Petite Danseuse' was almost a pleasure, because I was dressed in ballet costume and could pretend that I was Maman."

"Tell me again about 'Mischief,' the one you sold."

"It was an oval portrait, painted at about the same time as the angel and the shepherdess. I held my head *comme ça*," she said, illustrating, "and wore a scarlet cloak. But I was much too fair to make a convincing Gypsy."

"I must reserve judgment until I see the result, but in my opinion you are the perfect gamine." His voice was devoid of any inflection, so detached that his remark hardly seemed to be a compliment.

After he left her, Rosalie went upstairs to her room and watched from the window seat until she saw his travelling coach roll by.

Absence and distance would alter the easy relationship that had developed during his stay in Bibury, perhaps even destroy it, she thought sadly. By taking his money she had accepted him as an employer, and now she found it impossible to regard him as anything else. He'd never really been her friend, and she had always known he couldn't be her lover.

Their temperaments were so different—his was calm and steady, her own was emotional and variable. In addition to lacking the refinement and the social graces he expected in a female, she was shamefully uneducated. He was a duke, descended from dead kings and queens; royal blood flowed in his veins. She was only a dancer, her gowns sewn with false gems, consorting with imaginary lords and ladies in an endless masquerade.

However kindly and generously he treated her, they would forever inhabit separate realms. The fact that he'd invited her to live at his castle for several weeks wouldn't alter that harsh and disturbingly hurtful truth.

8

When you do dance, I wish you
A wave o' the sea, that you might ever do
Nothing but that.

—WILLIAM SHAKESPEARE

"Tell me how to say, 'That woman is ugly,'" Lord Swanborough urged his governess. "If you please," he added with an engaging grin.

Having learned how persistent he could be, Rosalie promptly answered, *"La femme est laide."*

"And fat."

"Elle est grosse aussi." Frowning at him, she said severely, "The duke did not send me here to teach you insulting expressions, my lord. Have you studied the list of words I copied out for you?"

"Yes." Ninian shoved at the thick fringe of black curls obscuring his brow.

They were wandering through the west wing, which contained spacious, elegant apartments and a magnificent ballroom decorated with plasterwork friezes and medallions. It was the most modern part of the castle, and the abundance of marble and gilding and pale silk draperies reminded Rosalie of Parisian splendors.

Nodding briskly at the earl, she said, *"Commencez, s'il vous plaît."*

"Now?" he asked in dismay.

"C'est obligatoire."

He began his recitation in a bored monotone, correctly translating the words Rosalie had assigned the previous day. Her efforts to impart the rudiments of French weren't

always so successful, but her pupil was so bright and quick
that she didn't entirely despair.

As soon as she had arrived at Haberdine Castle, she had
conferred with Jasper Duffield. Despite his profession he
was neither dull nor pedantic, but she was awed by his passion for ancient languages and his detailed knowledge of
obscure history. He didn't seem to disapprove of her true
calling, unlike the prosy chaplain and the provincial couple
who filled the positions of steward and housekeeper, and
thus she was able to maintain an easy rapport with him.

The tutor had searched among the books in the schoolroom and the library until he found a French phrase book
for travelers and a grammar text, formerly the possessions
of the earl's sister, Lady Miranda Peverel. Armed with
these, and her own well-thumbed copy of Jean Georges
Noverre's treatise *Lettres sur la danse et les ballets*, Rosalie had become a governess.

Accepting Mr. Duffield's advice, she gave Lord Swanborough informal, unstructured lessons. The castle itself
provided a wealth of ordinary, everyday objects for vocab-
ulary sessions. She taught her pupil the vagaries of irregular
verbs during long walks in the terraced gardens; he learned
his numbers by counting the hundreds of steps from the cellars to the attics. The kitchen staff had provided assistance,
admitting her into their domain for a study of food and
drink.

With no previous experience of English country houses,
she was astonished by the grandeur and antiquity of Haberdine. According to the scholarly Mr. Duffield, who haunted
the muniment room, its foundations dated from the reign of
William the Conqueror, the only remnants of the original
royal hunting lodge. In medieval times the building had
been converted to a fortress by the addition of the two solid
bastion towers flanking the entrance gate; the oldest part of
the castle still possessed a thick, nail-studded wooden por-
tal. A minstrel gallery, tapestry-hung chambers, and suits of
armor recalled the days when knights and their ladies had
roamed the corridors, and one meadow continued to be
called the Tilting Ground. The Marchants had purchased
the castle directly from the crown, but their own occupation

had been far from peaceful. At the time of the Civil Wars, the original Norman keep was irreparably damaged by Parliamentary forces and the stones now formed the chapel and the steward's house.

Scowling in concentration, Ninian continued, "Ballroom. *La grande salle de la danse*. Box. *La boite*. Button. *Le bouton*. Butter. *La beurre*."

"*Le beurre*," she corrected him.

"Is it? *Diable*!"

Startled by his unexpected talent for swearing in French, she demanded to know where he'd learned the expression.

"From you," he said blithely. "You lost your balance yesterday when you practiced that bouncing step, and that's exactly what you said."

"You must never repeat it, my lord!"

"Sometimes I've heard you say *sacrebleu*," he added, his blue eyes sparkling with mischief. "And *peste*."

"I should never have taken this position," she moaned.

Ninian grasped her hand. "Please don't leave me, mademoiselle! I'll be good, I won't say those words again."

His lordship's attachment to Rosalie had increased during her month at Haberdine, and she was worried that he wouldn't easily let her go. "I cannot remain indefinitely," she pointed out as gently as she could.

"Why ever not? Don't you like living here?"

"Very much. But I'm a dancer—I need a stage and an orchestra and an audience."

"When I come into my inheritance, I shall build a theater for you," the boy said grandly. "The finest in all the world!"

His offer made her smile, but she believed it was sincere. "Let's go to the Elizabethan wing," she suggested. "I've thought of another way to test your knowledge."

A row of paintings lined the wood-paneled walls of the gallery, and when Rosalie pointed to the silk gowns and velvet doublets and fine jewels of Ninian's Marchant ancestors, he identified their colors.

Pausing before a particularly fine portrait of a young lady with long, dark tresses and deep blue eyes, he said soberly, "This is my mother. She looks like that still, though she seldom smiles. She lives in Bath with a doctor, and before he cured her she was mad—*dérangée*. She's called Hermia."

"How pretty."

"It's a family tradition to name daughters for Shakespeare heroines. That's why my sister Mira's new baby is Juliet." He led her past the Countess of Swanborough's image and halted again when they came to a full-length study of a brown-haired youth with a gun under his arm and a spaniel at his feet. "That's Ger, with his dog."

It was an excellent likeness of Rosalie's employer. The artist Hoppner had captured the warmth of expression she knew so well, and the portrait conveyed the approachable quality so much at odds with his grace's exalted position. Reluctant to make any sort of comment that might reveal to Ninian how much she missed his guardian, she led him to the next picture and continued quizzing him.

On Christmas Eve the castle staff gathered in the chapel to hear Mr. Penfield read the daily collect. Garlands of holly decorated the brass altar rail, the scarlet berries brightening the somber vault of stone and wood. Rosalie shivered through the service; her fingers and toes were so numb with cold that she felt as stiff as the marble effigies of the entombed Marchants.

Fortunately the schoolroom, which doubled as her private parlor, possessed a large fireplace and a well-filled coal scuttle. After giving Ninian an abbreviated lesson, she dismissed him and began writing a holiday message to her aunt. Her task was interrupted when the upper housemaid, patently excited about the festivities belowstairs, brought her a letter from London.

Rosalie, spying Mary Grimaldi's familiar script, eagerly unfolded the page. But when she finished reading, her expression was pensive.

It wasn't that her friend's news was bad—quite the opposite. The Christmas pantomime at Drury Lane was extremely popular, and Clown Joey's portrayal of the fierce Vegetable Man had been acclaimed by all of London. His latest character appeared in more printshop windows than portraits of the Prince of Wales, and his innovative antics were discussed as often as the proposed Regency Bill.

Rosalie rejoiced in the actor's success, but not when she read the newspaper clipping enclosed with his wife's cheery note, a review of the first opera of the season. The critic vilified the management of the King's Theatre for presenting the plump-faced, matronly soprano as the tragic heroine Zaira. And he ridiculed Signora Bertinotti mercilessly, pointing to her girth as proof that she had greater talent for wielding her knife and fork than the prop dagger. Her performance had so displeased the exacting and anonymous gentleman that he neglected to comment on the ballet, which followed, merely noting that it had been *L'Épouse Persane,* a Rossi creation dating from the previous spring.

The descriptions of Grimaldi's triumph and the signora's failure not only rekindled Rosalie's desire to perform; they also prevented her from enjoying the servants' dinner and ball that evening. While footmen and maids were engaged in a rowdy country dance, she mentally composed a speech to Lord Swanborough to explain her immediate desertion.

But by the time she climbed into her bed she'd decided that she couldn't spoil his lordship's Christmas as hers had been spoiled. The news that she must return to London could be delayed for another day or so.

Ninian, granted a respite from his less than arduous studies, spent his holiday playing games—billiards, cards, charades. In the evening he and Rosalie and Mr. Duffield dined on roast goose and braised partridges, stewed carrots, salsify pie, and a plum pudding. After eating himself into a stupor, he went up to bed, saying he must be up early to meet the hounds.

At daylight he and his groom rode off to the Boxing Day hunt at Swanborough Abbey. He returned late, consumed another hearty meal, and after withdrawing to the library with his instructors he sought additional sustenance from hothouse oranges, sweetmeats, and roasted chestnuts.

Wiping his fingers with his handkerchief, he said in his abrupt and determined fashion, "Let's play Snapdragon."

"I don't know how," Rosalie replied.

"Easiest thing in the world," he assured her.

The student became the teacher, and soon she was leaning over a bowl of flaming brandy, deftly plucking out hot currants. Ninian, who had suggested the game, was the first to tire of it, but Rosalie and the tutor remained at the fireside to continue the contest long after he had stretched out upon the sofa with paper and pen.

A few minutes later he looked up and asked, "What's the French word for ravishing?"

"Ravissante," Rosalie answered absently, her attention fixed upon the hazy blue flame before her. Knowing that a quick, bold action was the best, she thrust her hand into the bowl and snatched up another hot currant, bravely placing it in her mouth.

Ninian lifted his head again. "What color are your eyes, mademoiselle?"

"Bluish green," Mr. Duffield offered.

"In French, please."

"Bleu-vert," Rosalie translated.

The Duke of Solway, who had stepped into the room unnoticed, declared, *"Elle a les yeux turquoise."*

"Gervase!" Ninian shouted gleefully.

As the tutor and governess rose from the hearth rug, their employer encouraged them to proceed with the game. "But 'Take care you don't take too much, be not greedy in your clutch! Snip! Snap! Dragon!'" Turning toward the sofa, he asked, "Why aren't you playing, Nin?"

"I'm writing a poem. In French," the boy announced impressively. "It's about Mademoiselle."

Rosalie gave up her futile attempts to smooth the creases from her skirt and explained, "I assigned the task to his lordship, though I never dreamed that I should be the subject of his verses." With a Gallic shrug, she concluded, *"On essaie de faire des progres."*

"It appears that you've made considerable progress," Gervase commented, "if Ninian is willing to spend Boxing Day engaged in studious pursuits."

"Where's Aunt Elizabeth?" Ninian asked. "Did she stay at Cavender Chase?"

"She's visiting in Derbyshire now, with Ophelia and

Hethington and their half-dozen children. We left Miranda and Justin immediately after the christening, and reached Hethington Hall on Christmas Eve."

"What does Mira's baby look like?"

"She's very tiny," Gervase reported. "Her eyes are blue like yours and nearly as dark."

"When will I see her?"

"There is talk of your visiting the Chase again at Eastertide. May I read your poem?"

Shaking his head, Ninian thrust the paper into his pocket. "Not till it's finished."

Sitting down beside his ward, Gervase asked, "Did you take my place at the servants' dinner?"

The youth nodded vigorously. "It was a grand feast! Afterward we all sang silly songs, and the footmen tried to kiss the maids under the mistletoe. There was dancing, too. I partnered Mrs. Brinkworth, but not because I wanted to. She asked me."

"How else have you been passing your time?"

"Learning French. And translating Latin." Ninian's black brows drew together in a frown. "Caesar's *Gallic Wars.*"

"Rough going?"

"Agony! Oh, I went hunting with Jap last week, and by myself today. We had some pretty fine runs. I'm at liberty from my lessons, and will be on Twelfth Day, too, for our party. I've been telling Mademoiselle about the ball Aunt Elizabeth and Uncle William used to give, and about the cake."

Gervase sighed. "Do you think of nothing but food? I'm not opposed to having a cake, but with the household still in mourning I doubt that celebrations would be appropriate."

"We needn't invite anyone else, it will be just ourselves—you and me and Jap and Mademoiselle. If we wear fancy dress we can call it a masquerade. A *bal masqué,*" Ninian added with a triumphant glance at Rosalie.

"There won't be much mystery about our identities."

"I don't care about that," his cousin replied. "*I'm* going to be Sir Francis Drake. Will you help me make a costume, mademoiselle? With so many boxes of cast-off clothes in the attic, I daresay we can find materials."

Rosalie glanced at the duke, whose thoughtful expression gave nothing away. "If his grace permits."

Ninian turned to his tutor. "What character will you be, Jap?"

"Oliver Cromwell, I think. Most of my clothes are black."

"Oh, but we can't have him here," the boy objected. "The Marchants were Royalists. You should be a knight—we've got helmets and swords and armor all over the castle."

Gervase curtailed the ensuing debate by saying that Mr. Duffield would make an admirable Cromwell. Then he asked Rosalie, "Have you made your choice?"

"There are two dancing costumes at the bottom of my trunk, so I have the choice of being a fairy or a shepherdess."

"You must come as Titania," Ninian said decisively. "The queen of the fairies. And what about you, Ger?"

"I'm keeping my character a secret," Gervase responded, "in order to provide one surprise on the night."

Assuming that he would wish to consult Mr. Duffield about his ward's studies, Rosalie convinced Ninian that he should go up to bed, and excused herself. To her surprise, the duke followed them into the great hall.

"Ninian," he said, "the length of your hair is a disgrace. In the morning I expect you to submit yourself to Webster's scissors."

"Must I?"

"I've already told you so." Watching his cousin climb the carved oak staircase, Gervase addressed Rosalie. "Tell me frankly, how does he get on with his French?"

She answered ruefully, "He's no worse a student than I am a teacher. He seems to enjoy our lessons and has acquired some useful words and phrases. When I leave Haberdine, as I must do soon, I won't consider myself a complete failure."

"You agreed to take part in our Twelfth Night revels," he reminded her.

"I did so in the hope that my participation will reconcile Lord Swanborough to my imminent departure."

Glancing up at the brass chandelier hanging above their heads, he asked her, "What has become of the kissing bough that usually hangs here?"

"The only one I've seen is in the servants' hall."

"A pity. This is exactly the place for it." Smiling, he said in a more intimate voice, "To assure myself that my ward has been behaving is not the only reason I've come to Haberdine. I've thought about you often, and I—" After abruptly breaking off this statement, he asked, "Has your ankle given you any trouble?"

"It's strong enough that I'm able to spend a part of every day twirling about your ballroom."

"Without any music? Or do you keep it here?" His forefinger grazed her brow.

She nodded in affirmation. His gray eyes were as near to blazing as she had ever seen them, and this light kindled a fire in her cheeks. Awkwardly she murmured, "It grows late, your grace."

"One more question, and then you may retire. Are you glad that I've come, or would you rather I'd stayed away?"

His question aroused an emotion she dared not define. Nor could she give him an answer. Alarmed by the tension between them, she broke away, moving wordlessly toward the ornate staircase. Not until she attained the safety of the upper landing did she recall that she'd failed to wish him a happy Christmas.

When Rosalie realized she was in love with the Duke of Solway, she did not immediately perceive the danger of her situation. Dancing, her primary concern for the whole of her life, had consumed her thoughts and directed all her actions to the exclusion of all else. Her tender regard for the Duke of Solway was so novel that at first she reveled in it. The physical manifestations—an erratic heartbeat and hectic pulse—were not unlike those she felt before stepping on the stage.

Her dancing was unaffected, but mental disquiet had a disastrous effect upon her ability to sleep and eat. However fatiguing her daily practice sessions, at night she lay awake for hours at a time, reliving every encounter with her employer, however insignificant. Increasingly rigorous exercise demanded adequate nourishment, but despite a noticeable improvement in the dishes since the duke's return her appetite faltered, especially in his presence.

When the weather permitted, he and Ninian rode off to join the Swanborough Abbey hunt. Upon their return, which usually occurred around midday, Ninian settled down to his Latin studies, followed by a French lesson, and Gervase conferred with his steward. He rarely received company, and his only dinner guests were other sportsmen from neighboring estates in Rutlandshire or Leicestershire. On those occasions Lord Swanborough and his instructors were served their evening meal informally, in the schoolroom.

Rosalie, Ninian, and Jasper Duffield spent one rainy day in the attic rooms, hunting for suitable raiment for Sir Francis Drake and Oliver Cromwell. All were so caught up in the pleasures of opening trunks and trying on discarded garments that they forgot to watch the clock, and the ring of the changing bell caught them unawares. Scurrying to their rooms, they washed smudged faces and combed out tangles and replaced soiled clothes with clean ones.

Rosalie joined the small group assembled in the great hall, avoiding the stern and disapproving eye of the chaplain when he wondered aloud about what had detained Lord Swanborough. She was relieved that the duke appeared to be unconcerned about her tardiness, or his ward's.

Later that night, after the dour cleric retreated from the library, Gervase drew a chair close to hers. "I heard the laughter coming from the garret this afternoon."

"Were we so noisy?" she asked, meeting his gaze uncertainly.

"Yes, and I hope you will be again. This house isn't as gay as it should be at this season."

When he asked what kind of celebrations she'd been accustomed to in France, she answered, "Very few. Although religious rites were discouraged when I was very young, Maman did take me to Mass on Christmas morning. And we had a *bûche de Noel* with our dinner. This time of year is the busiest for stage performers, with so many pantomimes and spectacles and ballets. Until now I've never been at leisure to enjoy the festivities."

"Haberdine was bustling with wedding preparations a year ago," he told her. "My cousin Miranda and Viscount Cavender were married in the chapel on New Year's Eve, so all our family were together. My father wasn't well, but he concealed it from us—I suspect he knew it would be his last Christmas. I've never felt his absence more acutely than I have done this week. This house harbors so many memories that the prospect of coming here was more than my mother could bear. Very likely she'll remain with my sister at Hethington Hall until the London season begins, when she removes to Solway House."

Ninian growled, "I can't think why she'd want to do that. Except for Sadler's Wells and the Serpentine, London is detestable."

"I'm not especially fond of it myself," Gervase said.

"But why not?" asked an incredulous Rosalie. "I think it's a splendid city. The houses may not be as grand as some in Paris, but the shops are every bit as good, if not better. There are so many parks and gardens and theaters and exhibitions that one can never be bored—there's always something to do. On holidays there are processions and illuminations, and every night all the streets are lit up so beautifully."

"And by day are nearly impassable because of all the carriages, drays, and hackney coaches," Gervase countered. "I grant you, Mayfair and Kensington are pleasant, but in too many districts you'll find criminals lurking behind every corner and hear beggar children crying from hunger. The workhouses are overflowing, as are the houses of correction, and there's scarcely an empty cell in the debtors' prisons." Smiling at her, he asked, "Haven't you discovered yet that the town cannot compare with the country?"

She was hurt by his apparent disdain for her opinion, and reflected that the disparity of taste matched the inequality of their stations. How foolish it was, she chided herself, to yearn for someone so far removed from her in birth, intellect, and experience. Instead she should concentrate upon the more attainable of her dreams, returning to the opera house stage.

The oppressive fog on New Year's Day could not deter Ninian from his hunting.

"The scent will lie high today," he explained to Rosalie when she took her place for breakfast. Bounding out of his chair, he urged his tutor to hurry. "Tom Webb must have our horses ready. We're frightfully late—the hunt will be halfway to Stoke End covert by now—and I'm not waiting for Ger. He can catch up to us later."

Rosalie toyed with her food, consuming very little, and drank a cup of coffee far too weak for her Continental palate. Not so long ago she had been accustomed to taking all her meals alone; now it depressed her.

Going to her room, she put on a hooded cloak her aunt had provided and the half boots she'd procured locally, from a cobbler so charmed by her dainty dancer's feet that he begged the privilege of making her a pair of kid slippers as well. Hoping to banish her cares, she strolled down the hill to the village, a long street of solid stone buildings: cottages crowned with thatch, a church, several shops, and the Solway Arms. From the number of horses, carts, and gigs in the innyard, she surmised that a number of people were inside, toasting the arrival of 1811.

She decided to explore the remnants of the ancient forest of Haberdine. Mr. Duffield had explained that most of the trees had been felled centuries ago to create farms, but a few small tracts of woodland still formed the boundaries of the duke's vast estate. Coming to a broad, open field grazed by sheep, she saw a medieval barn which brought to mind the tutor's observation that the landscape continued to reflect the feudal system which had shaped it.

Because the cart track winding through the trees was the shortest and swiftest way from Great Melden to Little Melden, she encountered several pedestrians. A man and a woman accompanied by a large brood of noisy, red-cheeked children. Then a pair of lads and their dog hurried by, calling out wishes for a joyous New Year.

The sky had darkened to a deeper gray, and the air

seemed to grow more frigid as a result. To avoid walking all the way back to the village, she followed a narrow footpath which she hoped would lead directly to the castle. But her sense of direction was so poor that she sought assistance from the next person she met, a shabby individual carrying an axe.

"If you walk on," he answered gruffly, "you'll soon find yourself at the old tilting ground." Narrowing his eyes, he said, "You must be that Frenchwoman, the young lord's governess."

"I am."

"My boy was killed in Holland more'n ten year ago. He was fighting the French."

Striving to moderate his resentment, she said sympathetically, "He must have been very brave."

"He was that," the man corroborated, continuing on his way.

Rosalie proceeded along the path, shivering from the intense cold, but she halted once more when she saw Gervase coming toward her. Startled, she cried, "I thought you went hunting!"

"I've been hunting for you," he responded. "Parry said you left the house nearly an hour ago, and I was worried that you might be lost."

"*Mais non,* your grace." She hoped he would think her breathlessness a natural result of a long walk. The wind blew harder, causing bare branches to scrape against one another. "Such a mournful sound," she murmured, flexing her frozen fingers.

Staring intently at the treetops, he said exultantly, "There it is."

"What?"

"The very thing I've been searching for. Come closer and I'll show you."

As soon she carried out his request she was drawn into an embrace that was firm yet gentle, passionate yet tender. His arms held her more securely than any of her dancing partners, and at the touch of his lips upon hers a searing warmth replaced the wind's icy sting. This kiss was quite unlike the one she had received that long-ago night at

Sadler's Wells. Then she had been desperate to escape him—now she dreaded that he might let her go.

Without releasing her, he said softly, "Look up."

Rosalie tilted her head back, and tiny white flakes settled upon her brow and cheeks. "It's snowing!"

"Keep looking, it's on the highest limb."

"I see nothing. Only a—a clump of something."

"That's mistletoe," he told her.

"Are you sure?" she said, disappointed. "The kissing bough in the servants' hall is so pretty, with its red velvet ribbons and gold tassels."

"Clearly I must teach you to appreciate the starker beauties of a wood in wintertime, my little opera dancer."

But Rosalie, missing the gauze and tinsel, the soft lights and painted screens of her own rarified realm, doubted that he could.

He was smiling, as if pleased with himself, or with her. "You are surely thinking this season has a strange effect upon me, and I can't deny it. How cold it has grown! If this weather continues, Ninian will be able to go skating on the pond. But don't let him persuade you to try it—we can't risk another accident." Touching her on the shoulder, he said with a hint of regret, "We'd best go back to the house."

His words and actions, as disturbing as they were gratifying, seemed to prove that her feelings were requited. But what if he was only trifling with her out of curiosity, to determine how receptive she was to his advances? The uncertainty tortured her.

They separated in the great hall, Gervase going to the library and Rosalie hurrying up to her room. She needed privacy to recover her equilibrium, for their encounter in the woods had been singularly unsettling.

Hoping that work would bolster her spirits, she changed into a multicolored dance costume and pink hose, and made her way to the ballroom. At first its size had intimidated her, and more than one slip had taught her the dangers of the highly polished floor, but otherwise it was an ideal place for rehearsing.

As was her habit, she started by copying the poses of the bas relief gods and goddesses. Then, using a chair back as a makeshift barre, she began her preliminary exercises, her eyes watching for mistakes in a tall pier glass framed in giltwood.

Moving to the center of the room, she performed Lison's "Ribbon Dance" from *La Fille Mal Gardée*, her favorite ballet. Its plot was refreshingly simple, and she was particularly fond of its characters, not the allegorical or mythological beings of most ballets, but ordinary humans entangled up in a dispute over an arranged marriage. She hoped one day to repeat the role of lovely Lison, who renounces her betrothal to a rich and foolish young man favored by her mother and plots with her sweetheart Colas to avoid a marriage of convenience.

Jean Dauberval had first staged the ballet in Bordeaux, the site of his celebrated dancing school, and the debut performance had taken place two weeks before the fateful storming of the Bastille—the very day of Rosalie's birth. The celebrated choreographer had created his heroine with Delphine de Barante in mind. He had expected her to perform his promising new work in Paris after recovering from her confinement, but the dancer never had an opportunity to interpret the part she had inspired. By the time Delphine returned to the stage, the Revolution had brought more serious, politically significant ballets into vogue.

The first time Rosalie had danced Lison, Armand Vestris had been her Colas. He'd been an engaging youth in those days and popular with his fellow students. But Delphine, an exacting critic, informed her daughter that he lacked the greater talents of his father Auguste and his grandfather Gaetano, forever known as *Le Dieu de Danse*. She would have been even less impressed with the mature Armand, thought Rosalie, who was now a self-centered, overly confident performer, determined to trade upon his famous name.

But, she reminded herself, she had a similar motive for calling herself de Barante. It was unfair to condemn Armand out of envy, just because he'd achieved a success which eluded her.

Pleased with her execution of an *entrechat six*, she concluded that the long weeks of rest had done no harm, only good. Her former flexibility had returned; she was capable of soaring *battements*, deep pliés, and graceful *ronds de jambe*.

Her dancing was good enough for the opera ballet, she had no doubt of it. She would be satisfied with any available position, however lofty or lowly—*première danseuse*, *soloiste* or *coryphée*. For just as she had promised her dying father that she would guard her virtue, she had assured her beloved mother that she would continue to perform.

Gervase entered the ballroom quietly and stealthily, concealing himself in an alcove so he might spy upon the girl whose poppy red skirts swirled with her gyrations, revealing a petticoat the color of coral.

In the months since she had danced into his life, he'd often wanted to kiss those alluring lips, to hold her small body against his pounding heart. Now he deeply regretted the impulse that had prompted him to take advantage of the mistletoe. Kissing her a second time had been both unwise and unfair. But in future, when she was no longer Ninian's governess, he need not be constrained by the restrictions of an employer. He would then be able to speak freely about his feelings, and discuss the arrangement he had in mind.

During his stay in Shropshire she had persistently invaded his thoughts. Their separation confirmed what he'd first suspected while visiting her in Bibury. He wanted her. So much that he had risked offending her with that impulsive and ill-timed overture.

"*Peste!*" The dancer, oblivious to his watchful presence, pounded her forehead with her palm and muttered, "*Chienne stupide, et gauche!*"

Gervase hadn't noticed her error and could not fathom why she'd called herself a stupid, clumsy bitch. Slowly rising upon her toes with one pink leg stretched out behind her, she was the personification of grace.

But her labored breathing and fleeting grimace of pain warned him that she'd passed the limit of her endurance. Lacking the authority—and the right—to make her stop, he slipped out of the ballroom unnoticed.

The apology he owed her, like his declaration, would have to wait.

9

Thy mummeries; thy Twelfe-tide Kings
And Queenes; thy Christmas revellings.
—ROBERT HERRICK

Six days of unceasing snowfall kept the duke's household indoors, and by the twelfth day after Christmas the castle grounds were buried beneath a thick white blanket. Vague rumors about delayed mail coaches and tales of stranded travelers were communicated to Haberdine by the servants, who heard them third or fourth hand. Ninian, hoping that Rosalie's departure might be delayed indefinitely, made no secret of the fact that he desired a continuation of the cruel weather.

Unable to ride with his hounds, he'd kept busy organizing the festive dinner and masquerade, which would take place in the evening. All that day he sought his governess's approval of the last-minute additions to his menu and relied upon her to help him decorate the room he'd chosen for their party.

Mr. Duffield found Rosalie in that tapestry-hung chamber late in the afternoon and sat down to watch her attach a pair of wings fashioned from gauze and wire to a spangled frock. Firelight illuminated her face as she bent her tawny brown head over her work.

Breaking their companionable silence, he said, "Haberdine won't be the same without you, mademoiselle. I trust we'll meet again one day, for I intend to see you dance. But his lordship's aversion to London is so violent that I can't say how soon I'll be able to go there."

"Peste!" Rosalie muttered when she stabbed herself with

the needle. Removing a lace-edged square of linen from her pocket, she dabbed at the spot of blood on her finger. "Did you find any theatrical news in the papers?"

Mr. Duffield shook his head. "I was reading the accounts of the proposed Regency Bill. A change of government seems unavoidable. The King's Tory ministers are so inimical toward the Prince of Wales that he'll want to replace them with Whigs if he comes into power."

"Is he so political? I thought he preferred gaming, and chasing middle-aged matrons and building expensive houses to state affairs." She reached for her scissors and snipped the silvery thread. "Finished at last."

"With the paste tiara we found in the attics and the wand his lordship made from the shaft of a broken candlestick, you'll be a splendid Queen of the Fairies." Mr. Duffield cleared his throat, as he often did when he wished to make a serious observation. "The earl is greatly attached to you, Mademoiselle de Barante. He tries not to show it, but he's fretting over your decision to leave."

"I will miss him," she admitted. "But he has his Latin and Greek and history to occupy him, and after the snow is gone he'll be able to hunt again."

"The Duke of Solway also holds you in very high esteem."

Avoiding his gaze, Rosalie studied the gauzy material spread across her lap. "I am honored by his grace's good opinion, though I've done nothing to deserve it."

The tutor was intelligent and perceptive enough to guess her secret. He must also be aware, as she was, that her hopeless and impossible love for the Duke of Solway would result in heartbreak and remorse.

Her final preparations for the evening party included coloring her cheeks and lips with rouge and darkening her eyelashes with a burnt cork, as she did before a stage performance. The sparkling tiara made her feel regal, and she promenaded before her dressing table mirror, admiring herself. Recalling her conversation with Gervase just after he had kissed her, she thought again that she was entirely susceptible to fantasy—her existence was governed by it.

Gervase Marchant, titled and wealthy, could afford his

preference for reality. The treasures of his country had not been plundered by angry, hungry people, or sold to wealthy foreigners. No angry mob had attacked the palatial homes of his friends, or flung them into prison to await an appointment with the guillotine. The scales of his conscience had never been weighted down by innate loyalty to aristocratic patrons and the opposing need to placate the agitators who had replaced them in society and the government.

To aid her recovery from the agonies of her past, she'd allowed herself to be seduced by that imaginary world she inhabited on the stage. Beauty, however artful or illusory or transient, was more desirable than ugliness. She needed the gentle glow cast by oil footlights, the heavenly music of the orchestra, and all of the seductive theatrical magic.

When she joined Lord Swanborough in the tapestry room, he complimented her extravagantly. "I say, Jap, won't Ger be pleased when he sees Mademoiselle?"

"Undoubtedly, my lord," the tutor replied. Meticulous research had enabled him to put together a costume suitable to the Lord Protector. He had put on the black gown from his university days and wore a round hat with a wide brim, to which Rosalie had affixed a silver buckle.

While waiting for his cousin to appear, Ninian speculated on what character he'd chosen. Adjusting his false beard and moustaches, he said, "I told Ger he should wear armor—the breast plate and helmet that belonged to an ancestor, the one who trounced Oliver Cromwell's army at the Battle of Solway Marsh."

But Gervase had spurned his ward's suggestion. He had robed himself in a floor-length garment of green velvet, loosely bound at the waist by a gold sash. Beneath it he wore a lawn shirt and red satin breeches. A heavy chain encircled his neck, and jeweled rings adorned his fingers, and his head supported a pinchbeck crown.

After a painstaking inspection, Ninian was still at a loss. "Who *are* you?"

"I've guessed," Mr. Duffield announced. "His grace has come as Oberon."

"How clever of you, Ger! I wish I'd thought of that!"

"You are quite magnificent in doublet and hose," Gervase comforted him, "and the sextant completes the portrait. However, you failed to seek my permission before removing it from the glass case in the muniment room." With a smile at Rosalie, he added, "Shall we take our places at the table, fair Titania?"

Accepting her consort's outstretched hand, she let him escort her to her chair. He had entered her realm of make-believe, and for this one night they were equals.

During the meal Ninian's companions teased him about the disproportionate number of sweets he had included with every course: gingerbread, fruit tarts, lemon custard, macaroons, and glasses of whipped syllabub. The last item to appear was the Twelfth Night cake borne by Parry. At his master's command, he set it down before Rosalie, who was invited to cut it.

"This is so pretty I can't bear to spoil it," she said mournfully, gazing at the spun sugar icing and the candied cherries. *"Eh bien,* if I must."

"Divide it into four equal pieces," Ninian instructed, handing her the knife. While she quartered the cake he exchanged a complicitous glance with his cousin, and when he passed the plates around he examined each slice carefully.

"It tastes as delicious as it looks," Rosalie said after her first bite. She raised another forkful to her mouth, lowering it quickly. Embedded in the cake was an unidentifiable object, something green which resembled a tiny pebble.

"You've found it!" Ninian cried excitedly. "A pea is always hidden in the cake, and the lady who finds it is queen for the night."

"But I'm already a queen." Watching him stab his own piece with a knife, she asked suspiciously. "What other items are concealed?"

"A bean," said Gervase, holding it up.

"Diable! I wanted it." When Ninian realized that the others were staring at him, he mumbled an apology.

"You promised not to use that word again," moaned Rosalie, her face hot with chagrin. "I never *taught* him to say it," she defended herself to the duke.

He chuckled and said, "As Pope observed, a little learning is a dangerous thing."

"Which pope?" she wondered.

Mr. Duffield shook his head. "Not the prince of the Roman church, mademoiselle. His grace refers to the great English poet, Alexander Pope."

Mortified by her ignorance, she blushed again.

After dinner they moved to the tapestry room. Ninian, who had adorned the mantel with holly boughs, led the master and mistress of the revels to their thrones, a pair of ornately carved and gilded chairs. He explained to Rosalie that possession of the pea and bean conferred the right to decree the evening's entertainments.

"Which game would *you* most like to play?" he asked.

"Snapdragon," she answered promptly, remembering that it was the duke's favorite.

Afterward they derived considerable enjoyment from forfeits, followed by speculation. Gervase persuaded a reluctant Rosalie to favor them with a pantomime. While her audience shouted out characters, she personified Queen Charlotte, the butler Parry, and lastly a drunken sailor, Ninian's mischievous suggestion.

To ensure her pupil's satisfaction, she insisted upon playing Blindman's Buff. After he completed a brief turn as Blindman, his cousin and his tutor succeeded him. Rosalie, swiftly captured by Mr. Duffield, was the last to submit herself to the blindfold.

Tying the silk scarf over her eyes, Gervase asked solicitously, "Too tight?" She shook her head, and he spun her around, slowly at first, then with greater speed until he finally released her.

Dizzy and off balance, she waited for her senses to be restored. The room was not large and there were only three players, so she anticipated no great difficulty.

Hearing frantic footsteps, she moved forward. Her outstretched hands brushed the damask curtains, and when she ascertained that no one was concealed behind their folds, she continued her sightless search.

A soft laugh made her pause, but while she was trying to determine its origin, a muted commotion from the hall confused her. Someone emitted a sharp gasp, followed by a low groan which broke off abruptly.

The sound of the door opening prompted her to cry out, "*Arrêtez!* No one is permitted to leave while the game is in progress!"

"Pray forgive my intrusion," said a cool, unfamiliar voice, unmistakably that of a female.

Disconcerted, Rosalie ripped away the blindfold. She was horrified to see a middle-aged woman standing directly in her path.

The candlelight lent a sheen to her sable mantle and muff. Her lavishly plumed bonnet was black, as was the skirt visible beneath the dark furs, both indicative of fullest mourning. She stared down at Rosalie from a superior height, her silvery eyes clouded with anger, and her arched brows expressive of aristocratic disdain.

When Gervase approached her, crown in hand, she asked him, "Who is this person?"

"Mademoiselle de Barante. She is teaching Ninian to speak French."

"Is she capable of doing so?"

The earl popped up from behind a sofa. "*Certainement, ma chère tante.* She made my costume, too. Can you guess who I am?" He replaced his drooping beard and brandished his sextant.

The Duchess of Solway's expression softened. "The suspense of knowing whether I've guessed right or wrong would be more than I could bear. An illustrious naval hero, I should think, from the look of you. Raleigh?"

"Sir Francis Drake!"

"And who might this be?" she asked, glancing at the gentleman standing in the corner.

"Jap is my tutor. He's Oliver Cromwell. Ger and Mademoiselle are Oberon and Titania."

Not knowing what else to do, Rosalie knelt down for a plié in the fourth position, the traditional stage curtsy. "*Je suis enchantée de faire votre connaissance,* Madame la Duchesse."

"I daresay." Tugging at her gloves, the lady addressed her nephew again. "Ninian, come and give me a kiss before

I go up to my room. And Gervase, I must ask that you come with me. We have *much* to discuss."

"As you wish."

The duke's parent maintained her disapproving silence even after they entered her upstairs suite, where a fire was being hastily kindled by a chambermaid. After placing her gloves on a console table, she removed her bonnet and wrap. The hovering abigail took them from her and immediately withdrew into the dressing room, motioning for the maid to follow her.

Not until she was alone with Gervase did the duchess address him. "What sort mischief have you been getting up to? And who is that painted, half-dressed creature downstairs? You can never convince me that she is a governess."

"She's an opera dancer," he said baldly. "Her given name is Rosalie Delphine Lovegrove, but she is known professionally as Mademoiselle de Barante."

She shook her graying head. "If that is meant as a jest, I don't consider it an amusing one."

"It's the truth."

"Then I can only conclude that you've taken leave of your senses."

Sensitive to any remark about madness, which had plagued his father's family, he moved away from her. "Had I been informed of your intention to come to Haberdine, I would certainly have provided a full explanation beforehand."

"Do so now." She sat down upon a chair, her chin remaining high and her back erect.

From earliest childhood Gervase had been close to his mother, but since becoming a man he'd concealed from her those aspects of his life that were likely to provoke disapproval. With regard to Rosalie, his efforts had succeeded all too well. Choosing his words carefully, he explained how he and his ward had become acquainted with her.

"Her mother was a Parisian dancer and her father an English violinist—lawfully wed," he added, lest she make the same erroneous assumption he had initially. "Both are dead now. Mademoiselle de Barante has supported herself by performing at the King's Theatre, and more recently at Sadler's Wells. Because I inadvertently brought about the injury which caused her to lose her place, I felt honorbound to provide temporary support. The only way I could to do it logically, and respectably, was to employ her as a French teacher until she resumes her work."

"It would surprise me greatly if she ever chose to work again," his mother said caustically. "Your chivalry is laudable, but in my estimation you've carried it to excess. From what I saw of her—which was entirely too much for my comfort—she has made a full recovery. Yet she is still living with you."

"It is her stated intention to leave within the week."

"She will go tomorrow," the duchess declared.

Gervase shook his head. "I cannot allow that while the roads are so bad."

"I traveled here from Hethington Hall without mishap," she countered. "The London turnpike is in a fair state, and the mails and stagecoaches are running again. I don't dispute your right to befriend whomever you please, but I refuse to associate with a dancing girl, or countenance her presence in this house. Give her money, promise her an expensive trinket, but get her away from Haberdine."

"She's not my mistress," Gervase stated firmly.

"Thank heaven for that," his mother breathed. "She would be far worse for you than that atrocious Titus woman."

Her criticism of his taste offended him, and only through a concerted effort did he maintain his composure. "You should save your lectures for Ninian, who has taken quite a fancy to her."

"I'm sorry to hear it. My dear, I don't mean to dictate to you, for you are your own master. But I must implore you to do as I've requested."

Reluctantly he said, "I'll speak to Mademoiselle de Barante in the morning."

"You'd better not wait," she advised him. "And don't look so tragic, my dear. Females of that sort always land on their feet."

When Gervase returned to the tapestry room, Ninian reported that Mademoiselle had retired. "Is Aunt Elizabeth angry because of our party?" he asked.

"She's weary from the long drive," Gervase replied. He knew he should prepare the boy for Rosalie's immediate departure, but he couldn't bring himself to disappoint another person that night. "There is something I must attend to, but you may stay up for as long as Mr. Duffield allows."

Going directly to the steward's office, he gathered together as many banknotes as he could find and stuffed them into the deep pockets of his velvet robe. Slowly he made his way to the distant part of the house traditionally allotted to the family governess, and tapped gently upon the door of Rosalie's room, his heart heavy with regret.

He knew she'd just been washing the paint from her face, for it was still dewy with moisture and damp curls clustered at her temples. "Meet me in the schoolroom," he said in a low voice, "and bring your candle."

Going to the dark chamber across the hall, he waited until she arrived with a flickering taper. He took it from her and placed it upon the scarred table where he and his siblings had learned their lessons. "Please sit down. I won't keep you long."

"I can guess what you are about to say," she told him, "and I can save you the trouble. I've already made up my mind to leave in the morning."

When she shivered, he realized that her shoulders and back were exposed to the chilly air—she was still wearing the diaphanous fairy costume. He removed his heavy velvet robe and wrapped her in it, saying, "I bear full responsibility for that unfortunate scene a short while ago. When I informed my mother that I'd engaged a lady to instruct Ninian, I left out certain details of your history. I also concealed the truth of your profession."

Smiling faintly, she said, "Many weeks ago I warned you that I'm not a proper person for Lord Swanborough to know. Has the duchess been telling you as much?"

"I disagree with both of you. Your success as Ninian's governess has been considerable, far greater than I thought possible. He has minded you and Duffield better than any member of my family. Not only does he admire and respect you, I believe he is also fond of you." After a pause he continued, "My mother is less concerned about your influence on Ninian than the danger you pose to me."

One white hand flew to her cheek in dismay. "I didn't think of that!"

"No? How could you not think it?"

"But you are a duke, and—and I'm only a dancer."

"That didn't prevent us from becoming friends."

Her gaze was steady and her voice calm as she said, "I believe you seek more than friendship."

"Yes," he confessed, relieved that he could finally speak openly and candidly. "From the night we met I've known that you are as virtuous as you are desirable, Rosalie. I didn't have seduction in mind when I persuaded you to come to Haberdine. And not until I joined you here on Boxing Day and saw you again did I become aware of the nature of my regard for you. But because you were my employee, I couldn't court you in the way I wanted to."

"You did in the wood," she reminded him.

"I don't regret kissing you, I'm not that honorable."

"You mustn't talk that way—not tonight!"

"If not this night, when?"

"Never! Because I cannot give you the answer you expect." Her subsequent words came fitfully, in short bursts. "I don't want to become your *chère amie*. My profession is too demanding and fatiguing. Every day I attend classes, and rehearsals, and the performances sometimes continue past midnight. I couldn't give parties and entertain your friends. I'm not witty or dashing or fascinating. And I don't know anything about pleasing a gentleman."

When she had exhausted her objections, he said quietly, "I don't require that you become a slave to my whims. It's my habit to avoid social gatherings, so you needn't serve as my hostess. I've got only one good friend, and he's such a handsome fellow that I'd just as soon you *didn't* entertain him. The qualities I demand in a mistress are constancy and honesty, nothing more or less." But her sad eyes and wistful face were proof that his speech had failed to move her. Kneeling beside her, he took both her hands in a firm grip. "Rosalie, I'd try so very hard to make you happy."

"But you wouldn't be happy with me. We have nothing in common. I spent but a few months at a convent school, and dancing is my sole accomplishment. I read only novels and poetry. You are educated, your ancestors were kings and generals. I'm descended from English farmers and French lawyers." She drew a long, sobbing breath and bowed her head. "But there is another reason that I must refuse you, and I don't know how to explain."

"Try," he urged, tightening his hold upon her. "You can tell me anything—everything."

"I suppose the place to start is with Maman," she began tentatively. "She was the daughter of a respected attorney in Rouen, who was rich enough to provide her with dancing masters. Her talent was such that Madame Montansier, the proprietress of the local theater, decided to take her to Paris and when she agreed to go her family disowned her. She never saw them again, or tried to communicate with them, though they must have been aware of her success. She performed at Versailles and won the favor of the Queen."

"Yes, so you've told me."

"She was young and beautiful and popular, the toast of Paris. My father was one of her many admirers, but she scarcely noticed him. She'd fallen desperately in love with another man and was to him what you ask me to be. They lived together, and though their affair lasted several years, he did not treat her well nor was he *fidèle*. She expected to become his wife, and when he abandoned her, she was destroyed by grief."

Gervase broke in at this point. "I can guess what happened next. She sought comfort from your father."

"*C'est vrai*. And she was so grateful for his kindness that when he proposed she agreed to marry him. Theirs was a hasty union, but it turned out to be a happy one. My mother's gratitude became a love so strong that she forgot the other man. In addition to receiving acclaim as a dancer, she was revered for being a dutiful wife and a devoted mother—a shining example of the virtues of the new republic."

When she paused, Gervase asked, "How did you learn

about her unhappy past? I can't imagine that she told you about her lover."

"Papa did, when he thought I was old enough to know. It was his way of explaining the facts of life for opera dancers."

Now comprehending the deeper meaning behind her story, Gervase said, "I can understand that you might be reluctant to live as your mother did before her marriage. But surely you know I'm not so heartless as to desert you?"

"It isn't that." Her greenish eyes locked with his. "I won't be your mistress because of my *father*. When he lay on his deathbed, I promised him I would never give myself to any man but my husband. That, Gervais, was my sacred pledge, and I will not break it. Not even for you."

There was little comfort to be had from her wistful conclusion, which indicated that she was not entirely indifferent to him. Staring down at her fingers, still entwined with his, he heard himself say, "I'm sorry—sorrier than you can imagine."

"*Moi aussi*. You aren't angry?"

"Only disappointed." Releasing her hand, he dipped his hand into the deep pocket of the robe and withdrew the money he'd collected.

"You gave me what I need for the journey to London before you left Bibury," she reminded him. "I've still got all of it and I know there's more than enough for a post chaise."

"You must take this as well—consider it your salary if you prefer."

"*Non*, it is too much."

Ignoring her protest, he continued, "You can hire lodgings in town and live comfortably until you find another situation. Should you require anything at all, I want you to let me know. Will you?" He expected resistance and was glad that she nodded.

He slipped his arms beneath the folds of velvet and pulled her close. Her body was yielding, and when he kissed her mouth he discovered that his longing for her, if not his love, was indeed reciprocated.

"Go to bed," he said at last, separating himself from her.

Her lips, now warmed by his, brushed against his cheek. "*Adieu,* Gervais."

She took the candle with her, leaving him equally bereft of light and hope.

10

Each step trod out a Lover's thought,
And the ambitious hopes he brought.
— RICHARD LOVELACE

Rosalie stood before the building that occupied the corner of Haymarket and Pall Mall, her fingers curled around a pair of dancing slippers. The arches and pediments of its facade reminded her of a temple and she, an aspiring vestal, doubted her worthiness to enter. During her years as a humble coryphée, she'd always used the stage door.

"What are you waiting for?" asked James d'Egville impatiently. "We cannot linger, for Rossi is waiting. And nothing could be worse for your muscles than this brisk wind and chilling damp."

London was caught in the frigid grip of winter. The Thames waters were frozen, enabling intrepid pedestrians to walk on ice from Battersea Bridge as far as Hungerford Stairs. In the days since Rosalie's return, the weather had moderated slightly: the heavy snowfall of last week had been succeeded by rain showers.

Rosalie hurried through the sacred portals of the King's Theatre in d'Egville's wake.

Recent events had demonstrated that fate could be generous as well as cruel. A soloist in the ballet had requested a leave of absence necessitated by pregnancy, and Signor Rossi needed an immediate replacement. The term of employment would last for the remainder of the opera season, which ended in August, but as her mentor had pointed out, a temporary appointment often became a permanent one.

Together they had worked diligently to prepare her for

today's examination. Determined to make up for the weeks she'd lost, Rosalie had visited d'Egville's dancing academy. He'd spent the better part of a morning supervising her exercises at the barre, barking out intricate combinations of steps, and hadn't stopped until her entire body was shiny with moisture. Then she had listened stoically to his critique of her performance, so scathing that she was reluctant to return the following day.

Her mother had often warned her that the dancing profession was one of practice, sweat, rehearsal, and worry, and the past week had proved it.

Somehow she'd found the time to locate a lodging in Panton Street, only a short distance from the opera house. And she'd engaged Peg Reilly, the downtrodden girl who had waited upon her in Islington, as her servant. The princely sum Gervase had provided was largely intact and would keep her in comfort until Easter, when the Sadler's Wells theater opened. For if Rossi deemed her unsuitable, she would have to return to Islington and Mr. Dibdin.

"I've already discussed the terms of employment with Michael Kelly," James d'Egville told her as they proceeded through the lobby. "He agrees to a salary of eight pounds a week, and you'll have a dress allowance of fifty pounds." Opening a door, he ushered her into the cavernous auditorium. "Remember to hold your arms high for the arabesques," he said under his breath, "it will make you appear taller. And don't forget to smile."

Although Rosalie was familiar with the theater, its proportions were overwhelming after six years at the more intimate Sadler's Wells playhouse. The auditorium, vast enough to accommodate over two thousand spectators, seemed even larger when empty. Only the chandeliers nearest the stage were lit, and after her eyes had adjusted to the darkness she discovered that the decor was different from what she remembered. The alterations included new upholstery for the seats which matched the scarlet curtains of the boxes. The lighter hues of the frescoed ceiling were completed by the panels of the box fronts. The ones on the ground level had been painted gray with decorative medallions, those directly above were embellished with trompe l'oeil marbling, and the next highest had bas relief figures on a silver ground. The fourth and fifth tiers and the gallery above were unadorned.

A pair of gentlemen stood in Fop's Alley, a broad central aisle separating the rows of red-cushioned benches, conversing with each other in rapid Italian. One was Signor Rossi, who turned his head to say, "Here they are. D'Egville, I have decided to revive your ballet *Le Jugement de Paris,* and it must be ready in only two days!"

Rosalie's friend answered calmly, "Mademoiselle de Barante is already familiar with the piece, for she danced it several years ago. I've been teaching her the role of Juno."

"Molto bene." The ballet master acknowledged the aspirant's presence by saying, *"Signorina,* you will be showing me that you dance as well as your mother, no?" When she removed her heavy cloak to reveal a thin muslin gown and pink stockings, he said approvingly, "You do not need to make the change of clothes—d'Egville has warned you how much I am misliking any delay. I summoned Vestris, but he takes so long a time in the dressing room."

Relieved to know that Armand would be her partner, Rosalie felt this was a favorable omen. She was putting on her slippers when he materialized, clad in tunic and hose.

After kissing both of her cheeks in the French fashion he said gaily, "What a prophet I am, *chérie*—now I see you in the place you belong. We perform together again!"

They made their way to the stage, already arranged for the first act of the current opera, and he explained that the side pieces and painted backdrop represented an Oriental palace. Taking her position, Rosalie was content to be back in her own comfortable setting, where castles were built of wood and canvas rather than stones and mortar.

A pounding heart and a dry throat were the first signs of her habitual stage fright. As she waited for the music to begin, the larger purpose of reestablishing herself in the company suddenly seemed less important than proving that d'Egville's faith was not misplaced. She knew her *épaulement* was intact—her head, neck, shoulders, and arms moved as gracefully as ever—but her jumps were sadly *terre à terre* and her footwork was less accurate than either of them liked.

Rossi angled his dark head toward the other Italian, now seated before the harpsichord. "Signor Pucitta, it will be the *pas de deux* of the shepherd Paris and the goddess Juno."

The sound of her feet brushing the wooden floorboards threatened to drown out the soft strains wafting from the orchestra pit. She concentrated on the music, matching her movements to its rhythm, her performer's smile growing more genuine with each success of her will over the laws of gravity. She placed her hand upon Armand's outstretched arm, letting the other rest upon his firm shoulder, and raised one leg behind her for the *arabesque penchée*. A moment later she darted away from him, her toes skimming the stage, and he pursued her by vaulting himself into one of his celebrated *jetés*.

Inspired by his brilliance, Rosalie completed a tricky *bourée* without cheating, as she'd done when practicing with d'Egville. Armand's eyes flashed as his stocky, muscular form left the earth yet again, and it occurred to her that when he danced he was almost handsome.

His next feat, an *entrechat huit,* provoked a sharp comment from Rossi, whose disembodied voice called out from the front row, "Allegro—faster! No, no, try again. You want to be quick, lively! We will attend to it later. Signor Puccitta, continue."

The coda was grand and stately, demanding less energy from the dancers, and the pas de deux ended with another supported arabesque.

While Signor Rossi and James d'Egville conducted a whispered dialogue, Rosalie stood beside Armand, her chest heaving. She was too weary to think clearly, but instinct told her that she'd performed reasonably well for a dancer who had been away from the stage for two months. Her technique hadn't entirely deserted her, and the troublesome right ankle remained wonderfully steady and free of pain.

"I am satisfied, *signorina*," the ballet master announced, "even though you are small to be Juno. Go down to the tiring room and someone can make the costume fit. I will advise Signor Kelly to draw up a formal contract, if you accept our terms."

Exultation deprived Rosalie of speech, but before withdrawing to the wings she managed a nod signifying assent.

"Wait, Vestris," Rossi commanded as Armand followed her off the stage. "I am wanting to see the *entrechat* once more. Your elevation is not what it could be."

The Frenchman's scowl indicated that his professional pride was offended by the comment.

As Rosalie peeled off her leather slippers, their insides damp with perspiration, she puzzled over Armand's displeasure. A true artist, her mother had often said, must strive to vanquish the ego and recognize those weaknesses which required improvement. Distressed to discover that fame and adulation had altered her friend, she made a silent vow never to let vanity impede her ability to learn, especially now that her dream had become a reality.

A chorus of London church bells were striking the hour of two as the Duke of Solway's town coach and the vehicles bearing a Parliamentary delegation reached the columned forecourt of Carlton House.

A mere two days after Rosalie de Barante's departure Gervase had also deserted Haberdine Castle, citing his need to take his seat in the House of Lords. It had been an act of rebellion, a demonstration of his unwillingness to be ruled by family expectations. He hadn't stated his intention of seeking out his inamorata, and if his mother had guessed that duty was not the only reason for his journey she'd been astute enough not to make any comment. Perhaps she didn't care, so long as he refrained from conducting his amours in her presence or beneath his ancestral roof.

He already knew that Rosalie had not returned to the Tottenham Street theater, the one she'd left so abruptly after her October accident. His hopeful visit to Islington had been similarly unrewarding: Sadler's Wells remained closed until Easter, and Mrs. Dibdin was quite certain that her husband hadn't engaged the French dancer for his summer season. Mary Grimaldi had been unable to help him, and she'd seemed so preoccupied by some private concern that he regretted troubling her with questions.

It was imperative that he find Rosalie. While he didn't expect to overcome her scruples by admitting the depth and strength of his attachment, he wanted her to know that his proposal had been prompted by more than a transient physical desire. He had cheapened his offer of protection by failing to explain that he was in love with her. Madly, fiercely, agonizingly in love.

Before joining the group of officials, he gazed across Pall Mall at the Italian Opera House. To dance there had been Rosalie's stated ambition—possibly he could solve the mystery of her whereabouts by seeking her there.

Reluctantly he'd interrupted his search for the dancer to participate in the frenzied political debate being waged by the Government and the Opposition over the proposed Regency. Without understanding how it came about, he had become embroiled in a conflict rife with intrigue.

Spencer Perceval, the Prime Minister, was determined to restrict the powers of the Prince of Wales. The Whigs, anticipating a swift rise to prominence in a new ministry, were eager to placate His Royal Highness and protested the limitations. Gervase, taking his seat in the House of Lords some days after the final division on the question, had followed his father's example of enlightened Toryism in subsequent votes, thereby endearing himself to the party. His new and unsought prestige had resulted in Lord Camden's invitation to join the deputation of Lords and Commons bound for Carlton House, where they were about to hear the Prince's response to the provisions of the Regency Bill.

Grey and Grenville, the Whig lords most likely to head the next government, were brimming with self-importance and ill concealed triumph when the doors were opened by a footman in the Prince's livery. As a crowd of noblemen and ministers assembled in the octagonal vestibule, the major domo intoned, "My lords, gentlemen, His Royal Highness is prepared to receive you now."

From his position at the rear of the procession, Gervase cast a fleeting glance at a marble bust staring down from a pedestal. It was Charles James Fox, the Prince's political hero, who had labored for a Whig supremacy but hadn't lived to enjoy it.

Entering the circular drawing room in the wake of his illustrious companions, he discovered that their royal host had summoned his friends among the Opposition to witness this momentous occasion. Richard Sheridan and Lord Moira were present, as was the Duke of Cumberland, whose scarred face was more grim than the proceedings seemed to warrant.

Presently in his forty-ninth year, George, Prince of Wales was less handsome than in his youth. An excess of French food and French spirits had broadened his figure, and his features were rapidly vanishing beneath fat. His bulging blue eyes scanned each member of the party, and when they fell upon Gervase, he said, "It is my pleasure to welcome you to Carlton House this afternoon, cousin. You have never been here, I think."

"I've not been so honored, Your Highness."

"Some other time you must permit me to show you my many treasures. I deeply regret that the business at hand prevents my doing so today."

Conscious of the stares of all the other gentlemen as they puzzled over an obvious overture, Gervase made a deep and reverent bow. He could not account for it himself, having encountered the Prince but a few times in his life. By tradition all peers above the rank of baron were officially designated as cousins by the King, but the present monarch had only the remotest blood connection to the aristocracy. Was the Prince's familiarity an early attempt to establish himself as his father's substitute?

After a brief exchange of civilities, Lord Camden began reading Parliament's final resolutions. For the term of one year, the Prince could create no peers. The Queen would be responsible for the care of His Majesty, assisted by a council, and crown property would be administered by trustees.

Gervase, feigning attentiveness, examined the towering columns of red prorphyry and the blue silk draperies. Now he understood why many people referred to Carlton House as the grandest palace in all of Europe. The Prince had certainly created a suitably royal residence for himself and an appropriate repository for his most precious works of art.

When Lord Camden reached the conclusion of his address, his voice increased in volume. "The lords spiritual and temporal express their hope that His Royal Highness, out of regard to the interests of His Majesty, will be prepared to undertake the weighty trust proposed to be vested in him, subject to such limitations and restrictions as might be provided."

The attention of every person in the room turned toward the portly individual in the blue coat and tight white breeches.

The Prince dutifully recited the acceptance composed by his Whig advisers. "Being determined to submit to every personal sacrifice consistent with the regard I owe to the security of my father's crown and the welfare of his people, I do not hesitate to accept the office and situation proposed to me." He paused, then added, "My lords and gentlemen, you will communicate this answer to the two Houses, with my most fervent wishes and prayers that the Divine Will may extricate us and the nation from our present position by the speedy restoration of His Majesty's health."

At the conclusion of the ceremony, Gervase stepped aside so the others might precede him out of the room.

Upon reaching the courtyard the distinguished gentlemen scattered in several directions, some departing for Westminster, others hastening toward such Whig strongholds as Holland House and Melbourne House to report on what had passed. There would be no rejoicing in Tory circles; it was almost certain that after his swearing-in the new Regent would topple his father's ministers from their lofty perch.

The rain showers of the morning had abated; the heavy clouds were lifting. Gervase sauntered purposefully across busy Pall Mall to find out if Rosalie had returned to the King's Theatre.

He posed this question to the box keeper, who shrugged and replied helplessly, "Mr. Taylor is confined to the Rules of the King's Bench Prison, and 'is secretary Masterson doesn't tell me nothing. One of the ladies of the ballet was given leave for a lying-in, but whether a Frenchie replaced 'er I can't say. Most of our dancers are Italian—Angiolini,

Mori, Peto. But that Madame Nora is a Portugee, so is Monroy."

"Mr. Read, would *anyone* here know if Mademoiselle de Barante has applied to the management?"

The man shook his head. "The stage manager—that's Mr. Michael Kelly—will very likely be at Drury Lane today. And our treasurer Mr. Jewell departed after the midday rehearsal. Tomorrow is an opera night, so you might come back then and see if she's dancing."

Gervase, having already decided to do so, was dismayed to learn that his own box might not be available. "How can that be? It's my personal property. My father purchased it twenty years ago, when the theater was rebuilt."

His informant gave a guttural laugh. "Aye, in theory it's yours. But last year, when 'er grace stopped attending, she gave Mr. Ebers permission to let the box. Any member of the public can 'ire it by going to a certain bookseller in Bond Street. It may be too late to recover your seats, for they're 'ard to come by for a Saturday performance even if the Cat—when Madame Catalini isn't singing."

As Gervase retreated, Mr. Read called after him, "Your grace might take this, if you're interested in backstage matters." Turning around, he saw that the boxkeeper was holding out a newspaper. "It's the *Examiner,* crammed with gossip about stage performers. Mr. Jewell left it behind, and I was going to throw it out with the rubbish."

Gervase left the theater, the paper tucked under his arm. His carriage was waiting at the corner, and before climbing inside he commanded his coachman to take him to Elston House. Damon, he knew, retained possession of his opera box and would no doubt oblige him with a seat.

The vehicle moved forward. Gervase, who relied exclusively upon the *Morning Post* and the *London Gazette,* settled back against the cushions to study the unfamiliar newspaper. He was scanning the back pages absently when his eyes fell upon a promising paragraph beneath the heading "New French Dancer to Perform."

Mr. William Taylor and Mr. Michael Kelly, managers of the Italian Opera House, announce that they have engaged

MADEMOISELLE DE BARANTE to perform in the opera ballets for the remainder of the season. On Saturday, 12th January, she will essay the role of Juno in Mr. d'Egville's popular ballet *Le Jugement de Paris*. The new soloist is the daughter of the celebrated *danseuse* Delphine de Barante, who formerly graced the stage of the Paris Opera.

Smiling, Gervase removed a penknife from his coat pocket and cut out the notice. He wasn't sure which made him happier, the prospect of seeing her again, or the knowledge that she'd found her way back to a theater where her talents would be recognized, and appreciated.

The Duke of Solway and the Marquis of Elston navigated their way through the crowded lobby of the King's Theatre until they reached a box located on the bottom tier, on a level with the pit and slightly lower than the stage.

In common with the other gentlemen attending the opera, they wore long-tailed coats, embroidered waistcoats, and satin breeches. Their cravats were tied in the most intricate styles, and snowy ruffles extended from the sleeves of their coats, falling over their white kid gloves. Diamonds studded Gervase's silver knee buckles, and a dress sword hung from the crimson sash at his waist. He, like his friend, carried a *chapeau bras* under his arm.

Gervase studied the female component of the audience, equally splendid in low-cut gowns and flashing jewels, with far less interest than Damon. The marquis ogled the ladies, who waved their fans to and fro as they chattered to one another or flirted with their elegant escorts.

When the first act ended, Gervase asked if the soprano was a superior artist, or merely adequate. "She isn't much to look at," he commented.

"Nor are many other opera singers, with the notable exception of Angelica Catalini," Damon replied. "Bertinotti's voice hasn't the power of the Cat's, but it has a quality of sweetness. In my opinion, the management have chosen an inappropriate piece for her introduction to the public—I should think she's better suited to comic roles. I believe her prospective husband, a musician, has been commissioned to create a new work for her."

The opera dragged on to its tragic finish and Gervase, eager to see the ballet, was relieved rather than saddened when the suicidal heroine raised her dagger for the last time. He wondered whether Rosalie was nervous as she awaited her entrance. Had she found friends in the company, or did the others treat her as an outsider, a newcomer? Did she ever think of him, or remember their times together in Bibury and at Haberdine? Before the night was over, he hoped to have the answers to those and many other questions.

During the ensuing interval, Damon moaned softly, prompting Gervase to ask, "What's amiss?"

"That bovine fellow we met at Sadler's Wells is parading up and down Fop's Alley. What was his name?"

Gripping the padded rail, Gervase said grimly, "Beckmann."

"Can that man in the powdered wig be his father? By his appearance he is a gentleman of the old school, although a green velvet coat seems a bit excessive even for the opera."

"His father is dead, that's how he came by his money," Gervase recalled. He glowered in the direction of the young fellow who had discomfitted Rosalie on the night of her accident.

He clenched his gloved hands, tense with anticipation. The curtain rose to reveal three goddesses and their respective courts posed before a backdrop of Mount Ida, its peak obscured by pillowy painted clouds. The soloists performed a lively *pas de trois*, each one striving for the golden apple, and when the shepherd youth Paris appeared, they pantomimed an appeal, begging him to choose the fairest.

Armand Vestris danced first with Rosalie, who made an enchanting Juno in her sleeveless Grecian tunic. Narrow bands sewn with pearls supported a high-waisted bodice, artfully draped to reveal one bare breast. The elaborate arrangement of her hair made her appear exotic and unfamiliar to Gervase—curling tongs had imposed strict order upon her shorter curls, and the longer ones were crimped into ringlets.

The *scène d'action* continued, with the *danseur* partnering Mademoiselle Monroy, a warlike Minerva. His last and longest *pas de deux* was with Venus, the lovely Fortunata Angiolini, to whom he awarded the apple.

Although the spectators applauded graciously when the ballet ended, the occupants of the boxes and the pit abandoned their seats immediately after the curtain dropped. Damon explained that they were eager to take part in one of the most exclusive assemblies in London, a postperformance supper in the concert room.

"Do you intend to pay your compliments to Mademoiselle de Barante?" he asked Gervase as they skirted the multitudes of people in the box lobby. "As the holder of a ground level box, I am entitled to move freely behind the scenes. My guests also."

"Does she have her own changing room?"

"No, she hasn't the seniority for any perquisites. There's so little space backstage that the choristers of the opera and the ladies of the corps de ballet, poor souls, must share quarters. Never fear, I'll help you find your pretty friend— Lord Swanborough's friend, I should say," he added slyly.

Gervase accepted the offer of assistance politely but unenthusiastically, for he would have preferred a private reunion with Rosalie. They joined the other bucks and beaux thronging the subterranean corridors, chatting up the female performers. After peering over many a shoulder and being jostled more than once, Gervase glimpsed Rosalie. Benjamin Beckmann and his well-dressed companion had already cornered her.

"Blubbery bastard," Damon muttered.

Beckmann's bulk made the dancer appear more fragile than ever, and Gervase fancied there was a hunted expression in her wide eyes.

"Your invitation to dine is most generous, sir," he heard her say in a strained voice, "but it is so late." She fidgeted with the pearl trim at her waist.

"Don't refuse me," Mr. Beckmann pleaded. "You won't be sorry—and we'll not be entirely alone. See, I've brought someone who wishes to talk with you. Come forward, Lemercier, let me present you to Mamselle de Barante."

Turning to the man in the green velvet coat, she asked, "You are Monsieur Lemercier?"

He bowed his powdered head in confirmation.

"I received your letter," she said, oblivious to the presence of the duke and the marquis as she stared at the Frenchman. "I am happy to meet any friend of my mother's."

"*Pauvre* Delphine," he sighed, swaying slightly. "How like her you are, *ma belle*—I hoped it might be so."

Rosalie reached out to him, placing her hand on his arm. "Monsieur, you are ill."

"*Non, non,*" he protested. "*Je suis hébété*—I am dazed to look upon your face at last, after so many years of wondering what happened to you. And to her."

She gazed at him in confusion. "Have we met, then? *Je regrette,* but I do not remember. Was it in Paris?"

Large tears slipped down the man's shadowed cheeks as he replied, "*Non,* for I was in Vienna at the time you were born. It is so—so *difficile* to explain to you a secret my Delphine concealed for so long, and with success. I am not bitter that she married her Englishman. She had no other choice when I left Paris, but she was always mine and so are you." Gripping her hands, he said, "*Ma chère* Rosalie, I must kiss your sweet face—that is my right. For I am your true father, Etienne Lemercier."

11

I know not how t'attain the wings that I require
To lift my weight that it might follow my desire.
          —SIR THOMAS WYATT

"But this cannot be—*c'est impossible!*" Mrs. Hughes exclaimed, her thin face incredulous. The former dancer had come to Panton Street to hear Rosalie's report on her performance only to find her preoccupied with what had happened afterward. "Delphine must have married Mr. Lovegrove many months before you were born."

"She did," Rosalie agreed. "But that in itself doesn't disprove this gentleman's claim. Maman had a lover before she was wed—I expect you even knew him."

"*Certainement.* It was *une grande passion.* She used to be so angry when her *cher* Etienne flirted with me." Seeing Rosalie's dismay, the Frenchwoman asked sharply, "Is that the name of this man?"

"Etienne Lemercier."

Mrs. Hughes stiffened. "So he is here in London? But I thought—" Breaking off, she regarded Rosalie speculatively. "His willingness to acknowledge you is unusual, for most men deny paternity."

Rosalie had hoped her mother's friend might discredit Lemercier's assertion, but instead she was confirming her worst fears. "Not this one. He announced that I was his love child in the presence of the Duke of Solway and Lord Elston. And I should not be at all surprised if that horrid Mr. Beckmann spreads the tale all over town."

Shock had blunted her recollection of all that had transpired after she emerged from the emotional Frenchman's embrace. Gervase, whatever he may have thought, brought the uncomfortable scene to an abrupt end, removing Mr. Beckmann with a curt command to procure a hackney. With consummate gallantry he'd escorted her to the waiting vehicle, nodding his understanding when she refused to let him see her safely home.

Not that she would be ashamed to have him visit her lodging, of which she was justly proud. The large bedchamber contained everything necessary to her comfort, and the sitting room was tastefully arranged, with dark blue curtains and a handsome Turkish rug. Delphine de Barante's porcelain image smiled approvingly from the mantelpiece ledge, as if satisfied with her daughter's new abode.

The pantry was spacious enough to admit a cot for Peg Reilly, whose chief duties were brewing tea, cooking simple meals, and the daily marketing. The girl wore her fresh white cap and serviceable olive green gown with a pride that had been notably absent when she'd worked at the shabby house in Islington.

As her maid carried off a tray of food and drink, none of which Rosalie had touched, she told Mrs. Hughes about her intention of receiving Monsieur Lemercier that afternoon. "He begged me to, and I couldn't refuse."

"*Non,*" the other lady said ruefully, "that would be unwise. But you need not meet him alone, *chérie.* Shall I ask my husband's lawyer to advise you, or do you rely on your protector for assistance?"

Disliking her friend's implication, Rosalie said hastily, "But his grace of Solway is nothing to me, madame."

"*Bien sûr,* that is not my business, and I know you will conduct your *affaire d'amour* with great discretion—as Delphine did hers." After a thoughtful moment, the Frenchwoman continued, "If Lemercier should be telling a lie, he might be persuaded to recant. Especially if you have the support of this English *duc.* I am convinced he ought to be present."

"I'd rather not ask him."

The plumes of Mrs. Hughes's bonnet swayed when she shook her head in reproof. "*Quelle sottise!* Is a foolishness to be so timid. Begging favors of gentlemen is an important and necessary task. How else does one manage to survive? The opera paid me well, *c'est vrai*, but my lovers were more generous. From each I received a large settlement."

"The duke is *not* my lover," Rosalie repeated.

But she had accepted money from him, she reminded herself. Her cosy, handsomely furnished flat was proof that French practicality had outweighed any English prudence she possessed.

Reluctant though she was to impose further upon her benefactor, she also respected the opinion of her worldly-wise friend. Shortly after Mrs. Hughes departed, Rosalie sat down to compose a note to Gervase, glancing occasionally toward the figurine occupying the mantelshelf as though it could provide the answers to her many questions.

When Peg left to perform her usual errands, she carried with her the note bound for Solway House. Rosalie, not altogether certain that its recipient would respond to her summons, sat down to wait and worry.

Gervase arrived in less than an hour, his promptness earning him a warm and grateful welcome. Her relief at seeing him again was so overpowering that she could not spurn the comfort he offered.

While he held her close, she burrowed her cheek into his white muslin shirtfront and murmured, "Thank you for coming, Gervais." But his strong embrace had revived a deeper misery and reminded her that he had expectations she could never fulfill.

"I'm glad you wanted me to," he said, encircling her waist with a firm arm and leading her to the sofa. "When do you expect Lemercier?"

"At any time," she told him, sitting down.

He remained on his feet, observing her silently for several seconds before saying, "Since last night I've thought of you constantly, considering all that occurred at the theater. And I remembered what you told me on Twelfth Night about your mother's lover. Isn't there a possibility that the Frenchman could be he, and that you could be his daughter?"

"As much as I would like to say no, I cannot. Lemercier wrote to me—his letter was the one that arrived the day I went fishing with you. In it he said only that he knew Maman and Papa in Paris, and wished to meet me. His claim may turn out to be false, though one cannot doubt his conviction. And even if he speaks the truth, at least this awful uncertainty will be over. My being baseborn won't harm my career."

"From what I observed last evening, nothing could do that." His praise brought a fleeting smile to Rosalie's troubled countenance. "It is a pity that your triumphant return to the opera has been overshadowed by this event." He went on to voice his concern that her new position might be too demanding physically.

"Signor Rossi does work us very hard at rehearsals for his new ballet, but I need to discipline myself after practicing on my own for so long." When asked if she found the members of the company congenial, she nodded. "Oscar Byrne's father used to direct the ballets at Sadler's Wells, so we were already acquainted. I met some of the other male dancers years ago, during my earliest days in the corps, or knew them in Paris. Nearly all are French—Armand Vestris, Boisgerard, Deshayes, Bourdin, Moreau— and when I return home at night, poor Peg has to remind me to speak English!"

"What about your female colleagues, have they treated you well?"

"Not very," she admitted. "Most of them are Italian, and all are inclined to be wary of newcomers. I have made one friend, little Charlotte Dubochet, the youngest member of the ballet company. I daresay you've heard of her sister, Harriette Wilson, the courtesan."

"And Fanny and Sophia. All three are notorious."

"Charlotte is a pupil in Boisgerard's dancing academy. When I watch her practicing the role of Cupid, she reminds me of myself at that age, for she truly loves to dance and is quite talented."

"You seem to be drawn to children," Gervase commented. "It amazed me that you could manage Ninian so easily."

"I trust he's well."

"When I left Haberdine, he was still struggling with Caesar's *Gallic Wars*. My mother was agreeably surprised by his proficiency in the French language."

Rosalie had not forgotten how insignificant she'd felt in the presence of the haughty, disapproving duchess. And the knowledge that the parent of the man she loved considered her a wanton would forever be a source of pain and regret. One week only had passed since her conversation with Gervase in the dark schoolroom, but so much had happened since then that it could have been a year ago.

She suspected him of trying to divert her from her problems when he encouraged her to tell her impressions of London's rival prima donnas. She preferred plump Bertinotti, recently engaged to a violinist from the orchestra, to the beautiful Angelica Catalini, whose greedy French husband demanded huge sums for her rare appearances. Her description of Signor and Signora Cauvini, a tempestuous married couple, made Gervase laugh.

"They squabble constantly, in very rapid Italian, during rehearsals for the new opera. Signor Pucitta composed the music for *Le Tre Sultane,* which is quite lovely, and Catalini sings it with the voice of an angel. I hope it will be acclaimed but expect our largest crowds next month, when she repeats *Semiramide*. It's one of her most popular parts."

Her discourse was interrupted by a knock at the door, followed by Peg's hasty tread in the hall. She rose swiftly, her eyes meeting Gervase's, then she crossed to the looking glass above the mantel to make sure her hair was in order.

When she turned around, she saw that Gervase was smiling. "What amuses you?"

"You looked so very French just then, patting your curls and adjusting the lace at your throat."

"I may well turn out to be more French than I knew," she said, striving for a cheerful rather than a despondent note.

Etienne Lemercier entered the room. Rosalie judged him to be in his middle to late fifties, but the powdered wig and the deep crevices about his eyes and mouth made him appear somewhat older. His attire, albeit less formal than the previous night, conformed to Continental fashion and was characterized by elegant ostentation.

With as much aplomb as she could muster, she presented him to Gervase.

"You were at the opera last night, Monsieur le Duc?" he asked. "At the time I had eyes only for *ma belle fille,* but I recall seeing you."

"Pray be seated," said Rosalie, indicating the chair nearest the fire. She returned to her sofa, expecting Gervase to join her there, but he moved to a window. "Monsieur Lemercier, because I've always believed myself to be the daughter of Richard Lovegrove, your insistence that you are my father is difficult to comprehend."

"I intend to explain, then it will be clear to you. I lived with Delphine de Barante in Paris, and for more than two years she was *une maitresse fidèle.* Often I angered her with my own transgressions and dissipations, and there were scenes. Eventually I became so impatient that I ended our affair, never guessing that she was *enceinte.* Her pride, or her shame, must have prevented her from telling me then, and later she did not know where to find me. I had wealth enough to travel, so I left Paris for Vienna, and within some months the Revolution broke out. I was a careless young man, too fond of my pleasures and expensive diversions to return to a land of strife and death."

"It is as well you did not," Rosalie murmured.

"Not until the year before last did I journey to Paris. A sentimental desire to know what had become of my Delphine took me to the Opera. I met there a lady who remembered me, one of the character dancers, and from her learned about my mistress's hasty marriage to the Englishman, and of the little daughter they passed off as his. *Mais, ce n'est pas possible,* if your mother gave birth in 1788."

Encouraged by the discrepancy, she informed him that in fact she hadn't been born until July of the following year.

"Are you so positive, or is that what Delphine and the musician told you?"

She sank back against the sofa cushions. "I can't imagine they would have lied."

"Out of consideration for your feelings, they could have concealed the truth," Gervase suggested.

"I bring no proof of what I believe," Lemercier continued, "for my search produced none. I even visited Delphine's church, but the register of marriages and births had been removed or destroyed. Many who might have confirmed my suspicions had vanished. I learned that Pascal Boyer, the editor of the *Journal des spectacles,* was a victim of the guillotine. And I was unable to locate Madame Montansier, who must have guessed whose child you were, or the Abbé de Bouyon."

"My godfather." Rosalie's hands clenched involuntarily. "He was killed during the Great Terror. The *canaille* dragged him from his house and hung him from a street-lamp."

"*Chère* Rosalie, how I wish I could have removed you from all the danger and destruction." After a pause, he continued, "I do not doubt that the violinist was good to you, or that he treated you as his own. But he has been dead many years, and cannot be hurt by your accepting me as your father. You did not even take his name."

"Occasionally I use it in my private life," she informed him, looking to Gervase for corroboration.

He stepped forward and asked, "Monsieur Lemercier, what was your motive for contacting Mademoiselle de Barante?"

The Frenchman regarded him blankly. "Motive? I only wished to meet the child of my mistress Delphine, to know her. Is that not permitted?"

"Now that you have succeeded in your object, what are your intentions? Will you return to France?"

"England is now my home, Monsieur le Duc. For almost a year I have lived here, all the time trying to trace Delphine's child. Other emigrés will confirm this—Monsieur Beckmann, *aussi.*"

Rosalie, curious about his association with that gentleman, asked how they had met.

"I went to the Sadler's Wells a few months ago, after hearing that it had a ballet troupe. My stage box was the one rented out by the *bouffon* Grimaldi, and that night I shared it with Monsieur Beckmann. When he described to me a Mademoiselle de Barante who had been part of the company, my heart filled with joy. After the performance I asked the actors and dancers for additional information, and they referred me to Madame Grimaldi. Though she would not tell me or my *avocat* exactly where you had gone, she kindly offered to forward our letters." With a sad smile for Rosalie, he concluded, "If you desire that I keep away and tell me so, I must comply. But I hope you will not, for I am a lonely man in a strange country, without wife or children or family."

Rosalie responded, "Your story raises more questions than it answers, and it is too soon for me to give you any answer."

She could not dislike him, nor was she impervious to the easy charm that must have captivated her mother so many years ago. But she could not yet acknowledge him as her parent, despite the increasing probability that he was.

"If I really am his daughter," she told Gervase after the Frenchman's departure, "I don't know how I shall bear telling Aunt Tilda. She won't love me any less for not being her blood relation, but I am her last tie with Papa— that is, we *thought* so," she concluded pensively. "I have always called myself de Barante, yet I always knew that I was equally a Lovegrove. Now it seems my name could be Lemercier. Difficult though that is to accept, it is even worse to imagine that I might be a full year older than I supposed. For a dancer, that is a fearsome discovery!"

Even in February, the meticulously landscaped grounds of Solway House provided their owner with a pleasant refuge. The water in the marble fountain behind Solway House was turned off for the winter and the branches of the ornamental trees were still bare, but the gardeners were busily pruning the banksia roses growing along a high wall. Although the erratic sunshine failed to warm Gervase as he wandered along the evergreen yew hedge, it raised his spirits. So did the white and yellow crocuses blooming in the borders.

During the past month he's seen Rosalie several times, most often from his box at the King's Theatre. Because the House of Lords sat late into the night, he invariably missed Tuesday night performances, but every Saturday he was there, sitting through hours of operatic tragedy or comedy in order to enjoy the dancer's brief appearance in the ballet.

His initial hope that Rosalie might no longer feel constrained by the deathbed promise she'd made to David Lovegrove was exceedingly short-lived. Integrity and honor were her most notable virtues, apart from virtue itself. She would not become his mistress, she'd told him so quite plainly, and he cared too deeply for her good opinion to enact some ruthlessly persuasive seduction.

As yet he'd found no opportunity to inform her of the powerful feelings that had him soaring to heights of happiness and tumbling back down into the depths of despair every hour or so. His first visit to Panton Street had been twice repeated, with disappointing results. On one occasion Mrs. Grimaldi had been with Rosalie, and the next time he encountered a former colleague of David Lovegrove's, an elderly musician from the King's Theatre orchestra.

The most recent attempt to see her had been the least successful. Hoping to amuse her with a description of a solemn ceremony he had witnessed in the Crimson Drawing room at Carlton House, he'd gone to her house at midday. After Peg Reilly informed him that her mistress had just departed to attend a rehearsal, he had returned to Solway House to prowl the garden pathways.

Lord Elston found him there, and took him to task for his failure to attend an evening party the previous night.

"But unlike my beauteous hostess, *I* didn't really expect to see you. Georgiana Titus was desolated by your absence, for which I hold myself partly responsible. I should have warned her not to give it on an opera night. However, I didn't come to tease but to discuss a matter of importance. Two of them, in fact."

"Oh," Gervase said indifferently, his mind still dwelling upon Rosalie.

"You might have told me about your most recent encounter with royalty rather than letting me read it in the newspapers. I wish I'd known you mean to attend the Regent's first levee. I'm your best friend, your crony, your boon companion, yet you said nothing at all. After affronting me so grossly, you don't deserve my advice, but

I'll offer it anyway. As one whose experience of our Prince far exceeds yours, I warn you to be cautious in your dealings with him."

"I intend to be," Gervase assured him.

"He is notoriously demanding and dangerously fickle. Just ask Grenville and the other Whigs, who were engaged in forming their new administration when they learned that their hopes and efforts were all in vain. But I'm sure that you, His Royal Highness's newest confidant, know all this."

Gervase nodded as they passed beneath the intertwined branches of the laburnum arch. "The political status quo is preserved, and the King's Tory ministers will keep their places."

"And the Prince is always motivated by self-interest, to say nothing of pure selfishness. He wants something from you, and everyone knows it. Speculation has been rife from the day you went to Carlton House with the Parliamentary delegation. Do you know what is being said?"

"I'm not sure I want to," he said grimly.

"Yours is a family of distinction, but even more to the point, Tudor and Stuart blood flows in your veins. The Prince Regent is known to have an abiding interest in the romantic rulers who were supplanted by his plebian forebears from Hanover. He also has a daughter approaching marriageable age. An English duke, one with a royal heritage, would be a more popular choice as her husband than any German princeling."

Gervase emitted a sharp laugh. "Are you implying that the Prince regards me as a prospective son-in-law? If that's the role the gossips have chosen for me, they've outdone themselves on absurdity! I've never met Princess Charlotte of Wales, and considering all I've heard about her I don't particularly wish to. Besides, her grandfather's madness combined with my Aunt Hermia's mental instability must be regarded as serious impediments to an alliance."

"Nevertheless, keep on your guard against palace intrigues. Unless, of course, you aspire to the position of consort."

"I can think of nothing more distasteful to me—or my

family. Mother would be appalled, and I've worried her quite enough lately."

Damon exhibited his most wicked smile. "Your obsession with the opera dancer alarms the duchess, does it? And while we're on the subject of Mademoiselle de Barante—"

"I'm in no mood for another of your warnings," Gervase said firmly.

"I wouldn't presume to interfere to that extent," said the marquis, wagging his golden head. "Do you remember asking me last autumn if I was familiar with a work by Jean-Baptiste Greuze?"

" 'Mischief,' " Gervase said quickly. "Yes, I did."

"I thought you might like to know that just such a painting is on view at Mr. Christie's rooms in Pall Mall. I noticed it there earlier this week and recognized the subject immediately. That was the other important thing I came to tell you."

Gervase ordered his carriage at once, unconcerned about exposing himself to mockery from Damon, who insisted upon accompanying him to the auction house.

But his friend exhibited remarkable restraint, merely saying in his languid way. "I perceive that your interest in Mademoiselle de Barante is more than casual."

"I refuse to discuss my connection with her," he stated as they were borne southward along Park Lane. But he thought better of it, not wishing Damon to draw an incorrect conclusion. "Trust me, she is undeserving of any censure. And whether or not she permits me to become something more, I am forever her friend."

"Obviously you wish it could be more than friendship. Poor Gervase—with all the opera dancers who would welcome your attentions, you had to choose the only one who is unattainable. But your taste, I must admit, is in all other respects impeccable."

When the two noblemen entered Mr. Christie's showroom, one of the employees stepped forward to offer assistance.

"I believe this establishment has acquired a painting by Greuze, and I should like to examine it," Gervase announced.

"Ah yes, the little Gypsy girl. I would have been most happy to show it to your grace, but I fear it went under the hammer yesterday and was sold."

"Sold?" he repeated.

"It failed to fetch the price we had hoped," the gentleman explained. "Even so, the seller, who had acquired it from the original owner, made a substantial profit. The painting had an interesting history, for it was formerly the property of a Parisian lady who posed for several notable artists, including Fragonard. I understand that she was a famous dancer."

"I'm interested in knowing the identity of the purchaser," Gervase said.

"If your grace will grant me but a moment, I shall examine the record."

Damon drifted away to inspect a framed landscape displayed on an easel, while Gervase waited impatiently for Mr. Christie's assistant to return. He wished he'd learned about the painting sooner, for then he could have attended yesterday's sale and placed a bid high enough to secure it for himself. For Rosalie, he amended, because it was on her behalf that he'd wanted the elusive picture.

The man returned to report that the Greuze had been acquired for two hundred guineas.

"Is that all?" Damon asked over his shoulder.

"It is not regarded as one of the artist's better efforts, my lord."

"But a charming study nonetheless. I daresay you could still have it, Gervase, if you offered the new owner three hundred."

The assistant shrugged. "I can't say with any certainty that he would be willing to relinquish it so soon after adding it to his collection, but your grace could inquire."

"I intend to do so," Gervase said with decision. "Who is he, this admirer of Greuze's lesser works?"

"A French gentleman, now a resident of London," their informant replied. "His name is Lemercier."

12

Whatever subjects occupy discourse,
The feats of Vestris or the naval force.
—WILLIAM COWPER

"You are dismissed. And remember, everyone, tomorrow evening it is necessary to dance *con brio, con spirito!*"

Rosalie, her confidence shaken by one of Signor Rossi's sharp rebukes, was relieved that the morning rehearsal had ended. Utterly dispirited, she followed the other soloists to the lower regions of the theater, retreating to a dim, out of the way corner to repeat the intricate *enchainement* she'd muddled on the stage.

She didn't care that the bodice of her muslin gown clung damply to her heated flesh, or that her feet ached, and she ignored the twinge in the small of her back whenever she elevated her leg. Only by improving could she maintain a place in the company and keep her part in *Asiatic Divertissement,* a new ballet with music by Michael Kelly, in which she would portray an Asian court lady.

Armand Vestris and Oscar Byrne exited their dressing room and paused nearby to continue an ongoing conversation. She listened to them absently as she attempted a *pas de basque.*

Said Byrne, without lowering his voice, "Concern about his debts greatly impaired his judgment. He and his wife made up their minds to share a dose of poison in order to escape their financial troubles."

"A sad end for *le bouffon* Grimaldi," was Armand's comment.

Rosalie's body went rigid when she heard the comedian's name. "Grimaldi can't be dead!" she cried.

In a calming voice Byrne replied, "No, he still lives. But he attempted suicide, and so did his wife. They swallowed some laudanum before going to bed t'other night, but didn't even mix enough to put themselves to sleep. When Mary asked, 'Joey, are you dead yet?' he replied, 'I don't think so—are you?' and both began to laugh. To hear him tell it, 'twas a great joke. After eating a good supper and drinking quantities of wine, they felt a great deal more cheerful and decided to live on."

This tale was followed by some gossip about Grimaldi's regular visits to a Clerkenwell pawnbroker. Armand was clearly amused by it, but Rosalie regarded both of Byrne's anecdotes as pathetic rather than humorous. Her last chat with Mary Grimaldi had been some weeks ago, and she felt guilty about neglecting someone who might require a friendly word and possibly monetary assistance.

She returned to her lodging house for a hasty wash and a fresh gown, and set out for Baynes Row in a hackney coach. Along the way to Islington she spied comforting signs of spring's approach—a clump of wild primroses whimsically planted in the windowbox of a town house, and the waving daffodils in Clerkenwell churchyard. When she arrived at the Grimaldi residence, she gazed across Waterhouse Fields toward the New River, Islington Spa, and Sadler's Wells—reminders of her earliest encounters with Gervase and his cousin.

Mary Grimaldi, delighted by Rosalie's unexpected visitation, welcomed her with a warm smile and a fond embrace. "Just look at you!" she exclaimed. "Such a modish bonnet, and quite a pretty shawl—you're doing very well for yourself, I see. No regrets about leaving the aquatic theater?"

"Only one, that I so seldom see you and your family."

"And we also miss you. Don't we, Joe?" Mary smoothed her son's dark hair, then returned her attention to Rosalie, saying, "You must tell us what it's like, dancing in the opera ballets, and about all your admirers."

"I'm not here to talk of myself," she objected. "I want to know how things are with you, Mary."

Her hostess expelled a heavy sigh. "You've been hearing rumors about us. I'm not surprised—my husband *will* tell tales on himself to provoke a laugh. Joe, my dear, why don't you amuse yourself while Mama and Miss Rose are talking, and in a little while we can have tea and cakes." When her child resumed his play, Mary said quietly, "We're buried in debt. Between us, my husband and I have three salaries yet are quite unable to meet all our expenses. I do try to economize, but when it comes to Joe I find it very hard not be indulgent."

Rosalie studied the little boy as he manipulated a mechanical monkey; a turn of the key at its back made the head bob from side to side. It, like the other playthings scattered upon the hearth rug, must have cost Joe's fond parents a considerable sum.

"I greatly fear we shall be forced to let Tippety Cottage go, and that will break our hearts. Joey discharged his groom and gave up the horse and gig. Now he has forbidden me to make any alterations in this house or hire more servants. In the hope of settling with our creditors, he will put his affairs in the hands of a solicitor, who will doubtless demand additional sacrifices from us."

"But at least it might help you out of your difficulties," Rosalie said encouragingly.

"Joey and I share the blame for managing so badly," Mary acknowledged. "We both committed our resources to our son's education, our primary expense. First we sent him to the local school, then we provided French and Italian lessons, and now he has a private tutor. Lately we've engaged a music master—he plays the violin beautifully for a boy so young. The Byrnes and the Fairbrothers, who put all of their lads and lasses on the stage, think us mad to bring him up a gentleman instead of a theatrical performer. But he's very clever, is our Joe, and could make something of himself."

The child, hearing his name, looked up.

"Come and sit by me," Rosalie invited him, patting the cushion of the settee. "Now tell me, what do you most want to be when you grow up? And don't say you aren't sure, because I made up my mind before I was eight years old."

Joe grinned. "I'm going to be a clown in the panto, just like my pa." He wound up his toy again, and made it bow to her. "Papa was younger than me when he went on the stage—he played the part of a little monkey. I can, too. Watch!" Pulling at his ears, he copied the simian's expression.

"Don't make faces," his mother reproved him gently. "Be a good lad now, and tell Cook to make us some tea. Perhaps later Miss Rose will talk French to you. Dear me," she moaned softly as he scampered out of the room, "suppose he really *does* become a player? It's such a hard life, not the one Joey wants for his child."

"It's only natural that he should want to perform. When I was young and saw my mother dancing, I longed to do it, too."

"And I was just the same," the clown's wife acknowledged. "I come from a family of actors and actresses. So does Joey. Old Grimaldi set him to stagework as soon as he could toddle about. I'll speak with him tonight," she said decisively. "Perhaps he will agree that it's foolish to beggar ourselves turning Joe into a gent if he'd rather train to be a comedian."

When Rosalie returned to London, she instructed the hackney driver to convey her to Piccadilly. She spent the rest of the afternoon in the shops on both sides of that fashionable thoroughfare, searching out dress materials for a forthcoming role.

She rejected velvets and satins as too heavy and stiff, and silver tissue as too expensive. After finding a turquoise gauze woven with strands of gilt thread, she chose a length of white sarcenet for an underskirt. The same establishment sold ribbons and other trimmings, and she was tempted by a spool of shiny gold braid and matching silken tassels. Her seamstress, Madame Ferrier, regularly performed miracles and with such items at her disposal would certainly create a costume to arouse envy in all the other dancers.

The shop assistant was already sweeping the floor in

preparation for closing when Rosalie paid for her purchases. The proprietor tied up her last parcel and asked if she wanted her goods delivered. She declined; she lived so near that it was no trouble to carry them herself.

Rounding the corner of the Haymarket and Panton Street, she noticed a curricle and pair waiting at the curb. To reach her door she had to walk past the groom holding the horses, and he leered at her, winking slyly. Despite a strong inclination to put out her tongue, she disregarded him.

Her feet dragged as she climbed the two flights of stairs to her floor. Monday always seemed the longest day of the week, and she was glad to be spared the effort of a performance. Before the next rehearsal she would perfect the *enchainement* for Rossi, and dance it faultlessly at tomorrow's performance.

Recalling that this was Peg's afternoon off, she shifted the packages to one arm and reached into her netted reticule for her key. While she was fitting it into the lock, a large figure moved out of the shadows.

"Mr. Beckmann!" Her startled cry was followed by the sound of her key hitting the wooden floor.

He stooped down to recover it. But when she held out her hand, he only grinned and held it just out of reach.

"If you please, sir, let me have that key."

"Allow me."

When he had unlocked the door, he followed her into the cramped vestibule. She placed her parcels on the parlor table, silently praying that Peg would soon return.

Before she could ask the gentleman's purpose in coming, he stated proudly, "That's my new curricle in the street. I happened to be tooling it down Haymarket, past the opera house, which made me think of you. I'm here to invite you on a little excursion I have in mind. High time we became better acquainted, so what do you say to a drive out to Salt Hill? The Windmill is a snug inn, and its dinners are fine enough for the chaps in the Four-in-Hand Club."

"I'm not able to go away with you, Mr. Beckmann," she said firmly. As much as she disliked him, she couldn't bring herself to be rude.

"My horses can cover thirteen miles in an hour, and we'd be there within two, maybe less. We'll lie abed as late as we please tomorrow morning, and I'll get you back to the theater in time to dance. I'd like to take you down to Brighton, too, but that can wait till the opera season ends."

"You misunderstood me. To put it more plainly, I do not *want* to go. Not to an inn, and definitely not to Brighton."

"Come now, don't play the coquette with me," he said impatiently. "We both know you've got no other prospect but me, not now that your fine duke has deserted you for that royal wench. That's who Solway's chasing, didn't you know? Young as she is, the Regent's daughter is as troublesome as her mama, and the only way to be rid of her is to arrange a marriage as soon as possible. But don't break your heart over his grace, for I'm here to take his place in your affections—and your bed. I may not have a golden coronet or a castle, but you can depend on me to stick by you."

At the end of this preposterous speech he put a pudgy hand upon her arm. Unnerved by the hot, greedy light in his pale eyes, she edged away. "Come no closer, Mr. Beckmann," she warned, flattening herself against her bedchamber door.

"I'll wager you're not so damned skittish with Solway," he said grimly. "Why are you set against me? I'm rich enough, you'll live in grand style under my protection. I should've thought you'd be grateful to me for helping your old father find you. It's more than the duke ever did."

Rosalie groped behind her back for the brass doorknob, twisting it surreptitiously. "I am not grateful at all," she declared with considerable heat, "nor will I be your *fille de joie. Jamais!*"

He came to an abrupt halt, and she seized the opportunity to make a swift escape. She slipped inside her room, slammed the door in his face, and slid the bolt into place with shaking fingers.

Her pursuer let out a loud, derisive laugh. "What a sly one you are, mamselle—like all the Frogs. I don't object to playing games, if that's what you prefer."

Rosalie did not reply.

His heavy tread made the floorboards creak. "I'm going now, but I'll be back. Remember, I've still got your key!"

His arrogant assumption that she would welcome his advances had alarmed her as much as his implication that the Duke of Solway had been her lover. And now, if Beckmann told the truth, Gervase was involved with the Prince Regent's daughter. That could well account for his failure to call upon her in recent weeks. Not so long ago he'd stopped by often, albeit at irregular intervals, to show her a letter from Lord Swanborough or vent his growing frustration with his political allies and adversaries.

Peg Reilly returned at dusk and found her mistress locked in the bedchamber. Outraged by Rosalie's tale of persecution, she offered to sleep on the sitting room sofa in case Mr. Beckmann should make good his threat to return.

"You must send for a locksmith first thing tomorrow, Miss Rose. And if that nasty, thieving man tries to get at you again, he'll discover that you're much cleverer than he *thinks* he is!"

Spring had come early, but in the first week of April its rapid progress was inhibited by a chilling easterly wind. The dismal change in the weather matched Rosalie's low spirits. Mr. Beckmann had not approached her again, but he continued to prowl Fop's Alley. And backstage gossip confirmed his allegations about the Duke of Solway and Princess Charlotte of Wales.

Rumors of a royal engagement had supplanted the Regent's retention of the King's ministers as a favorite topic of conversation in theatrical as well as social circles. The Heiress Apparent was only fifteen, and some performers professed to be shocked by the duke's apparent courtship. Armand Vestris, whose roving eye had lighted upon the fourteen-year-old Lucia Bartolozzi, a recent addition to the dancing academy, could not understand this objection.

No one bothered to ask Rosalie's opinion, which was just as well. She preferred to keep it to herself.

Because the King's Theatre suspended its performances during Passiontide and Easter Week, she faced a fortnight of inactivity during which to mourn Gervase's defection. In an effort to divert herself, she sent a letter to her aunt in Gloucestershire, begging her to visit, and was disappointed when Matilda regretfully refused; a string of social commitments would tie her to Bibury until summer.

On Easter Day, Rosalie went to the Roman Catholic chapel near Golden Square, where she joined a crowd of emigrés. Many were strangers; others, like the hedonistic Armand, she knew quite well. The priest's singsong Latin and the heady scent of incense carried her back to her early childhood, when attendance at Mass had been regarded as a dangerous act of defiance. During the service her attention was caught by a gentleman wearing a white wig. When he turned his head to gaze back at her, she saw that he was Etienne Lemercier.

"So much I have heard about your English *duc*," Mrs. Hughes told her after the service. "*Pauvre petite,* you should have snared him when you had the chance. If he marries *la princesse,* her stuffy relations will be careful to keep him away from the opera!"

Her dismay was heightened when Etienne Lemercier approached her to ask if she would dine with him that evening, accepting her polite refusal with a nod, as though he'd expected it. She regretted causing him pain but was still unable to offer him the filial companionship he desired.

Although she had hoped to sleep luxuriously late on Easter Monday, she woke with the sun and lay in bed brooding until Peg brought her breakfast tray.

She forced down mouthfuls of boiled egg until the shell was half empty and swallowed a piece of buttered toast, but the food seemed to stick in her throat. For the remainder of the morning she altered the white tunic she'd worn for her debut as Juno, which she would use again in *The Loves of Mars and Venus* later in the month. Never fond of needlework, she was glad to set it aside for a titillating novel. All afternoon she lounged upon the parlor sofa, her stocking feet supported by a cushion, and devoured *Les Liaisons Dangereuses*. She was so absorbed in her reading that for long periods she was unaware of the incessant chopping sound coming from the pantry, where Peg was preparing cabbages for soup.

An abrupt tap on the door recalled Rosalie to the real world. She sat upright, tense and wary, and reminded herself that Peg had instructions to send Mr. Beckmann away should he return.

"It's you," she breathed in relief when Gervase entered. His habit of appearing just when she was convinced that he'd never return bewildered her. And past experience had taught her that the peace of mind his presence bestowed was transitory, and would not outlast the visit.

He handed his hat to the beaming Peg and asked, "Are you displeased to see me?"

"Of course not, only I'm embarrassed that you've come at a time when my rooms smell of cooked cabbage." Instinctively her hands flew to her tumbled hair, although his broad smile indicated that disheveled appearance appealed to him.

"The soup is ready, Miss Rose," her servant announced, "and I've sliced the bread. Shall I lay two places?"

Rosalie turned to her guest. "I've dinner enough to share with you."

"I accept with pleasure. But you weren't expecting a guest, so you must permit to let me make some additions to the meal." Turning to Peg, he presented her with a handful of coins. "Go to the pastrycook shop across the way and purchase some meat pies and hot cross buns and fruit tarts. I prefer gooseberry, if any are to be had. Choose whatever you like for yourself."

Peg bobbed a curtsy. "Aye, your grace, and thank you."

"Sadler's Wells playhouse opens tonight," he told Rosalie when they were alone.

"Yes, I know."

"I've sent my footman Robert there to secure a pair of box seats. May I escort you to Islington to see how well Mr. Dibdin is managing in your absence?"

She knew it was folly to accept but lacked the strength to do anything else. Conscious of a painfully intense longing to be in his arms again, she knelt down to search for her slippers.

He sat down on the sofa and picked up her discarded

novel. "By Choderlos de Laclos. I know his name but never read this work. What is your opinion?"

"It's a troubling tale. And a tragic one."

"And shocking, *n'est-ce pas?*"

"Only to the English," she retorted.

Throughout dinner, she managed to stifle her nagging questions about his budding relationship with Princess Charlotte. Surely if he was about to enter into an engagement, he wouldn't have visited her—unless, she thought in sudden panic, he had come to announce his marriage plans. The suspicion that he intended to break off their loose and ill-defined connection grew ever stronger, and she decided that his invitation to the playhouse was a characteristically thoughtful attempt to give her some pleasure before shattering her heart. Except that he could never know how deeply she cared for him, she reasoned with herself.

Her appetite, which had flagged of late, deserted her altogether. She was unable to finish her portion of the Perigord pie, a concoction of meat and truffles in a light pastry, and the play of candlelight across his aristocratic face was of greater interest to her than hot cross buns from the cookshop.

When he complimented the cabbage soup, she told him, "It is made from the recipe of *ma marraine,* my godmother. Because she was childless she mothered her actors and dancers and provided them with sustaining food, not trusting them to take proper care of themselves. She often served this soup—and a good thing she did. It helped to make her fortune."

"How?" he asked curiously.

"It has a heavy aroma, as you will have noticed. One night when the Queen was in attendance she smelled cabbages and was told that the manageress had made her famous soup. Her Majesty, who had not dined, sent a footman to ask if she might have a bowl of it herself. That is how Mademoiselle de Montansier won Marie Antoinette's favor and friendship. After the encounter she was invited to the *petits levées,* and eventually became *directrice* of the theaters at the royal palaces of St. Cloud, Marly, Fontainebleau, Compiegne. And Versailles."

"Where your mother sometimes performed," he said with a fond smile.

As Peg began clearing the table, Rosalie excused herself and left the duke to finish his wine.

Going to her bedchamber, she changed into a gown more appropriate for an evening at the theater. Standing before the looking glass in her chemise, she wondered if she might alter her destiny by inviting Gervase to come to her. She imagined his hands caressing her body, his gray eyes smoky with desire. But there was no certainty that she could keep him beside her for longer than a single night, and afterward she would be doubly shamed. Her guilt over a broken vow would be as hard to bear as the loss of her self-respect.

She took pains with her hair, piling the curls high and securing them with the gold combs she'd been given on her sixteenth birthday, after her mother had sold the Fragonard canvas. Inspired by Delphine de Barante's shining example of strength and dignity in the face of adversity, she prepared herself to accept Gervase's engagement as any friend would, with felicitations. She was a dancer, not an actress, but she trusted in her ability to make her best wishes sound genuine.

Her finest gown was rose-colored silk, its low neck adorned with creamy Valenciennes lace. In future, if he should think back to their final hours together, she wanted him to remember that she had looked beautiful.

During their drive to Islington, to give the impression of being gay and lighthearted, she said brightly, "What a pity Lord Swanborough isn't here to share the treat."

"He and Duffield are in Wiltshire—they spent Easter at Cavender Chase," Gervase told her. "Ninian's mother is also there, so they'll have another opportunity to improve their acquaintance."

"I'm glad." Rosalie recalled the day in the Elizabethan gallery at Haberdine, when the boy had shown her Lady Swanborough's portrait. "The only time he mentioned her to me, he said he'd met her but once."

"Yes. But her condition is much improved, and she wishes to be reconciled with her children." Looking at her, he said quietly, "I believe the French regard melancholy as a singularly English malady."

"*C'est vrai*. Even your King suffers from it. Our King," she amended, unwilling to appear wholly foreign.

"His Majesty's recoveries from previous spells have been remarkable, but this time he appears to be more gravely ill than ever before. When I was at Windsor with the Prince Regent I was privy to a gloomy report from the royal physicians."

Rosalie's blood ran cold at his acknowledgement of a growing intimacy with the court.

"My visit received a great deal of publicity, far more than was warranted. Fortunately it served to conceal the truth of why I went to Windsor—just as well, I suppose, for I did so in connection with what could become a serious royal scandal. I'll tell you as much as I can, if you promise never to breathe a word to anyone."

"No, never," she murmured through stiff, pale lips.

"Princess Charlotte has developed a strong attachment to her tutor. Not surprising, really, for the poor girl is constantly surrounded by females, dull ones at that, and the only gentlemen she's allowed to see are her royal uncles and the Regent's ministers. The Duke of York was the first to suspect her feelings. He told his brother the Regent, who was appalled to learn that his fifteen-year-old daughter regarded a commoner with affection. Remembering that I had attended both his swearing-in ceremony and the first levee, he summoned me to Carlton House and requested that I accompany him to Windsor."

"For what purpose?" Rosalie asked around the lump in her throat.

"I was excluded from his private discussion with his mother, but I believe he sought her permission for me to call on the princess. As best I can determine, in his mind I represent a more suitable alternative to a scholarly clergyman. But the Queen adamantly opposed him. Not long afterward, she visited Warwick House herself to scold her granddaughter for her waywardness. Princess Charlotte, who is as headstrong as she is volatile, took her revenge by drawing up a will leaving all her jewels, her books, and other private property to the tutor as a pledge of her high regard for him. She told me about it herself."

"Then you have been visiting her?"

"Not officially. Perceval, the Prime Minister, hopes I can counsel her to abandon her quarrel with the Queen before it becomes public, so I'm forewarned on those occasions when she takes exercise in the gardens of Carlton House. And I've escorted her and her governess, Lady de Clifford, to Blackheath, where she goes every Saturday to dine with her mother. The last time we were all entertained by some singers from the opera."

Rosalie nodded. "Naldi and Tramezzani—I heard of it, but not that you were there. Is Princess Charlotte pretty?" she asked, careful to keep her voice steady.

"Her skin is fair and her hair is reddish gold, like her father's. She has his large blue eyes, too. Her features are very expressive, and her figure voluptuous for her age."

This favorable account, coupled with the earlier description of the harsh treatment the Heiress Apparent received from her relations, reminded Rosalie of the heroine of a romantic fairy tale. And any lonely and persecuted princess would look upon Gervase, the head of the nation's most prominent and pedigreed family, as the perfect cavalier.

The duke's servant had acquired a pair of box seats which provided an excellent view of stage and auditorium, smartened up by a fresh coat of paint and chandeliers of gleaming brass. The crowded theater was typical of the first night of the season, but Rosalie was so preoccupied that she felt no satisfaction on behalf of the management.

There was no ballet that night, so she could not discover who had replaced her in the *corps*. The evening's entertainment began with a new harlequinade, *Dulce Domum, or England the Land of Freedom*. The curtain opened upon a cottage *ornée*, the honeymoon dwelling of Columbine and Harlequin. Bored with their quiet life, the newlyweds journeyed to foreign lands, a device which permitted Mr. Dibdin to draw comparison between Britain and enemy nations and turn the piece into a form of political propaganda. Joseph Grimaldi, as a strutting and bombastic Napoleon Bonaparte, was loudly hissed by the patriotic crowd.

The comedian reappeared later in his customary guise of Clown, to sing a merry ditty. When finished, he declaimed, "Oh, give me little England, where a man's head is his own freehold property, and his house is his castle. And whoever touches a hair of the one, or the latch of the other without leave, is sure to get the door in his face!"

The people cheered, ladies waving their handkerchiefs and the gentlemen their hats. Rosalie and Gervase joined them, similarly inspired by partisan sentiment.

The finale turned out to be *The Spectre Knight,* the popular aqua-drama from the previous season. Turning to her escort, Rosalie whispered, "I'm sick to death of this play and doubt it has improved since last autumn. Do you mind if I slip away for a little while? I'd like to speak to Mr. Grimaldi, before he departs for the Myddelton's Head."

"I'll meet you outside the stage door," Gervase replied.

The renovation of the theater had not included the areas most familiar to her; the narrow, twisting hallways were as dim and dirty as ever. Grimaldi, his swarthy face washed clean of the white and red paint he'd worn onstage, greeted her with surprise.

"How are Mary and young Joe?" she asked, eager for news of his family.

"Both are very well. Now that my son has made plain his inclination for a career on the stage, I've begun instructing him in tumbling and mime. It's not what I'd have chosen for him, Miss Rose, but I cannot deny a vain desire to see my success repeated. The Grimaldi name has been synonymous with pantomime since my father's time, so I'm not altogether displeased that the association will continue for another generation."

She exited the building, pausing to speak with Mr. Wheeler, gently puffing on his pipe as he guarded the door.

Gervase was waiting for her, and when he recommended a stroll through the grounds she readily assented, for the weather was pleasant and mild. She let him lead her across the greensward and farther away from the glow of the oil lamps marking the carriageway. A gentle breeze stirred the branches of the towering elms and caused the daffodils along the paths to tremble.

Gervase said softly, "Listen to that nightingale. It's the first one I've heard this spring." Speaking over the song-bird's trilling aria, he added, "The ideal accompaniment for a love scene, don't you agree?"

Her shining eyes and upturned face expressed her willingness to oblige him. A few kisses under the stars were all she could aspire to, and she was determined to have them before it was too late. His exploring lips helped her forget that they were soon to part, and in his sheltering arms she felt entirely weightless, capable of soaring over the tree-tops.

"Would you fly away with me tonight?" he murmured against her cheek. "For the rest of the week you're at liberty from the opera house. Like Columbine and Harlequin, we might hide ourselves away in some secluded, secret place, where no one knows us and no one could find us."

This invitation was far more appealing than the similar one tendered by Mr. Beckmann. How difficult, how terrible to give him up without sampling the passionate pleasures his eyes and mouth and seductive words promised her.

"Don't ask me again, Gervais, unless you wish to break my heart."

"Keeping your precious heart intact is more important to me than anything in all the world." He looked as if he might speak again, but when he did it was only to suggest that they return to the carriage.

Throughout the return journey to London they said very little. Rosalie, understanding that the time for words was behind them, wondered what their fate might have been were he not a duke or she a dancer.

All too soon they reached Panton Street. He assisted her out of the vehicle, and when he pressed her hand in farewell she was more certain than ever that she'd been given her final chance to refuse his increasingly tempting offer.

Rosalie knelt upon the unrelenting wooden floor, holding her portion of a long floral garland supported by a line of white-clad nymphs. Tonight she was part of the corps; only one female soloist was needed in this new ballet about Mars and Venus.

Armand Vestris and Fortunata Angiolini, lovers on the stage as in life, skipped and swayed before her. The dancer's diminutive body matched the movements of her stocky and athletic partner, and her pretty face testified to her rapture at their togetherness.

The music, so light and bright, clashed with Rosalie's somber mood. From her position she had an excellent view of the royal box and its occupants. The Prince Regent sat in the center, flanked by his current favorite, Lady Hertford, and his brother the Duke of York. Behind them were two individuals unknown to Rosalie, and one whom she knew much too well for comfort. The Duke of Solway's presence would doubtless lend credence to the popular belief that he was the Prince Regent's chosen candidate for the hand of the Princess Charlotte.

Not even Rosalie's devotion to her precious art had enabled her to forget the nobleman she loved no less for having lost him. It was a terrible strain, dancing as though she hadn't a care and smiling brilliantly all the while, when her well-trained body felt utterly leaden with despair.

13

Stay near me—do not take thy flight!
A little longer stay in sight!
                    —WILLIAM WORDSWORTH

Rosalie stood in the wings drinking in the sublime notes of
the lovelorn Fiordigili's lament. She thought it a great pity
that the fashionable people avoided benefit performances,
for this new production of *Cosí Fan Tutte* was one of the
season's best.

Therese Bertinotti-Radicati's portrayals of tragic heroines had not been well received by the critics, who compared her unfavorably to Madame Catalini, but Rosalie
suspected that they would praise her in this lighter work.
The singer's voice was particularly well suited to Mozart's
comic opera, but even so she'd excised two bravura arias
that she deemed too demanding.

Signor Naldi performed the *buffo* role of Don Alfonso
with his usual zest. Rosalie, who admired his vocal abili-
ties, was also exceedingly fond of him. Despite his leg-
endary hatred of France and her people, he never failed to
treat her kindly. And his wife, a former dancer, had been
acquainted with Delphine de Barante.

The popular tenor Tramezzani, with his manly figure and
dignified manner, made a romantic Guglielmo, and Signor
Cauvini sang Ferrando's ardent arias with a heart-wrench-
ing pathos. His magnificent but volatile spouse was per-
fectly suited to the part of Despina, the meddling maid, and
the mezzo soprano Madame Collini rounded out the cast as
Dorabella.

The gaiety and fun of the opera had infected all of the

performers, and merriment reigned backstage. Even the dancers had set aside their characteristic jealousy for one night, chattering to one another in the dressing room, and even Rosalie had laughed at some of the jests and pranks.

Because the company was small in number, she and her colleagues were needed to swell the crowd scenes. In the first act she'd made a brief and anonymous appearance as a villager, and now she was awaiting her cue to go on as a household servant in the final scene.

Her dress, pale green with emerald piping at the seams, was the one Madame Ferrier had made last autumn in the days preceding Rosalie's accident. The addition of an apron had transformed it into a maid's costume, and in place of a chemise she wore a creamy gauze shift. She had only to remove her overdress and tear away the kerchief covering her hair to be ready for the *divertissement* that would conclude the evening's entertainment.

As the trio of gentlemen finished their merry chorus of *"Cosí fan tutte!"* she moved aside to make way for their exit. The scene shifters went to work, transforming the sisters' bedchamber into the grand salon, and Rosalie took her place with the other supernumeraries. When the lilting music started, she spread a large square of brocade cloth upon the table where the marriage settlements would be signed, lighted some candles, and generally tried to look busy while Despina trilled her orders.

Her duty done, she darted back to the wings. Squeezing past the curtain and a web of ropes, she rushed to the wooden staircase and descended carefully, relying on the handrail. A broad figure at the bottom blocked her way, so she called out, "Move aside, if you please—I have a costume change!"

"Not so fast, my beauty."

She was too consumed with her mission to question Benjamin Beckmann's presence. "Pray excuse me, sir, for I cannot stop to talk." She tried to brush past him, but he grasped her arm.

"You won't snub me tonight." As he pulled her toward the stage door he said gruffly, "Hurry along now."

Rosalie resisted with all her might. "You're hurting me," she gasped and struggled to free herself.

"I wouldn't if you'd stop wriggling."

Her dread of another accident was so great that she let him drag her up the rain-slick stone steps to the carriage yard. A hackney waited, its door gaping open. "You can't do this!" she protested. "I'm dancing in the ballet. Don't you understand, you *must* let me go!"

Shoving her into the vehicle, Beckmann growled, "Not yet. We're going for a little drive together, you and I." He plopped down beside her.

His face, pink and bloated from good living, repulsed her and she edged away. "You're mad!"

"If I am, it's your fault," he retorted. "You've toyed with me for months, and now it's my turn to choose the game." He pounded the roof with his cane and the carriage lurched forward.

"This crude attempt to suborn me will not succeed," she said furiously. Staring out the rain-splashed window, she watched the King's Theatre grow ever smaller. "Take me back to the theater now!" she demanded. "If I fail to appear in the ballet tonight, I'll be dismissed from the company."

Mr. Beckmann stroked his curling side whiskers. "You've been flying too high, m'dear—the Duke of Solway was bound to become jaded in time. And perhaps you expected too much of him. Surely you didn't think so grand a fellow would stoop to wed the bastard daughter of a French opera dancer?"

Rosalie's cheeks flamed and her eyes blazed. A sharp crack on the head with his walking stick might restore his reason, but it was beyond her reach. So she struck out at him with her balled fist.

He ducked just in time to avoid the blow. "What a spitfire!" he crowed. "And just my taste. I prefer a lady who is every bit as lively as she is pretty."

She tried to direct her chaotic thoughts into useful channels. Somehow she had to escape, for the prospect of being ravished by this man was sickening. He thought he could overpower her, but agility of mind and body would surely win out over brute strength.

When the jarvey negotiated the sharp turn from Pall Mall to St. James's, she gripped the leather strap to prevent contact with her abductor's encroaching form.

"Why do you pretend to dislike me?" he asked plaintively, capturing her hand. "My pockets are deep, and I'm a generous man. I'll give you jewels and an allowance—you won't have to dance for your keep. You can go with me to all the race meetings, and to Brighton. You'll have such a pleasant time that you'll soon forget your duke."

Her flesh crawled when he stroked her arm.

His thick fingers roamed the front of her bodice, then fumbled with the dark green ribbons of her stomacher. With a groan of impatience, he tugged and ripped the thin fabric.

Preferring possible injury to certain rape, Rosalie gripped the handle of the door and wrenched it open. The moving pavement aroused even greater panic, and just when her nerve failed her the jarvey slowed his horse to avoid pedestrians in the street. Before he picked up the pace again she tumbled out of the hackney.

Stunned and breathless, she sprawled upon the wet cobbles, certain that the fall had shattered all of her bones.

From a great distance above came a stern command to lie still.

"Don't try to speak yet," someone else advised her.

Ignoring the advice of the two gentlemen who had witnessed her escape, she tried to sit up. She blinked to clear the tears from her eyes and examined a long, raw scrape on her arm. The thigh on which she had landed felt badly bruised. "I must go," she panted, fighting for the breath that had been jolted out of her. "He—he might come back."

"I hope he does," one man growled. "I'd like to teach him a lesson. Look at that, Rupert," he said, pointing down at Rosalie. "Her gown is torn!"

"Yes, Allingham, I see that it is."

The group of onlookers expanded as other gentlemen exited the club. Rosalie wondered what they must think of her painted face and scanty attire.

"I've never seen anything like it," said the man called Allingham. "Harburton and I were just crossing over to

White's when this female fell out of a moving hackney coach!"

When his friend helped Rosalie to her feet, she discovered that her precious ankles had survived. "What's the time?" she asked desperately.

"Past midnight, I should think."

By now the ballet had begun—it might well be over. With that realization her aching body sagged, and had the stranger not supported her she would have fallen again.

"Can't we escort you to your home?" he asked, his owlish countenance matching the concern in his voice.

"*Non*—oh, no," she said hastily. She dared not return to Panton Street; Benjamin Beckmann might be waiting for her.

When she had thanked the gentlemen and assured them that she was capable of walking unassisted, she limped up St. James's Street. The thin-soled dancing shoes hampered her ability to maintain her footing on the greasy pavement, and she made a slow and agonizing progress.

In missing a performance she'd committed the unforgivable sin and the punishment would be exceedingly harsh. In all likelihood Signor Rossi would banish her from the stage of the King's Theatre. No one, not even James d'Egville or Armand Vestris, would intercede on her behalf. Her career as an opera dancer was over.

She walked on, though she didn't even know where she was going, constantly watching out for the hackney bearing Mr. Beckmann. She contrasted his brutishness with Gervase's unfailing chivalry, and a sob escaped her. Even though his intentions were once the same as her abductor's, how happy she could have been with him—if she hadn't given her word to Richard Lovegrove never to become what her mother had been to Etienne Lemercier. She was often teased by the irony of her position: she had managed to keep the respect of the man she loved only by giving him up. And with all her heart she wished that she could have shared her life with him and become a part of his, and preserve her honor at the same time.

On reaching Piccadilly she found it occupied by an endless line of carriages, their lamps creating a trail of light

that extended as far as she could see. The coats of the
horses drawing the nearest coach glistened with moisture,
and the caped coachman on the box regularly adjusted his
three-cornered hat in an effort to keep the rain out of his
face.

Two persons were seated within. Rosalie spied the flash
of diamonds on the lady's white breast, and snowy ruffles
at the neck of the gentleman seated across from her. They
were obviously annoyed by their delayed departure from
Devonshire House.

Had the Duke of Solway attended the ball? For some reason it hurt her to think that he might have been drinking
champagne and dancing and flirting throughout her ordeal.
But it wasn't his habit to flirt, she corrected herself, he disliked large parties. In all probability he'd spent the evening
at home, composing a political speech. Or writing a letter to
his mother, who so despised opera dancers.

Even though she knew he couldn't really help her—there
was no remedy for the variety of blows she had suffered
tonight—to her he represented security and decency. An in-
sistent voice in her swimming head urged her to find him.

But Mayfair was alien territory, so she had to seek directions from a passing watchman. He held his lantern close to
her face, his voice heavy with suspicion when he asked,
"Wot would the loikes of you be wantin' with the Duke of
Solway?"

"My uncle works in the stables," she improvised, "and
my aunt sent me with a message."

Although the man shook his head in patent disbelief, he
pointed the way. "You keeps goin' down this street and
turns roight at Park Lane—if you gets to the Hyde Park
turnpike, you've walked too far. A little beyond Lord
Dorchester's house, on the corner of Park Lane and Mount
Street, you'll foind a great white building with gardens behind." Grinning, he added, "The mews, if you *really* wants
'em, are at the back."

She knew he expected a token of appreciation but she
had no coins to give him, only her heartfelt thanks. She
broke into a run, her battered limbs rebelling with every
step.

The duke's mansion was more imposing than she had expected. She paused at the bottom of its shallow front steps and gazed up at the shadowed facade and dark windows. Having come so far she couldn't turn back, but she feared what she was about to do would be viewed as a serious transgression by the sort of people who lived in this exclusive neighborhood.

Summoning the necessary fortitude, she approached the house and pounded upon one of the glass panes framing the door with her fist.

A wrinkled visage appeared immediately. "Who goes there?" its owner asked suspiciously.

"I must speak to the Duke of Solway," she replied, her heart pumping furiously from the combined effects of nervousness and exhaustion. When she heard him draw the bolts she let her breath out in relief.

The man did open the door but after studying her from head to toe adamantly refused to admit her. "His grace has retired," he said frostily.

"Tell him I've come," she pleaded, "for I'm certain he'll agree to receive me."

He twisted his head to say in aggrieved accents, "Mr. Parry, this—this *painted* person is asking for the duke."

"Oh, is Parry there? He will know me." She boldly stepped past him and walked up to the butler.

"Mademoiselle de Barante?" Parry's carefully neutral expression never altered, but his eyebrows twitched slightly as he took in her bedraggled appearance. "Step into the green salon, and I will inform his grace of your arrival."

He conducted her to a sumptuously appointed chamber and left her there with a branch of candles. She was too sad and anxious to care about her surroundings, but she couldn't help noticing a vaulted ceiling decorated with a frescoe of sportive gods and goddesses, green damask hangings, and the towering marble chimney piece at one end of the room. She doubted that the elegant room had ever sheltered so forlorn and pitiful a creature as herself.

When his butler first roused him from deepest sleep, Gervase was reluctant to rise. After he heard the reason his mind was still too groggy and dazed for speculation, but he scrambled into shirt and breeches.

The hall porter standing stiffly at the foot of the marble staircase regarded him with disapproval. "Return to your post," Gervase said curtly before he entered the salon.

The lingering fog of sleep dissipated entirely when he saw Rosalie. Her full skirts were splattered with rain and dirt, and part of her bodice was torn, revealing the white shift beneath. "What the devil happened to you?" he demanded.

"Oh, Gervais, such a night I've had!"

Answering the appeal in her anguished eyes, he wrapped his arms around her, laying his cheek against her wet curls. "Don't worry, you're with me now. You're safe."

"I know. It's why I came." In a firmer voice she said, "I will *not* weep, for if I do I'd never be able to stop."

Gervase led her to a hassock and sat upon the floor at her feet, chafing her cold fingers as he said, "Tell me, as calmly and slowly as you can, what has distressed you."

He listened in horrified silence to her fractured account of all that had occurred after Benjamin Beckmann took her away from the opera house. His grip tightened involuntarily when she explained that she'd eluded him only by leaping from the carriage.

"I was dazed, but not hurt," she assured him. "Some kind gentlemen came to my assistance—they even offered to take me home. But I couldn't go back to Panton Street, I was too afraid Mr. Beckmann might be lurking somewhere near my house. I did change the lock on my door, but—"

"You did *what*?"

"Mr. Beckmann stole my key."

After extracting the story of her importunate admirer's visit to her lodging house, Gervase said harshly, "You should have told me."

"What could you have done?" she responded wearily.

A cold rage possessed him as he reviewed Beckmann's tactics. He should have guessed on that long-ago night at Sadler's Wells that the man could be dangerous.

Rosalie, living alone, her movements regulated by her performing schedule, had been an easy target for a sly and determined individual like Beckmann. Unlike Gervase, he'd been too dense to perceive at a glance that the dancer's morals were not as light as her little feet. And he had been too puffed up with his own consequence to accept that she might spurn him.

"I suppose I'll have to swear a complaint against him tomorrow," Rosalie said. "Can you tell me how to go about it?"

"I don't want you worrying about that now." A pity, he thought, that he had no legal grounds to prevent Beckmann from troubling her again. Only a father or a brother could lodge a petition in the courts.

Or a husband.

Pushing that thought aside, he went on, "My housekeeper will prepare a room for you here. No," he said firmly when she shook her head, "you mustn't refuse. It's quite late and you're utterly exhausted. I want a doctor to examine you in the morning, to confirm that you've sustained no lasting injury."

Rosalie stared at him. "But I can't sleep in your house, Gervais. The man who answered the door wouldn't even let me in, and I'm sure Parry disapproves of my coming in the middle of the night."

With a chastening frown, he replied, "Rosalie, my servants are employed to wait upon me, not dictate to me. And for the time being, I refuse to concern myself with anything so mundane as what they might be thinking about either of us."

The Duke of Solway spent the following morning alone in the study. The only member of his staff to intrude upon his solitude was Parry, who kept him informed of Mademoiselle de Barante's activities. At midmorning the Welshman informed him that she had awakened, and an hour later he announced that one of the maids had just removed her breakfast tray.

When Gervase went to the room in which his lady love had passed the night, he found her sitting up against the pillows of the mahogany fourposter. Her unbound hair massed about her shoulders in tangled waves.

"You shouldn't be here," she reproached him, drawing up the sheet to cover herself. "If I'd known you were bent on creating a scandal in your own household, I wouldn't have let you keep me here overnight."

"There's no scandal in visiting a sickroom," he pointed out, sitting down on the edge of the bed. "How are you feeling today?"

"I won't let myself feel yet," she said with what he recognized as forced humor. "*Vraiment,* Gervais, you mustn't be caught among the sheets with an opera dancer." Her faint smile faded when she concluded, "But I was forgetting—I no longer have a right to that title. Last night saw the end of my brief association with the King's Theatre."

In his most teasing voice he said, "Surely it isn't so bad as all that. You can't expect to give a perfect performance every time."

Shaking her head, she said sadly, "You don't understand. I must not have been very clear last night. I never *did* perform—Beckmann dragged me away just before the ballet began. I was there for all the crowd scenes of the opera, so no one will believe me if I pretend I suddenly fell ill, much less if I explain what really occurred. The management will remember what happened last autumn. My hasty resignation from the Tottenham Street playhouse will be dredged up as further evidence of unreliability."

"Nonsense. One small mishap won't matter so much."

"But it will," she told him earnestly. "Mr. Kelly will fine me, and Signor Rossi is certain to dismiss me, for nothing is more unprofessional than failing to go onstage. I'm only a temporary replacement, not really a member of the company, and therefore expendable. James d'Egville will turn his back on me forever, and so will Dibdin. It could be years before another theater manager will take a chance on hiring someone with so tarnished a reputation as mine is now. And," she concluded with a catch in her voice, "no dancer has years to spare."

The tears filling her eyes reminded Gervase of how very young she was. She had begun preparing for her career practically in her infancy and became a professional before she ever learned her alphabet letters. She hadn't experienced a normal childhood or adolescence because her theatrical upbringing had forced her out of them so quickly.

She might not realize it now, while her pain was so fresh, but she had no cause for regret—he would make sure of that. He intended to comfort and cosset her, this tiny, brave girl whom he loved.

"If it would make you feel better," he said, blotting her cheeks with his handkerchief, "I'll speak with Kelly. I'll even visit the King's Bench Prison and tell Mr. Taylor himself why you were absent last night."

"It will do me more harm than good," she prophesied bleakly. "And if you become too much involved in my affairs, there's bound to be gossip. Think how dreadful it would be if your friends or family found out I'd slept here last night!"

Gervase abandoned the bed and went to stand by the window. "Have you considered what you will do if you can't dance at the opera?"

"I've thought of little else this morning." She managed a lopsided smile. "Lord Swanborough once said he would build a splendid theater especially for me when he comes into his inheritance, but I'm afraid I can't wait that long. My only recourse is to return to Paris."

"Paris?" he echoed.

"If I leave at once I could be there before word of this frightful mess leaks across the Channel. Etienne Lemercier can help me acquire a French passport." She walked her fingers slowly across the counterpane, her eyes following their scissorlike motion. "My mother's name will be my entrée to the Opera."

Fiercely he said, "You aren't going back to Paris."

"But if I don't find work soon, I'd have to creep back to Bibury and spend the rest of my days pining for—for something that can never be."

He sensed that she referred to something other than the ballet, and his suspicion gave him the courage to admit, "I'm grateful to that cur Beckmann for cutting your connection to the opera house so neatly. I can't bear the prospect of waiting until you wear out your knees or sprain another ankle. Rosalie, couldn't you learn to live without dancing?"

"Someday I'll have to. No career lasts forever."

He continued, "It is wrong for you and me to remain forever apart, yearning indefinitely. Rosalie, do you care for me? Enough to let me look after you for the rest of your life?"

She bowed her head. "Yes to the first question. And to the second one—if it were possible for me to be with you always, nothing could make me happier. But it isn't, Gervais."

"You think not? Then I will tell you how I spent my time while I waited for you to wake up. I've been writing letters—to my mother at Haberdine, to both of my sisters, to my cousin Miranda and her husband. I even wrote one to my brother Edgar, though God only knows when it will reach him in Spain. But I couldn't post them yet. They all announce that I'm madly, intensely, irrevocably in love, and I wanted you to know it first. I also explained to my relations that I hope to be married very soon. If you'll have me."

She stared back at him with wide, unfathomable eyes. "*Je suis danseuse.* Your family will wish for you *la grande alliance avec la princesse,* or to an aristocratic lady."

"Rosalie," he said softly, joining her on the bed, "I adore your habit of speaking French in moments of strong emotion, but I object to your talking such drivel. Marriage is the one way we can be together. If you cannot feel right about being my mistress, then be my duchess instead." He pressed her back against her pillows, and his eager mouth covered hers.

Then he touched her cheek, her shoulders, the rounded contours of her breasts, and discovered that her skin was marble-smooth and deliciously warm. Her blushes delighted him, as did her soft sighs and startled cries.

Gripping her forearms, he said, "Now that I've presented you with a highly honorable proposal, are you still so eager to go to Paris?"

Apparently too shocked to speak, she rolled her head from side to side.

"Good." He resumed his caresses.

"Gervais, you are too naughty!"

"Be quiet," he commanded. "Most men would have compromised you first and then proposed, rather than the reverse. You can lie back and enjoy this—and I hope you will. I've dreamed of doing it for months."

"Have you?" she breathed. Smiling up at him, she asked, "What else did you want to do to me?"

"All sorts of wicked things, which I'll be happy to demonstrate in a moment. But first, Miss Rosalie Delphine Lovegrove de Barante, or whatever you call yourself, I want an answer. Will you now make another of your unbreakable vows, and promise faithfully to become my wife?"

14

And having danc't ('bove all the best)
Carry the Garland from the rest.
            —SIR THOMAS WYATT

Tomorrow night, Gervase thought exultantly as he exited Rosalie's bedchamber, he would finish convincing her how thoroughly he adored her. Before descending the marble staircase, he swiftly tidied his garments and smoothed his hair.

More than a little disoriented from the haste of his betrothal, he forced his muddled brain to consider his next course of action. Meeting his butler on the middle landing, he smiled dreamily and said, "Please be the first to felicitate me, Parry. I'm going to be married."

The Welshman smiled. "You have my most sincere wishes for future happiness, your grace. I know the entire staff will be gratified by the news."

"Thank you. Mademoiselle de Barante and I have agreed that the ceremony will take place in the morning, at Grosvenor Chapel. I'm off to speak with the parson, and also to procure a special license." Extracting his pocketbook, he studied the contents. "Just when I'm in need of cash, I find myself short. By any chance have you got five pounds about you, Parry?"

His butler reached into his pocket and produced a single note. "If your grace requires additional funds, I can open the strongbox."

"This will serve for the time being. I'll be wanting the town coach this afternoon, and there are some letters on the desk in the study—they must be posted without delay.

The footman who takes them should also go to Mademoiselle de Barante's lodging in Panton Street and bring back her maid. And you might inform the kitchen staff to begin preparing for the wedding breakfast. Nothing too elaborate, but there should be meats and cakes—and plenty of champagne." Gervase continued down the stairs, then turned back to ask, "Am I right in thinking that Richards has a relative who keeps an inn somewhere on the road from London to the west country?"

"His youngest brother lives at Overton, beyond Basingstoke, His house is called the Peacock. Quite respectable, as I have been informed, and popular with the gentry."

"Yes, yes, that will do nicely. I'll send Webster down to Hampshire to make the necessary arrangements for me. For us," he added beatifically.

Before leaving Solway House, he drank a tumbler of brandy to calm his nerves. He had made a momentous decision—not a difficult one, but he couldn't overlook the fact that the immediate future would not be easy. His love for Rosalie was unwavering, deep and strong enough to sustain him in the face of public censure and familial outcry. But what of her? Would her feelings withstand the troubles ahead?

Shoving that uncomfortable question aside, he set out in his town coach for Grosvenor Chapel, just around the corner in South Audley Street.

"No need to walk them, Tim," Gervase told his coachman when he climbed out. "My business here will take but a few minutes." His servant's vigorous nod and toothy grin told him the tidings of his forthcoming nuptials had circulated in the mews.

The brown brick chapel was dark and empty and silent, but he found the warden in the lower regions. Yes, he assured the duke after consulting a leatherbound volume, the priest would be at liberty to perform a marriage ceremony on the morrow. But, he warned, his grace might have some difficulty obtaining a license on such short notice, as the gentlemen of Doctors' Commons were notoriously slow.

It seemed to take forever to reach St. Paul's. Gervase,

now afraid that he would be unable to secure the essential piece of paper, fretted and fumed throughout his journey, hands clenched tensely around the knob of his walking stick. He scarcely noticed the traffic clogging the Strand, and by the time he arrived in the churchyard he was in a fever of impatience.

He passed beneath the Dean's Court archway and begged directions to the Faculty Office from a stranger, who obligingly took him to the stone-paved hall. A crowd of other hopefuls were seated upon benches and standing about in small groups.

"Did you wish to speak with one of the advocates?" inquired a squat gentleman swathed in a long scarlet robe.

"I'm not sure," Gervase answered frankly. "Is this the Court of Faculties and Dispensations? I expect to be married tomorrow, and I've come for a special license."

"You must wait your turn, then."

"It is a matter of some urgency," he said loftily, presenting his card.

The man accepted it unwillingly, but after reading the inscription his attitude of disinterest was replaced by one of respect. "I can be of assistance, if your grace will follow me."

They removed to a smaller room. Sitting down at a table covered with green baize, the gentleman took a paper out of an upper drawer. Reaching for a pen, he asked, "What is your grace's full name?"

"Gervase William Marchant."

"In which London parish do you reside?"

"St. George's, Mayfair." He watched as the official wrote this down, then added, "The lady lives in Panton Street, but I don't know which parish that might be."

"St. Martin's. Her full name, please."

"Rosalie Delphine Lovegrove."

"Are you both of legal age?"

"Indeed."

When he had finished writing, the man sanded the document. "That will be five pounds," he said, curt and businesslike, and Gervase tendered Parry's banknote. "In general, applications for a special license do not receive such prompt attention. Your grace is fortunate that you chanced to meet me on my way in."

"I suspect I'm equally fortunate in possessing a title," Gervase said wryly, accepting the coveted paper.

His next destination was Number 32, Ludgate Hill, occupied by the noted jewelers and diamond merchants Rundell and Bridge. His assumption that he was unknown by the proprietors was refuted as soon as he entered their establishment.

The gentleman standing nearest the counter bowed exceedingly low. "Good day, your grace," he intoned before introducing himself as Mr. Bridge.

Not entirely pleased to be recognized, Gervase made a civil reply and expressed his intention of establishing an account with the firm. "As my father had."

Again the jeweler bowed. "From time to time my partner Mr. Rundell and I undertook commissions from the late duke. We should deem it an honor to serve his son in the same way." Moving behind the counter, he asked, "Is there anything in particular your grace wishes to look at today?"

"I've come to purchase a ring. For a lady."

Mr. Bridge's eyes sparked with interest. "We have many fine gems in gold settings. Which stone would you consider most suitable?"

Regretting his failure to ascertain Rosalie's preference, Gervase answered, "Something rare, and of the best quality."

The proprietor removed a velvet-covered tray from his shelves and set it down before his customer. "I have here pearls, diamonds of various sizes, some emeralds, a single fine ruby, and a rare sapphire." He presented the latter for inspection.

Gervase tried to imagine it on one of Rosalie's small, childlike fingers and decided that it was much too large. Shaking his head, he said, "I'd like to examine that ruby." Mr. Bridge took back the sapphire ring and handed him the other. The stone was a dark, clear crimson, and a delicate pattern of rose leaves was engraved upon the golden band.

"A recent acquisition, your grace, and worthy of the most discriminating buyer. It is known as the Rose of India and was cut in Antwerp. One of our own goldsmiths fashioned the setting to Mr. Rundell's design."

"Charming," Gervase opined. And splendidly appropriate for a lady called Rosalie.

In a single afternoon he had acquired a bride, a license, and a ring. The ceremony was arranged, and the accommodating Webster had orders to plan the wedding journey. Thus he returned to Solway House with a strong sense of accomplishment.

Greatly though he wanted to relate his activities to his betrothed, they had agreed to keep apart until the moment they would join hands before the altar of Grosvenor Chapel. Half afraid that she might change her mind, he would be careful not to grant her any opportunity to tell him so.

He learned from Parry that she had remained in seclusion all afternoon, and the news that Peg Reilly had arrived with her mistress's trunk and bandboxes struck him as a favorable sign. Apart from packing his own bags there was but one thing left to do, and that was locating a pair of witnesses. Preferably close friends, and discreet ones.

He conducted his search that evening at White's Club. Although some of his acquaintances were there, he saw none that he liked well enough to request their presence at his wedding.

While taking dinner in the coffee room, he overheard the party of elderly gentlemen at the next table bemoaning the proposed rise in the club's subscription fee.

"Eleven guineas? Pshaw," one fellow said, "what man among us cannot afford that?"

"A great pity that everyone should have to support the alteration to the facade," commented another. "We're all paying for that damned bow window, even though that upstart Brummell regards it as his own. The only chap who dares make use of it in his absence is young Elston."

"He has impudence enough for anything, that one. Takes after his father."

"Careful how you speak of him—he's here now, with Harburton. Drunk as a lord, by the look of him."

Gervase turned around and saw his friend standing on

the threshhold, one hand gripping the doorframe for support. His companion, dwarfed by his superior height, surpassed him in elegance of dress.

Advancing unsteadily into the room, the marquis cried, "Hullo, Ger! We'll join you."

As his friends sat down at his table, Gervase commented, "A bit early for you to be in this parlous state of overindulgence, isn't it?"

"It's my butler's fault, damn him. Said the vintage red port that my father laid down in '88 desperately needed to be drunk, so we imbibed as much as we could in one sitting, Rupert and I." When a waiter brought the duke's bill, Damon regarded him sunnily and said, "A pot of strong coffee for Mr. Harburton and myself, Mackreth."

"As you wish, my lord."

"You really ought to eat something," Gervase advised. "Bring a plate of biscuits, and some fruit."

With a brisk nod, the man absented himself.

Rubbing his brow, Mr. Harburton complained that he had a devilish headache.

"It'll be much worse tomorrow," Damon predicted. His blue eyes sought Gervase. "You'll never believe what Rupert saw on his way here last night. He was crossing the street with someone, I forget who—"

"Allingham," Mr. Harburton supplied.

"With Allingham, when the damnedest thing happened! A female leaped out of a passing hackney coach and fell at their feet. Imagine—right in the middle of St. James's! He'll dine out on that tale for a week at least."

Gervase frowned at the other gentleman. "I sincerely hope you won't, Rupert. I know the identity of that lady and would be very sorry if her adventure became widely known."

Damon's eyes narrowed in suspicion. "Would you indeed? Then she must've been your little opera dancer."

"An excess of wine has definitely hot hampered your thought processes," Gervase observed.

"And," his friend continued triumphantly, "I'll wager she was trying to avoid that beast we first met at the Sadler's Wells playhouse."

"Yes. But I'm not going to reveal more than those essential facts."

"Challenge him to a duel," was Damon's advice. "Can't have some crass *bourgeoise* plaguing the girl to death."

"Beckmann won't trouble Mademoiselle de Barante in future. Not after tomorrow morning, when she and I are to be married."

"Married!" Damon crowed. "D'you hear that, Rupert? Ger's getting married."

"Of course I heard," Mr. Harburton retorted. "I'm drunk, not deaf."

"Well, well, this is an unexpected turn of events. Will it be a private affair?"

"Extremely, but I would be very happy if both of you would stand up with me. The wedding will take place at Grosvenor Chapel, with a breakfast at my house immediately afterward."

"And then the long-anticipated pleasures of the honeymoon, eh?" the marquis asked slyly.

"We'll spend a fortnight by the seaside, at Weymouth."

"Look at him, Rupert—he's love-bitten!" Damon ran his fingers through his golden hair. "Where's that coffee? I've got to get sober—can't disgrace Ger at his wedding."

"I think we ought to have a toast," Mr. Harburton said solemnly.

Laughing, Gervase said, "Perhaps you'd better save the toasts for tomorrow."

"I've just decided what my gift will be," Damon announced. "A dozen bottles of my '88 port. I'll have Mimms pack it up and send it round to Solway House. What are you going to give him, Rupert?"

"I'm damned if I know. He's a blasted duke, and has far more than he wants or needs. Ah, here you are, Mackreth." Mr. Harburton sighed thankfully as the waiter poured out a cup of steaming coffee. Gripping the handle, he held it aloft and said grandly, "To the bride and groom."

Gervase had made it exceedingly plain to Rosalie that he expected her to remain at Solway House until their wedding. Before parting from her he'd suggested that she busy herself with writing the happy news to her aunt, and she had obediently requested pen and paper from the chambermaid. She sat down at a Sheraton dressing table and scribbled a hasty note to Matilda Lovegrove, investing it with all the joy one would expect of so fortunate a being as herself.

But grave doubts overshadowed her joy in announcing that she was the future Duchess of Solway. An abiding love for Gervase and a powerful desire to be united with him body and soul could not blind her to several painful facts. Her unworthiness for the position to which he would elevate her chafed at her. Her parentage was questionable and might remain so. Her experience of society was restricted to the highborn gentlemen who had sometimes ogled her at the opera. And she worried that the Marchant family, the Duchess of Solway in particular, would suspect her of entrapping him by some devious stratagem.

For most of the afternoon she wondered why she hadn't refused his offer, just as she had the previous one, finally acknowledging the lack of reasonable justification. No promise precluded her becoming his wife, no scruple stood in her way. And if she didn't marry him, what else could she do but carry out her threat to go to Paris? She had no desire to separate from him again, or to spend the rest of her life alone.

The arrival of Peg and the accompanying boxes gave her thoughts a new direction.

"You're going to be a duchess," the maidservant said over and over, as if unable to accept either the inevitability or desirability of it. When Peg recovered her composure she asked Rosalie which clothes should be packed for the wedding trip.

"I haven't even considered that," she answered abstractedly. "*Bien sûr,* I'll want my jade green cambric to travel in and the rose silk for evenings, and whatever else is clean and in good repair. I need as many of my chemises and petticoats as you can fit into the trunk, and all my shoes and slippers. Except the ones I wear—wore—for dancing. The duke said I might choose something out of his cousin's wardrobe to be married in. Most of the gowns she left behind are out of style, but I found this white silk." She reached for a garment draped over the back of a chair.

At Peg's urging she tried the gown on, but because it had been made for a slightly taller, slimmer woman it turned out to be a trifle tight in the bodice and too long in the front. Her maid was confident that she could remedy these faults and immediately set to work.

While Peg sat in the corner busily hemming, Rosalie sipped tea and sampled some of the sweets from her tray to please Parry, who had come to consult her about the wedding breakfast. The senior staff already treated her as the mistress of the house, which was endearing yet disconcerting.

Glancing over the menu the butler had prepared, Rosalie noted one omission. "The duke is especially fond of gooseberry tarts," she reminded him. "As for the other cakes, I suspect the cook knows his preference better than I." She handed back the list.

After he left the room she wandered to her window and gazed in the direction of Hyde Park, her eyes following the line of smart carriages rolling toward Stanhope Gate.

Mayfair was such a new and different world. Islington and Sadler's Wells were no longer a part of her life, and in future she would return to the Haymarket as a member of an audience rather than the company.

Never again would she undergo the rigors of a rehearsal, dancing to the accompaniment of a poorly tuned harpsichord, contorting her body as commanded in the singsong French ballet masters used when calling out instructions. But she had the comfort of knowing that she'd achieved her ambition: her career had ended where it had begun, on the stage of an opera house. And she did not regret being finally and forever free of that ruling compulsion to emulate her mother's greater success.

Cruel Mr. Beckmann, though he might not realize it, had precipitated an improvement in her circumstances. But it would take time to grow accustomed to so many changes all at once.

Still wounded in body and spirit, she went to bed at an early hour, half afraid she might not be able to sleep. But the variety of emotions she'd been experiencing had wearied her more than she knew, and the scented sheets and fat goosedown pillow were not only comfortable but wondrously soporific.

She was gently wakened by the chambermaid who brought her morning coffee. The promise of hot water for the copper bath roused her even more successfully than her favorite beverage, for her limbs seemed stiffer on this second day after her fall from the hackney.

When she removed her nightgown, she was mortified by a large dark bruise marring her thigh and the unsightly scrape on her arm. Gervase, she thought ruefully, was acquiring a sadly disfigured bride.

Her nervousness was nearly exceeded by Peg Reilly's, whose shaking fingers fumbled with the fastenings at the back of the white gown. But Rosalie was accustomed to dressing for a performance and no stranger to the fluttery anticipation she felt while preparing for her wedding. When she inspected her reflection in the mirror, she commented that she looked like she was on her way to a ball rather than a church. The silvery lace and shimmering silk looked odd in the bright sunshine of the new day.

She was ready when Parry came to conduct her downstairs to Lord Elston's waiting carriage. "The household staff have already lined up in the hall to see you pass by, which is the custom in his grace's family."

While making her way down the staircase, she smiled shyly at the servants. Some of the women were weeping sentimental tears; the men's faces conveyed polite interest. She was startled to find two footmen carrying a large and weighty packing case through the front door, and her progress was impeded by another pair with a similar burden.

Said Parry apologetically, "The port is a gift from the marquis. It would have been sent around to the tradesmen's entrance had he not brought it here himself."

Rosalie exited the house through the door she'd entered two nights before and made her way to his lordship's splendid equipage. Parry handed her inside, then shut the door upon her and Lord Elston.

"A delightful day for a wedding, Mademoiselle de Barante," her handsome escort commented as the team pulled away from Solway House. "The sun smiles upon this happy occasion."

Uncertain how to reply, she simply nodded.

"What a charming gown. White becomes you well."

"I'm afraid it's borrowed finery," she admitted. "I hope Lady Cavender won't mind that I was married in her cast-off clothes."

"Knowing Miranda as well as I do, I can assure you that she'd be delighted," he told her with one of his brilliant smiles. "You must be sure to tell her when you meet." They rode in silence until he said quietly, "You aren't anxious about what lies ahead, I hope. There's no reason to be, for Gervase has loved you a very long time. Longer than he dared admit to me, and I'm his closest friend."

"He is also close to his mother, I think. She will not be happy with his choice, my lord."

"That needn't concern you. Her greatest desire is for Gervase to take a wife, and the fact that he wed a lady both beautiful and virtuous should gratify her."

This was such a blatant attempt to soothe her alarms that they increased. "I pray your lordship may be right," she murmured.

He patted her hand. "When you know me better, you'll discover that I always am. Well, my dear, here we are. That's Rupert Harburton standing at the church door."

The name was familiar, and when he introduced her to the short, nattily dressed gentlemen she recognized him instantly.

"We meet again, mademoiselle," he greeted her. "But the least said about your trials the other night the better, eh? Come, the bridegroom awaits."

She preceded the two gentlemen into the chapel. Gervase turned away from the black-gowned cleric standing before the altar and came down the aisle to meet her. He wore a dark blue coat with large gold buttons, a white satin waistcoat, and pale gray breeches.

"How lovely you are," he said, gripping both of her hands.

The enormity of what they were about to do suddenly swept over her. "You are quite sure this is what you want to do, Gervais?"

"I want *you*," he replied. "I always have, and I always will."

The quiet calm of early evening had settled upon the Hampshire town of Overton, situated some fifty-two miles and seven furlongs from Hyde Park Corner. Long before the Duke of Solway's traveling chaise reached the Peacock, his grace's valet had already bespoken a private parlor, the best two bedchambers, and a dinner.

"Well done, Webster," said Gervase as he handed his bride across the threshold of their suite.

The upper parlor was comfortably appointed and scrupulously clean, and a chambermaid was there to wait upon Rosalie and unpack her trunk. Fatigued from the combined effects of a busy morning and the long afternoon journey, she was relieved when Mr. Richards, the landlord, informed her that no one else was stopping there that night.

"I shall leave you for a little while," Gervase told her. "You should rest before dinner, if you can."

"I'll try," she promised.

The maid helped her out of her traveling gown, taking it and the rose silk away for ironing. Rosalie stretched out upon the bed and closed her eyes, reveling in the stillness and silence after the incessant swaying and dipping of the chaise and the thunder of horses' hooves.

Her enjoyment of the wedding breakfast had far exceeded her expectations. Lord Elston's effusive merriment had been tempered by Mr. Harburton's calm graciousness, and their easy acceptance of her as Gervase's wife had quelled her instinctive fear of their disdain. The Solway House servants were granted a holiday in honor of the occasion and provided with food and drink belowstairs. Gervase presented each of them, from the lowly footboy to housekeeper with a gold half guinea.

Despite her pleasure in the day, the unknown, uncertain future was never far from Rosalie's thoughts. As she lay upon the bed, she wondered whether her mother-in-law, now a dowager duchess, would receive her letter from Gervase tomorrow or the next day. Her reaction was easier to predict.

Benjamin Beckmann would learn of the marriage from the duke's lawyer, who would also present him with a writ requiring him to keep his distance.

Later in the week an announcement would appear in the London papers, doubtless leading to cruel gossip and unpleasant speculation. Possibly it would rouse the anger of the Prince Regent, for she hadn't quite trusted Gervase's blithe assertion that His Royal Highness hadn't been serious about that rumored match with Princess Charlotte.

Her wedding day, which brought her the greatest joy of her life, would cause so many people to feel anger and pain and resentment. However much she wished it otherwise, she had to face that uncomfortable reality.

From the moment the priest had declared her to be Gervase's wife, she had embarked upon an uncharted journey. The rules and rituals her mother had laid down for her as a dancer were useless to her now. No longer would she consort with the performers from the Wells and the opera house, although she hoped to maintain her relationships with Mary Grimaldi and Mrs. Hughes. But neither had been her confidante, and she suspected that she was going to need one. If only, she thought drowsily, there was another female to whom she could confide her feelings, simple and complicated, and go to for advice. Her Aunt Tilda would be sympathetic, but she'd never been married nor had she moved in fashionable circles. And Rosalie doubted that any aristocratic lady would befriend a former opera dancer. She would suspect the motives of one who did.

Eventually she rose to wash and begin preparing herself for dinner. When she sat down at the dressing table to rearrange her hair, she saw her pale face gazing back, her shadowed eyes reflecting inner turmoil. Gervase, she told herself sternly, deserved much better than a wan and worried bride.

The chambermaid returned with the rose gown and helped her to put it on. The color warmed Rosalie's complexion slightly, in her silk and lace she felt rather more like the duchess she must become and less like a frightened coryphée only seconds away from her debut.

She stepped into the parlor. A tall branch of candles in the center of the table cast its light upon Gervase, already seated and holding a glass of wine in his hand. He gave her a reassuring smile as she took her place across from him and signaled to Webster to begin serving. An array of covered platters adorned the sideboard, and the aromas were tempting enough to encourage Rosalie to sample nearly everything set before her.

"More wine, your grace?" the valet inquired.

When she realized that he was speaking to her, she nodded, wondering how long it would take to become used to the unfamiliar form of address.

"How many miles are we from Weymouth?" she asked her husband.

"A little over one hundred and twenty—rather a lot of ground to cover in a single day. I'm thinking that we might take the time to look around the cathedral at Salisbury, and stop along the road tomorrow night as well. Webster will continue traveling ahead of us, and engage our rooms at an establishment Mr. Richards suggested, Woodyates Inn. It lies just over the Dorsetshire border, and he assures me that it's greatly improved from what it once was."

After a sip of wine Rosalie stated her approval of this plan.

"I'm glad you agree, for travel by easy stages is far more civilized than dashing about in a great hurry."

"But more expensive, *n'est-ce pas*?"

"You're supposed to enjoy yourself during this trip," he told her, "not count its cost."

She readily assented, being too ignorant to accurately judge what he owed for their rooms and the dinner and stabling for the horses, or the charges demanded by the postboys.

As soon as they finished eating, the valet summoned a waiter, who cleared the table with speedy efficiency.

"That will be all, Webster," said Gervase. "Consider yourself dismissed for the evening." He waited until his servant withdrew before saying, "Rosalie, don't look so terrified. If you'd rather not take advantage of our married state tonight, so be it."

"I don't feel quite as I expected to," she confessed, hating the way her voice shook.

"Happy, you mean?"

"Married," she explained. "I keep remembering that I'm as ill equipped to be your wife as I was to be your mistress."

He reached down to pull her out of her chair. "You are everything to me. I've never been so content as I've been all day, knowing that we shall be together for the whole of our lives. Nothing and no one can come between us." Taking her face between his hands he kissed her.

His lips convinced her that he what he said was true. "I never really believed in love until I met you, Gervais," she whispered. Almost breathless from bridal shyness, she let him lead her to the bedchamber.

Did he expect her to disrobe, or would he undress her? "I'm not sure about what to do," she confessed, her pallor giving way to blushes.

"Let me show you," he offered, reaching behind her to unfasten her gown.

When she was clad only in her chemise and he in nothing more than his shirt and breeches, she asked if he intended to blow out the candles.

He abandoned the task of loosening his cuffs to glance at her. "Would that make you feel more comfortable?"

Her heart raced and her legs felt as though they might give way. Sinking down on the bed, she answered candidly, "No," for at that moment she was incapable of feeling comfortable.

Laughing softly, Gervase pulled his shirt over his head. "Are you more reluctant to see me in a state of undress, or to let me look at you? Lest you forget, my darling dancer, those ballet costumes of yours left very little to the imagination."

Then he took her in his arms and attempted to restore her confidence with his kisses.

15

Then to the dance, and make the sober moon
Witness of joys that shun the sights of noon.
                              —WILLIAM COWPER

Rosalie examined her left hand, which was lying upon the
sill of the open window, and admired the play of sunlight
on her ruby ring. Then she leaned out of the open window
to draw in deep breaths of salt-scented sea air. A gentleman
bather had emerged from one of several machines on Weymouth's sandy shore, and she watched him descend the
wooden ladder and gingerly lower himself into the lapping
water.

During the fourteen days since she and Gervase had exchanged their vows, they had occupied a suite in Stacie's
Hotel on the Esplanade, indulging their desire for privacy
and each other. When out of bed, her fond husband could
sometimes be quite stubborn, but his determination to have
his way was always rooted in his determination to give her
pleasure or guard her from unpleasantness. After so many
years of fending for herself, she was learning to enjoy
being spoiled.

The previous night they had danced together for the first
time, at a militia ball held in the Royal Assembly Rooms.
At Gervase's request, Mr. Rodber, the master of cere-
monies, had kept their identities to himself, and the company had therefore demonstrated scant interest in a tall
distinguished gentleman and his graceful partner, who wore
the same white and silver dress in which she'd been wed.

Over coffee that morning they had debated—not very
heatedly—about whether to drive to Lulworth Cave in the

morning or the afternoon. Rosalie abandoned her arguments when she remembered that it was his habit to visit the receiving office at midday. Because he had offered no explanation for this, she assumed he expected an important communication, probably from his mother.

"Had you quite given me up?" he asked when he returned from his errand. "I was detained at the stables, where I stopped to hire coach horses for tomorrow's journey back to town." Smiling, he held up a letter. "This arrived today, from Bibury."

"You've opened it," she accused him.

"Only because it was directed to me."

Puzzled, Rosalie asked, "Why would Aunt Tilda write you? What does she say?"

"She hopes you'll pay her a visit that she may felicitate you in person. Apparently I'm included in the invitation, because she adds that the fishing is excellent in the summer months. It's what she wrote in the closing paragraph that is most significant. Shall I read it to you?"

Curbing her impatience to set out on their expedition, she nodded.

" 'In reply to your grace's query about whether the family received letters from my brother during the year preceding Rosalie's birth, I can tell you that he first informed our parents of his and Delphine's expectations in December of 1788, some four months after their marriage. I have the letter by me now, as well as the one he sent immediately after his wife's confinement. In describing his new daughter, he states with endearing certitude that she inherited *his* eyes, nose, and chin. How he could make such a claim about a newborn infant, I shall never know. And although my niece grew up to resemble her mother, the portraits of her in childhood remind me very much of David in his early youth.' "

Rosalie pried the letter from his hand and read the passage herself. Her eyes shone when she looked up at him. "I ought to have asked Aunt Tilda for information, but I was too afraid to admit my doubts about my parentage. I never guessed you might have done so yourself, Gervais!"

"It occurred to me that she was the only person who

could clear up the mystery that has been plaguing you. I daresay Lemercier never knew the precise date of your parents' nuptials, which is why he might conclude that you were his daughter."

"I'll have to tell him the truth, poor man." After studying the letter, she added, "Aunt Tilda also says I must collect the Fragonard and the three Greuze canvases. They are my dowry and must have some value."

His arms encircled her. "You, Rosalie, are by far my most valuable acquisition. But I shall be glad to have your Greuze paintings—we can put one in each of our houses, if you wish. Or would you rather keep them together?"

They continued their discussion during their drive out of Weymouth to explore the natural wonders a few miles to the east. The road wound through the verdant downs and patchwork farms of Dorsetshire. The rolling contours were dappled with sunshine and shade, and the thick grasses on the chalk hills rippled in the breeze coming off the sea. Rosalie was entranced by the beauty and majesty of the surrounding landscape, which affected her in the same way as beautiful and majestic music, and made her wish she could dance out her feelings.

Lulworth Cove was a placid pool of green seawater enclosed by steep limestone cliffs. After strolling along the pebbled beach, the couple climbed a steep, turf-carpeted hill where a man was gazing through a telescope.

"I'm watching the ships in the channel," he explained after introducing himself as Mr. Weld. "Here, ma'am, have a look."

He offered the instrument to Rosalie. Peering through its eyepiece, she saw sailing vessels large and small, gliding upon the waters.

Gervase asked Mr. Weld if there was a decent inn nearby where he and his wife might order some dinner.

"The Red Lion at Lulworth sets a fine table. Are you stopping in the neighborhood?"

"At Weymouth."

"Ah," the gentleman sighed. "I'm afraid it has been sadly quiet since the King ceased visiting. The townspeople erected the statue of His Majesty last year to commemorate the Jubilee, but he has never seen it. Nor will he, it seems. Well, sir, may you and your lady enjoy a fine dinner, and an uneventful drive through the countryside."

"Are there footpads in this district?" Rosalie wondered as she returned his telescope.

Mr. Weld smiled and shook his head. "Nay, only smugglers, and unless you're preventive officers in disguise, you've naught to fear from them."

Although the Red Lion was a small establishment, it lived up to the gentleman's good report and provided the duke and duchess with lobster and prawns, sliced cucumber, and gooseberry pie. At dusk they wandered back toward the cove, hand in hand.

"I wish we could remain at the seaside forever," said Rosalie.

"But if we delay our return to London, the world will say we're hiding ourselves in shame."

"Not 'we.' You."

"I'd prefer to take you Pontesbury," Gervase told her. "It is a true country house, comfortable yet unpretentious, and Shropshire suits me best in summertime. At Haberdine and Solway House I'm required to live *en prince*, but never at cosy old Pontesbury."

"It has been your home for many years, hasn't it?"

"Since I came of age. When we do go there, possibly in July, we can stop at Bibury to see your aunt."

After remaining silent for a short time, Rosalie said, "If we must live in town during the coming weeks, I hope you'll send for Lord Swanborough to join us. I'm eager to see him again and it sounds as though we won't be visiting Northamptonshire for quite a long time."

Gervase paused on the path and faced her. "Are you saying you want to take charge of Ninian?"

"He ought to reside with his guardian, Gervais. I know he professes to dislike London, but he must be lonely at Haberdine."

"He's got Duffield for company. And my mother."

His last three words resurrected the depression that struck her whenever she thought of the dowager duchess. For now that Matilda's letter had vanquished all doubts about her lineage, the existence of her formidable mother-in-law was the only blight on her happiness.

"If it's what you want," he said, "I'll send an express to Haberdine straightaway. But first you must promise me that you won't let Ninian drag you off to Sadler's Wells when you'd rather not go."

Tucking her arm in his, she asked, "Is that what he did to you?"

"Yes. At first I complained, but for some time now I've realized that I have cause to be grateful to him, young devil that he is."

He slipped his arm around her waist and they continued down to the beach. The night was clear and cloudless, and a multitude of stars twinkled overhead; waves crashed against the shore of the dark, deserted cove. Inspired by the romantic beauty of the setting, the Duchess of Solway lifted her trailing skirts and twirled about, performing an impromptu dance for her appreciative husband.

The scandal resulting from their hasty and private marriage had subsided before the newlyweds reached London, and they soon discovered that the chief topic of conversation among all classes of people was the forthcoming fête at Carlton House. The Prince Regent intended to acknowledge his father's birthday and mark his own rise to power with a grand celebration, and it promised to be the most lavish in the history of the monarchy. The guests of honor would be Louis Bourbon, the hereditary King of France, and members of his court of exile.

The public criticized the Regent for spending an excessive sum—fifteen thousand pounds, according to one report—on a single entertainment and many people believed its magnitude and expense was inappropriate during wartime. Others, recalling the poor King's illness, denounced it as an unfilial act. The outraged buzzing grew still louder when the date was changed to allow the painters, upholsterers, florists, chefs, and confectioners to complete their extensive transformation of Carlton House. The delay was welcomed by London's dressmakers and tailors, who worked day and night to accommodate those clients who had been favored with an invitation.

The day after their return to Solway House the morning newspaper announced that over fifteen thousand members of the British nobility had been so honored, in addition to ministers, foreign ambassadors, and princes. Rosalie's fears that she and Gervase were the only aristocrats excluded from the festivities ended with the arrival of a footman in blue and buff livery. But the receipt of the coveted card engraved with the Prince of Wales's feathers meant that she, like every other noblewoman in London, had to decide what to wear. No gown in her wardrobe was magnificent enough for the occasion, and she was unacquainted with the most elegant modistes.

The removal of her belongings from the lodging in Panton Street diverted her from thoughts of fashion for the space of one day. She readily shouldered the responsibility of finding new employment for Peg Reilly, who preferred not to follow her mistress to Park Lane.

"I'd not be comfortable around all them grand servants of the duke's," she said sadly. "Best that I seek a place in a smaller house."

Rosalie took her to Golden Square and had no difficulty persuading Mrs. Hughes to increase her staff.

Gervase, who had divided his day between his man of business and his club, brought home the latest *on-dits* about the fête and repeated them to his bride. The Queen and the royal princesses were not expected to attend. The Regent had not only invited Mrs. Fitzherbert, he'd even offered to pay for her dress, but after she learned that she would not be seated at his table she'd refused to go. Lady Wentworth, as eager as anyone to take part in the greatest social event of this or any season, had boldly questioned the delay of the invitation her rank entitled her to receive.

"Her friends told her that the Regent's secretary ran out of cards before he reached the *W*'s on his list," Gervase said. "To which her ladyship replied, 'That can't be the reason, for quite half the *whores* in the town have theirs already!' But the members of that sisterhood must be sadly disappointed," he added, "for the Regent's mother made him promise not to receive any ladies who had been unfaithful to their marriage vows."

"Well, that's a neat solution to my problem," Rosalie said merrily. "If I can find myself a lover I won't need a ballgown!" After her husband objected to this drastic plan, she said, "*Vraiment,* I don't know what I ought to do. This afternoon I visited two dressmakers, one in Oxford Street and the other in Bond Street, and both were too overworked to accept the commission. Why couldn't we have stayed in Weymouth until this foolishness was over and done? I'm tempted to beg assistance from Madame Ferrier, who used to sew my ballet costumes."

"Why don't you?"

"Perhaps I shall," she said thoughtfully. "She's the most skilful seamstress I know, and efficient. And I still have that length of gold-shot silk that was never made up."

The very next day Rosalie took the town coach to Pentonville. Gervase remained at home to study the reports from his land steward in Shropshire, but he was forced to set them aside at midday when his mother, Ninian, and Mr. Duffield arrived.

He received his parent cordially but with caution, and was relieved to find her in an amiable mood. But her desire for a private interview was made obvious when she sent Ninian from the green salon to wash and change out of his rumpled garments.

"You have been busy since we last met," the dowager duchess told her son. "No, don't worry, I didn't come here to fling recriminations at your head."

"I'm glad of that," he responded. "Which is not to suggest that I deserve any."

"It was very sudden, your decision to take a wife," she said, taking a seat.

"I've always known it was my duty to marry," he countered. "How many ladies do you suppose I've met since I attained my majority? Hundreds, I should imagine. I danced with all the pretty ones and flirted with the bold ones. I even believed myself enamored with a certain widow, greatly to your distress. So you will surely agree that I've had sufficient experience of the female sex to make a reasoned choice."

"And what were those reasons? You omitted them when you wrote the letter informing me of your intentions."

"After several months of uncertainty, I recognized that Rosalie de Barante was no passing fancy. I also discovered that my feelings were so strong that I could not give her up. To me, she is the personification of that line from the poet Cowper: 'Strength joined with beauty, dignity with grace.' I want her by my side for the duration of my life, and it is she who must be the mother of my children, not some lady I hardly know and cannot love." Impressed by his own eloquence, he hoped she would be also.

"The announcement in the 'Recent Marriages' column of the papers was a remarkable feat of brevity," she said. " 'The Duke of Solway wed Miss Lovegrove of Bibury, Gloucestershire' sounded well enough, but it makes me wonder if you meant to conceal the fact of her former profession."

"No, nor has it. I hoped that if people knew about Rosalie's English background they might accept her more readily than if they believed her to be French. Society as we know it may be surprised by our marriage, but I don't doubt that by end of this season my duchess will have proved her worthiness for that title. And after she has been seen at Carlton House, all doors will be open to her."

"You may be right."

Eventually they talked of other family matters, which occupied them until the dowager duchess decided to end her visit. "My sister expects me to bear her company for the next few weeks, and the retired situation of Hampton Court has a strong appeal for me. But I will see you again soon, I trust. And also your bride," she added with a fleeting but inscrutable smile.

Upon her return from her meeting with Madame Ferrier, Rosalie learned that Lord Swanborough and his tutor had arrived. Five months had altered Ninian, increasing his stature, and his deeper voice was another sign of maturity.

"Aunt Elizabeth decided to visit her sister," he explained,

"so she brought Jap and me in her traveling carriage. Even though *I* wanted to ride on the stage. After she and Ger talked she left for Hampton Court. Her sister has a grace-and-favor lodging there because she used to wait upon the Queen."

Rosalie was surprised that the duke had not persuaded his mother to stay at Solway House. Or had his invitation been refused? It was entirely likely, for the dowager duchess must be grievously disappointed in her son's marriage.

During an afternoon stroll through the gardens, Rosalie questioned the earl closely, trusting him to be candid. "Was your aunt disturbed by the letter Gervais wrote?" she asked.

Ninian hunched his broadening shoulders. "I don't know, she didn't say anything to me. Why should she be? For years she has wanted Ger to be married, and I told her there's no one nicer or prettier than you." He halted beneath the laburnum arch, laden with dangling clusters of gold flowers, and asked, "What do I call you now? You aren't a mademoiselle any longer."

"I won't be satisfied with anything but 'your grace,'" she said severely.

His dark blue eyes widened incredulously. Then he grinned at her. "Duchess you may be, but I can't believe you'll be as toplofty as Aunt Elizabeth."

"Tell me about your Easter visit to Cavender Chase," she encouraged him. "What do you think of your niece Juliet?"

"Everyone says she's going to be *beautiful*," he reported. "My mama was there, too. Justin and Mira gave a party, and an old gentleman told her she looked the same as she did on the day they met. That made her very happy."

He was still talking about his stay in Wiltshire when Robert brought her the news that a French gentleman had called and wished to speak with her. While Ninian embarked upon a nautical discussion with his favorite footman, she hurried to the green salon to meet Monsieur Lemercier.

Bowing deeply from the waist, he said, "Madame la Duchesse, I was honored to receive your messenger, and it is my pleasure to see you again. Words cannot convey my joy when I read the notice of your marriage in the newspaper. I only regret that your surname was given as Lovegrove."

"It was no error, monsieur."

She explained, as gently as possible, that she had incontrovertible proof of her parentage.

He was disinclined to accept it. "This woman you call your aunt is certain of these dates?"

"You may read her letter if you wish," she replied. "I never informed her of your claim, or apprised her of my recent doubts about my parentage. The duke sought this confirmation from her without my prior knowledge, and sorry though I am to cause you pain, I'm thankful that he did."

The Frenchman's powdered head drooped. "When I found you, I believed that you would accept me, in time. I wanted it more than anything, for I have no other remembrance of Delphine, *la grande passion de ma vie.* Perhaps this is a just punishment for my cruel desertion."

Rosalie looked to the delicate porcelain figurine on the mantel, having placed it there at Gervase's suggestion. It was one of her most precious keepsakes, but she also possessed the Fragonard painting, and many lesser relics which had belonged to her mother. Etienne Lemercier had nothing but the memory of her tears.

"Take this," she said softly, presenting her treasure to him. "*Certainement,* Maman would want you to have something of she treasured."

Gazing sadly at the object she had given him, he said, "Whenever I look upon it, I will think not only of my lost love, but also of the so beautiful *danseuse* who became a *duchesse*—and might have been my daughter."

Rosalie's pensive silence troubled Gervase later, when they left Solway House to attend a performance at the King's Theatre. It would be their first public appearance as man and wife, and he suspected she was nervous.

Fingering her necklace, a *rivière* of large topazes and small diamonds, she confessed, "It is so strange to be going to the theater with you, in your carriage."

"You've ridden in it several times," he reminded her.

"Yes, but this is different. And it will be stranger still to see an opera from your box seat rather than from the wings. I hope you don't mind taking me—fashionable people aren't expected to attend a singer's benefit. But Naldi was always so good to me that I owe it to him to be there. *The Magic Flute* is a Mozart opera, after all, and Armand is dancing afterward." With a little shake of her head, she said, "I must remember to call him Vestris now."

Despite the fact that it was a benefit performance, they found a long line of coaches in the Haymarket and a crowd in the box lobby. They reached their seats only moments before the overture began.

Gervase noted that Rosalie was rather pale, possibly because hundreds of people were studying her face, her dress, and her jewels. He shifted his satin-covered thigh closer to hers, seeking to reassure her with physical contact. The soaring violins matched his mood, for his mother had not berated him, and his wife did him great credit.

Now that their honeymoon was behind them, they were expected to maintain a stifling degree of propriety at all times except when they were alone. This was made even more difficult by his recurring impulse to take her to bed, which he was now lawfully permitted to do as frequently as he wished. He'd discovered that she was remarkably demure for a girl with French blood—but only up to a point. And while she gave every sign of welcoming his attentions, he didn't want her to think he regarded her only as a plaything. To him she was much more than someone he'd taken as his wife simply because she refused to be his mistress. That, he suspected, was what his mother believed.

He became aware of a change in Rosalie at the beginning of the opera's second scene. While the evil Monostatos preyed upon Pamina, she pressed her lips together and clutched the arms of her chair, entirely caught up in the action. And, Gervase realized in a flash of intuition, the heroine's situation had reminded her of Benjamin Beckmann's attack. Should he put their precarious dignity at risk by reaching for her gloved hand? He restrained himself, for her sake.

The subsequent entrance of Papageno the bird-catcher brought an appreciative smile to her face. Soon Tamino was playing the magic flute, enticing various wild creatures from the wood, and while bears, apes, and an ungainly crocodile cavorted about the stage, Rosalie's enjoyment was exactly as Ninian's would have been. Her spirits were as changeable as a child's, and he was learning to expect those rapid transformations from gravity to merriment.

Between acts she turned to him and said, "The Parisian productions of this opera were far more spectacular than this one. And except for Signora Bertinotti, the singers are sadly out of voice tonight."

"I'm sorry that you're disappointed. Shall we go, then?"

"Not before the ballet."

After the curtain descended upon the principals and the chorus, she exhibited signs of extreme agitation. "You're quite sure you wish to stay?" he probed, but her firm, decisive nod failed to reassure him.

His foreboding increased when the ballet began, and Rosalie's profound interest in what appeared to be an unremarkable piece of choreography wounded him. Her attention never left the stage, where Armand Vestris leaped and bounded with vigorous abandon. Did he imagine it, or were her eyes misted by tears of regret?

Watching his wife watch her former colleagues, Gervase felt guilty of a crime as foul as those Beckmann had committed against her. Marrying her had been an act of supreme selfishness. He had caged this airy sprite, and now she was earthbound, no longer free. In future she might hate him for it.

To his considerable relief, he detected no animosity in his bride when they drove through the lamplit streets to their Park Lane mansion. And the way she snuggled against him, seeking to rest her head upon his shoulder, soothed his alarms.

"Thank you for taking me," she murmured. "But I don't think I'll often ask you to."

"Was it so painful?"

"Yes. Because the opera was less than good, and Armand's ballet even worse—and the performers must have known it, too."

"I thought you were jealous of them."

"Oh no," she protested, "*pas du tout*. I felt only pity."

Stroking her curls, he said, "I have admired you as a mermaid, fairy, goddess, and nymph, but in none of your roles have you pleased me more than in that of duchess."

She sighed, then said softly, "*Cher* Gervais, you always give the answer I most need to hear."

16

My charmer is not mine alone.
　　　　—WILLIAM COWPER

June the nineteenth, the day of the Carlton House fête, dragged by for Rosalie. Gervase, who had always proved capable of calming her worst fears, decided to take Ninian out to Greenwich, no doubt thinking he was doing her a favor, but she missed them both terribly. It was well past dinnertime when they returned and she was already closeted with Madame Ferrier, who brought her finished ballgown to Solway House.

The gauzy turquoise silk of the overdress was lavishly embroidered with gold thread, and the Frenchwoman had appliquéd a chain of miniature golden cockleshells to the hem. She confided to her satisfied customer that it was the most magnificent garment she had ever created, and deserved to be seen by the Comte de Lille, the uncrowned brother of Louis the Sixteenth.

"It is a dress worthy of Queen Marie Antoinette herself," Rosalie said, a compliment which brought tears to the seamstress's eyes.

"When you see our King, Madame la Duchesse, you must tell him that all loyalists pray for our monarchy to be restored. It is dishonor to our country that he must live in exile here, while that Corsican *usurpateur* pretends to be our ruler!"

Madame Ferrier, after years of serving as a dresser in the theater, was as skilled with the comb as she was with her needle. She arranged Rosalie's curling tresses in an elegant coiffure, upon which she placed the heavy topaz and diamond crescent. She handed Rosalie the other glittering pieces of the parure, one by one, and fastened each clasp for her.

By nine o'clock that evening, carriages bearing more than two thousand invited guests clogged the streets of Mayfair. The congestion was increased by the crowds of common folk who gathered along the street to watch the procession. Gervase preferred to wait until well past ten before calling for his coach, and by that time Rosalie was almost paralyzed with anticipation.

Ninian had stayed up late to see them off. As he studied his cousin's court dress of dark velvet coat trimmed with silver lace, white satin knee breeches, and silk waistcoat, he commented, "I never saw you look so much like a duke. May I hold your sword?"

"Definitely not," Gervase said without hesitation.

"Why is Rosalie wearing Aunt Elizabeth's necklace and eardrops?" Ninian wondered.

"Because I asked her to."

Rosalie turned away from the pier glass. "The topazes belong to your mother?"

"At my father's death they became my property. You will have the use of them for as long as I live, and when I'm gone they'll pass to our eldest son." He picked up his *chapeau bras,* tucking it beneath one arm, and extended the other to his duchess.

After a meandering journey through the lamplit streets, the town coach discharged its passengers beneath the columned portico of Carlton House.

Gervase and Rosalie proceeded through the entrance hall, and upon entering the Crimson Drawing Room they joined a vast crowd of exquisitely dressed persons. Most of the gentlemen were clad in velvet and satin, and the coats of those in military dress displayed medals and sparkling decorations. The ladies wore silk and satin; white was the predominant color, making Rosalie conspicuous in her vivid blue-green gown. Jeweled tiaras supported their waving plumes, and Rosalie marveled at the number of emeralds, rubies, and amethysts that had been mined from the

earth to grace the necks and wrists of England's noble-
women.

Gervase conducted her through the Circular Room, the
Throne Room, and the Rose Satin Room, each one
crammed with people. An orchestra played continuously
but there wasn't enough space for dancing, and the music
was drowned out by the incessant hum of several thousand
voices. Rosalie knew no one, although her husband tried to
remedy that by occasionally introducing her to Lord This or
Lady That.

"Are you acquainted with everyone here?" she asked him
when they reached yet another anteroom.

"Oh no," he laughed, "nor do I want to be. Come, I must
present you to His Royal Highness."

The Prince Regent was receiving his guests in the Blue
Velvet Room. Its azure velvet hangings, carpet, and silk
chair covers were so liberally decorated with gold fleur-de-
lis that it was a suitable setting for the exiled Bourbons.

Rosalie curtsied to her host, who bore a disconcerting resemblance to the caricatures she'd seen in print shop windows. His scarlet coat was trimmed with gold lace and he
wore the shining star that designated his membership in the
Order of the Garter.

The Regent beamed at Rosalie, his broad smile plumping
his pink cheeks. "How delightful that such a charming creature has married into our nobility. You were born in France,
I believe—or so we have been told."

"I was, sir," she replied.

"Allow me to present you to my guest of honor, the
Comte de Lille." Turning to the portly individual at his
side, he said, "Monseigneur, here is one of your countrywomen, the Duchess of Solway."

The comte inclined his powdered head in dignified acknowledgement. He was a victim of obesity and gout, and
his movements were slow and ponderous. *"Et votre famille,
Madame la Duchesse?"*

Gervase replied for her, saying, "My wife's father was
an Englishman, and her mother was Delphine de Barante."

The Comte de Lille's sharp eyes studied Rosalie. *"La*

Belle Delphine," he said, nodding again. *"Une artiste du ballet, une danseuse magnifique. Bon, bon."*

Rosalie forgot her disappointment in the titular monarch's appearance and manner when she met Marie Thérèse Charlotte, daughter and only surviving child of Marie Antoinette. A dignified woman in her thirties, she was handsome rather than pretty. Her small mouth and prominent nose were legacies from her Hapsburg forebears. Rosalie perceived a faint resemblance to the French Queen, whose face was more familiar to her from portraits than memory. She wore a diamond tiara of such great height that it resembled a crown of state.

Standing at her side was her husband and cousin, the unprepossessing Duc d'Angoulême, elder son of the Comte d'Artois. The Duc de Berri, his more vibrant and flamboyant brother, bowed over Rosalie's hand and murmured extravagant compliments.

Her face was still pink with pleasure when the Marquis of Elston approached her. "My dear duchess, you've no idea how glad I am to have found you—and wouldn't believe how desperately I've been searching," he said, his alabaster face more animated than she had ever seen it. "Follow me, there's something you must see. You, too, Gervase."

They went with him to a corridor hung with gilt-framed paintings. One of them, which was achingly familiar to her, depicted a young girl in a scarlet cloak, her hair bound by a matching ribbon.

" 'Mischief,'" Rosalie gasped. "Gervais, it's the little Gypsy!" Tearing her eyes from the long-lost canvas, she turned to her husband.

"The Regent's most recent acquisition," Damon told them triumphantly, "purchased on the advice of Sir George Beaumont, who told him it had been privately sold by Monsieur Lemercier."

"Etienne Lemercier?" Rosalie asked. After a thoughtful moment, she said, "I suppose he decided to let it go after our conversation the other day. *Pauvre gentilhomme.*"

Said Gervase, "I only wish I'd had the opportunity to make an offer. I doubt that His Royal Highness will let the painting go now that it's in his clutches."

"To think that my face is hanging on the wall of a royal residence! Maman would be so proud!"

"And not merely your face," Gervase interjected dryly, focused on the low décolletage of the girl in the picture. "I'm not best pleased that the Regent can gaze upon my bride's charms whenever he chooses."

Unlike his friend the duke, Lord Elston was acquainted with the majority of the guests. While he and the Solways strolled through the extensive gardens behind the house, he entertained them with wicked gossip about many of the individuals thronging the grounds. Canvas awnings had been stretched over many of the walks, from which hung suspended illumination and fragrant festoons of flowers.

When Gervase went in search of some champagne and the marquis paused to greet an attractive female, Rosalie walked on alone, relieved to have a moment to herself. The combination of crowded, overheated rooms, the ceaseless buzz of voices, and the weighty crescent she was wearing had given her a fierce headache. Assuming that her husband was lost among the mob, she wandered toward a shadowy grove of trees in the hope of finding some cooler, fresher air.

While weaving among the well-tended shrubs and topiary, she met another solitary lady in gray silk and pearls, and politely stepped aside to let her pass.

"Those topazes become you far more than they ever did me," said the woman.

Rosalie stared up at the proud, well-preserved face she remembered so well. "Your grace," she choked, dropping a hasty, off-balance curtsy. "I—we didn't know you were here."

"In such a crush as this, it is no wonder," replied the Dowager Duchess of Solway. "What has become of my son?"

"I don't know," Rosalie admitted. "I was about to look for him."

"Let him find you," the older woman suggested. "I will keep you company until he does so, for I have many things to say."

17

When at their dance's end they kiss.
—ANDREW MARVELL

This woman, thought Rosalie miserably, was every inch a duchess. Tall and regal with patrician features, she possessed an impressive air of command and an enviable assurance. How disappointed she must be in a successor so small and ordinary, and only half English.

Having no other choice, she accompanied her mother-in-law to a pair of empty chairs at the edge of the terrace. She felt even more vulnerable than she had at their first meeting, and prepared herself for similar unpleasantness.

"I hope you haven't felt slighted by my apparent neglect," the older woman said as they sat down together. "I intended to pay my duty visit the day I brought Ninian to London, but you were out and Gervase discouraged me from awaiting your return. He felt you were not yet ready to meet me."

She would have voiced a polite protest had she not suspected that this grande dame preferred uncompromising honesty. "It is true, your grace, although I never told him so."

"Is it because you believe me opposed to the marriage? On principle I would have been, had anyone asked my opinion beforehand."

"I didn't entrap him," she said in a rush, determined to clarify that point, "for I never imagined that he would want to marry me."

"It's just as well that he did. I much prefer having a former opera dancer for my daughter-in-law than I would the Princess Charlotte of Wales. You have spared me that indignity. As antecedents go, yours are respectable enough. According to Gervase, your father's family were Gloucestershire gentry."

"Yes, but the Lovegrove properties are not extensive, and my future inheritance consists of a few small farms and a house in Bibury village. I have nothing in the way of a fortune. My father was a professional musician, and Aunt Tilda taught singing at a Bristol seminary. Of my maternal relations I know very little. My French grandfather was a wealthy *avocat,* but I wasn't told any more than that. He disowned Maman when she went on the stage."

"Your mother performed at the Paris Opera, I have been informed. And also Versailles?"

Said Rosalie with pride, "She did, your grace. The Queen admired her very much. She had a great interest in children, too, and often invited Maman to bring me to the Tuileries. I was little more than a babe, but I do remember her holding me." Lifting her chin, she added, "This occasion is not the first time I have been presented to royalty."

For the first time the duchess smiled. "My dear child, you needn't be so uncomfortable. I'm not your enemy, and there will be no repetition of that deplorable scene at Haberdine. I admit, at that time I was concerned that my son's feelings for you would result in sorrow, or worse, bitter disillusionment. His happiness is of paramount importance to me."

"*À moi aussi,*" Rosalie murmured.

The fine silvery eyes studied the younger woman's face. "What I should like to know, if you can answer so intimate a question from a virtual stranger, is the reason you accepted his marriage proposal."

"I was so tired of refusing him. More than once he asked me to be his—his *fille de joie,* but I could not. It was agony for me to hurt Gervais."

"Had you not been in love before?" the duchess asked gently.

"No more than a little. And never with one such as he. If he had proposed to me at a time when I was able to think more clearly, I might not have agreed to marry him. I knew it was not *comme il faut* for dukes to marry dancers. But I was *très désolée*. My career had ended so badly and stupidly and, I didn't know what I would do except go back to Paris, and that he would not permit. I think to him I was *l'âme perdue*—a lost soul. So when he said that he wanted me to be his wife, I consented. We were married the very next day."

"It cannot have been easy making so swift a transition from performer to peeress. You haven't regretted your choice?"

"*Jamais.* How could I, when I have Gervais to love me, to help me? Before knowing him, I did not like to think of a life without dancing, and now I could not live without him. I have discovered that I have a talent for marriage also. It is very like a *pas de deux*," Rosalie elaborated. "There is a need for a sense of balance and timing. One must give support to the partner, and also rely upon his support. Gervais and I are learning each other's moods and habits just as dancers learn their music."

The duchess surprised her by saying, "I would have liked to see you perform. My nephew says that you are exceedingly gifted."

Smiling reminiscently, Rosalie said, "Everything is his fault. My meeting Gervais was the result of Lord Swanborough's mania for the aquatic spectacles at Sadler's Wells."

"He *is* a naughty boy. Has he been behaving himself?"

She laughed. "I wouldn't say that, your grace. He can be an exacting charge, but I enjoy having him at Solway House. My childhood was so odd that I have no notion of how to manage children properly. It is something about which I will require much advice."

"You'll find your way, I have no doubt. And I suspect your theatrical past will serve you very well in your new position, for it also demanded discipline and courage. Now that we have become better acquainted, I realize that Gervase has done very well for himself. And though I'm sure he'd rather spend the summer in seclusion, fishing and reading and doting on his bride, I hope he will remain fixed in town."

"He has said we will."

"Excellent. Otherwise our friends and acquaintances will believe you are an embarrassment to the Marchant family, or worse, some sort of adventuress. Although five minutes in your company would quickly disabuse them of that notion."

Following the other woman's lead, Rosalie climbed to her feet. "You will visit us, then?"

"As often as I may." The duchess took both her hands, clasping them firmly. "Had you remained on the stage, you would never have been more than what you were, an opera dancer. Now you are a wife and a duchess, the mistress of many houses. One day you will become a mother. And already you are a daughter I am proud to have."

Rosalie began another curtsy, but the duchess shook her head.

"No, no, I do not wish for formality between us." Patting the young woman's cheek she said, "After tonight, I hope you will cease to fear me, Rosalie. Gervase is wise enough to let us find our own way to friendship, and he's very patient. He gets both virtues from me."

And also his *beaux yeux,* thought Rosalie, answering her mother-in-law's smile with a radiant one of her own.

Two hours after midnight the Regent's guests assembled in the rooms on the garden level and under the marquees for their dinner.

Rosalie was amazed that she and Gervase should be seated so near their host, among the foreign princes and ambassadors, British ministers of state, and such honored female guests as the Duchess of York, Lady Hertford, and Lady Charlotte Campbell. The high table, extending the whole length of the Gothic conservatory, was laden with gold tureens, covered dishes, and goblets.

The upper servants of the royal household were clad in dark blue livery, and while they served the wines for the first course Rosalie examined the principal decoration. A channel of clear water flowed from the large basin near the Prince Regent's place and meandered down the middle of the table, exciting the admiration of the diners. Several picturesque bridges adorned this miniature river, which had a sandy bottom and was banked with rocks and green moss.

When Rosalie noticed the gold and silvery fish swimming about, she leaned close to Gervase and whispered, "Poor creatures, they'll not survive the heat from all these candles."

The meal was composed of innumerable delicacies, mostly French and all of them rich and heavy. It began and ended with toasts—to the Regent, his guests, the armies in the Peninsula, and the future restoration of the Bourbons. Rosalie, uncomfortably aware that the hands of the great clock marked the fourth hour of a new day, prayed that no more speeches would follow.

The Regent rose, glass in hand. "We would be remiss if we failed to acknowledge a marriage which lately took place," he announced. "It is a union symbolic of the great friendship between the hereditary rulers of the two greatest nations of the world, England and France. Your Majesty, my lords and ladies, I give you the Duke of Solway and his lovely duchess!"

Several hours later, when the newlyweds lay in bed discussing the event, Rosalie asked her husband, "Why would the Regent make such an announcement? You might have married his daughter, after all."

"There was never any chance of that," Gervase contradicted her. "The toast was simply one of the Regent's attempts to appear affable and charming. And it was a masterly way of acknowledging the Comte de Lille. More of a compliment to him than to us," he mused as his fingers drifted through her unbound hair.

"Well, it's something to tell our children, and our grandchildren. That is what your mother said afterward."

"I'm quite sure they'd rather hear about Clown Grimaldi, and your adventures in Paris—posing for the painter Jean-Baptiste Greuze, and dancing for Napoleon Bonaparte."

"I danced for you *aussi*," she reminded him.

"And also for me."

Their lips touched in a protracted kiss.

Resting her head upon the pillow they shared, Rosalie observed wearily, "The sun is already rising, Gervais. Do you think Ninian will let us lie in bed all day?"

"If he doesn't, I'll make sure he regrets it," the Duke of Solway replied, closing his eyes.

Historical Note

The personnel and productions at Sadler's Wells and the Italian Opera House are authentic, based upon descriptions from newspapers of the period and theatrical memoirs. The collection of London's Theatre Museum in Covent Garden provided a wealth of historical and visual information and contains many Grimaldi artifacts and memorabilia.

Joseph Grimaldi retired from Sadler's Wells on 17 March, 1828, during his forty-ninth year. His farewell performance took place at the Theatre Royal, Drury Lane, on 28 June, his final appearance on any stage. During the following season his son Joe performed some of his most popular parts at Covent Garden. Three years after his dismissal from that company the young man injured himself on another stage and died shortly afterward, aged thirty. His mother Mary, already in poor health, survived him by only two years. Joseph Grimaldi the elder lived until 1837.

In 1813, Armand Vestris married the sixteen-year-old performer Lucia Bartolozzi, and the following year he was promoted from *premier danseur* to ballet master at the King's Theatre. After separating from his wife he continued to work in various European capitals until his death in 1825. Madame Vestris later became wildly popular with early Victorian audiences as an actress, singer, and theater manageress.

I would be remiss if I failed to acknowledge another source of inspiration for *Dangerous Diversions*, the works of Jean Baptiste Greuze in the Wallace Collection, Manchester Square, London.

I dedicate this work to the many individuals who made a meaningful contribution, little though they may realize it. The following have earned my abiding gratitude:

Michael Deep—actor, musician, comedian, playwright, lifelong friend, and modern incarnation of Joseph Grimaldi, about whom he, too, has studied and written.

Marilyn Darling, an inspiring teacher of ballet, who opened my eyes to the fascinating history of dance. And Linda McInnis, at whose side I struggled and sweated through many a session at the barre.

Robert and Margot Pierson, for a memorable visit to Bibury. And my cousin Justin Evans, who kindly gave me a tour of Harrow.

My patient and supportive parents, for all those years they transported me to and from rehearsals and classes.

Lastly and mostly, my husband Christopher, for his involvement and encouragement.